WILD SCOTTISH EMBRACE

A slow grin spread over Alexander's face. "Scottish lads are weaned to the sword and given the taste of battle before they can reach the stirrups, yet we are never taught how to resist a beautiful woman's seductive ways."

"Oh," Maura said, unable to cover her embarrassment. "I shall try to remember that when I am ready to take a man."

Alexander threw back his head and laughed. "Here I thought to shock you, and instead you are taking lessons from my words."

"Have you been teasing me then?"

"Aye, you are very perceptive, lass." Alexander laughed deep in his throat, then he pulled her towards him. His cape enclosed her in a warm cocoon against his body as his lips descended on hers. . . .

SURRENDER TO THE PASSION

LOVE'S SWEET BOUNTY (3313, $4.50)
by Colleen Faulkner

Jessica Landon swore revenge of the masked bandits who robbed the train and stole all the money she had in the world. She set out after the thieves without consulting the handsome railroad detective, Adam Stern. When he finally caught up with her, she admitted she needed his assistance. She never imagined that she would also begin to need his scorching kisses and tender caresses.

WILD WESTERN BRIDE (3140, $4.50)
by Rosalyn Alsobrook

Anna Thomas loved riding the Orphan Train and finding loving homes for her young charges. But when a judge tried to separate two brothers, the dedicated beauty went beyond the call of duty. She proposed to the handsome, blue-eyed Mark Gates, planning to adopt the boys herself! Of course the marriage would be in name only, but yet as time went on, Anna found herself dreaming of being a loving wife in every sense of the word . . .

QUICKSILVER PASSION (3117, $4.50)
by Georgina Gentry

Beautiful Silver Jones had been called every name in the book, and now that she owned her own tavern in Buckskin Joe, Colorado, the independent didn't care what the townsfolk thought of her. She never let a man touch her and she earned her money fair and square. Then one night handsome Cherokee Evans swaggered up to her bar and destroyed the peace she'd made with herself. For the irresistible miner made her yearn for the melting kisses and satin caresses she had sworn she could live without!

MISSISSIPPI MISTRESS (3118, $4.50)
by Gina Robins

Cori Pierce was outraged at her father's murder and the loss of her inheritance. She swore revenge and vowed to get her independence back, even if it meant singing as an entertainer on a Mississippi steamboat. But she hadn't reckoned on the swarthy giant in tight buckskins who turned out to be her boss. Jacob Wolf was, after all, the giant of the man Cori vowed to destroy. Though she swore not to forget her mission for even a moment, she was powerfully tempted to submit to Jake's fiery caresses and have one night of passion in his irresistible embrace.

Available wherever paperbacks are sold, or order direct from the Publisher. Send cover price plus 50¢ per copy for mailing and handling to Zebra Books, Dept. 3389, 475 Park Avenue South, New York, N.Y. 10016. Residents of New York, New Jersey and Pennsylvania must include sales tax. DO NOT SEND CASH.

Highland Rogue

Casey Stuart

ZEBRA BOOKS
KENSINGTON PUBLISHING CORP.

As always, to my family for their support and faith, and for my husband, Bill—always for Bill.

And for Michael Crawford, the Angel of Music, *whose beautiful voice inspires, possesses, and awakens the imagination. He transports you to another time, makes your spirit soar and your dreams take flight—all with a song and a magical voice.*

ZEBRA BOOKS

are published by

Kensington Publishing Corp.
475 Park Avenue South
New York, NY 10016

First printing: May, 1991

Printed in the United States of America

There's no such thing as chance;
And what to us seems merest accident
Springs from the deepest source of destiny.
          J. Christoph Friedrich von Schiller

Prologue

The dawn was slow in coming over the Scottish Highlands. Against the pale sky, Alexander MacLaren's silhouette stood out tall and ominous, as the wind moaned restlessly through the parapets, matching his own restless mood. He had just promised his friend, Donald Gordon, that he would try to rescue his daughter from Cromwell's clutches, a feat no ordinary man could perform.

"I thought I'd be finding you out here," Simon MacLaren said as he joined his brother. "Colin just told me what Donald wants you to do. Is it possible?"

"I dinna know until I try it. The lass is at Beaumaris Castle preparing for her wedding to one of Cromwell's officers."

"Well, if anyone can do it, I'd wager you can," Simon said, knowing his brother was no ordinary man. He was the MacLaren, the chief of Clan MacLaren, a rugged lord known far and wide for his bravery.

"And what if the lass does not want to be saved?" Alexander questioned, turning to look at his brother.

"Because of the Gordon feud with the Campbells, Donald hasn't seen his daughter since she was two, and to my knowledge she has never even attempted to see him. She could very well be happy with Cromwell's arrangements for her marriage."

"Aye, it could be that her sympathies lie more with the English than the Scots by now," Simon agreed. "The Campbells saw to it that she had a place at Court as soon as she was old enough. From the rumors I've heard, the lass stood in high favor with excellent prospects for a wealthy marriage, but I'm certain they didn't think it would be to one of Cromwell's officers."

"True. Even the Campbells couldn't have guessed that Cromwell would have King Charles executed. From what Donald's contacts tell him, the girl had been left behind to help care for the King's children when the Queen fled to France, and Cromwell upon seeing her decided she should be married to one of his officers."

"Do you think he knows the lass is Donald Gordon's daughter?" Simon asked.

"Aye, I'm sure of it, and I'm sure he also knows the lass is Donald's only heir. That would put all of the Gordon land in English hands when Donald dies. That is something I intend to see never happen. I just wish the hell I knew what the lass's thoughts are on the whole matter. 'Tis one thing to scale the walls of Beaumaris Castle to save a lady in distress, but quite another to contend with a raving female who has no desire to be saved."

"Sticky situation, I agree," Simon said leaning his elbows on the wall as he looked out over the mountains. "When do we leave?"

"*We* dinna. I am going alone."

6

"God's blood, Alex, you canna be serious."

"I'm very serious. I willna put you in danger when it is I who have given my word to Donald Gordon."

"One man stands a slim chance of helping the girl, but the three of us . . ."

"Could get killed," Alexander interrupted his brother.

"We live with that danger every day of our lives. Why should this time be any different?"

"Because she is a Campbell," Alex growled. "I willna put you and Colin in danger over a Campbell."

"'Tis ironic, I agree, but if you go we all go," Simon persisted.

"We will have to leave Scottish soil, Simon, where we'd stand very little chance of getting help once we are in England."

"'Tis exactly the reason Colin and I need to be with you, Alexander. Now no more arguments. Together we will save the lass. Besides, I hear she's more than pleasant to look at."

Alex's deep laughter rumbled over the hillside. "So that is why you suddenly want to play hero. So be it, little brother. The MacLarens shall rescue the damsel in distress."

My friends forsake me like a memory lost.
John Clare

Chapter One

Maura Campbell stood deathly still as one of the servants finished fastening the tiny buttons on her ivory velvet wedding gown. She struggled against the panic rising slowly in her throat as the time for the ceremony drew nearer. It didn't help matters that her mother continually mumbled that someone would help them. Maura knew there was no one to help them. The King was dead, at the hands of Oliver Cromwell, and his family were in hiding in fear of their own lives. Her own Campbell relatives seemed content with her fate, even though she had pleaded for their help. No, there wasn't anyone to help her. In less than an hour she would be wed to Lord James Randolph, one of Cromwell's officers, and a man known for his cruelty, particularly to the Scottish people.

"Maura . . . Maura . . ." Anne Campbell suddenly closed her eyes and began to moan.

"Mother, what is it? What is wrong?" Maura asked, kneeling in front of her mother.

Anne Campbell stared into her daughter's beautiful violet eyes, unseeing. "There is black . . . and mountains . . . the Highlands. We are traveling in wind and rain, but we are safe . . ."

"What is it, m'lady? What is wrong with her?" one of the young servants asked.

Suddenly the terrible trembling inside her ceased and Maura felt numbed by a strange calm as she listened to her mother. "'Tis all right, Elspeth, do not be frightened."

She knew her mother had the gift of second sight, even though Anne usually didn't like to admit it. A few months before, her mother's premonition had saved the Queen from being trampled to death beneath a team of runaway horses, and for weeks before King Charles had been imprisoned, her mother had felt the impending danger, even though she couldn't precisely say what it would be. Now, if her mother was seeing mountains and them traveling . . .

Maura realized the servants were staring at them. "Everyone leave us except Elspeth," she said, excluding the young servant girl who had become her friend and confidant. "I will send for you as soon as my mother has composed herself."

No sooner had Elspeth slid the bolt across the door, then a tall figure dressed in black climbed into one of the tall casement windows.

Maura felt a childish urge to rub her eyes to see if she was dreaming, but she knew from the expression on her mother's face that she was not.

"Maura Campbell?" the figure asked.

"Aye. Who are you?"

"I am a friend of your family, lass," he answered. "I am here to help you. Now come quickly. We dinna have much time."

"Mother, get your things," Maura ordered.

"No," Alexander said abruptly. "I am here to take only you."

"I will not go without my mother."

Alexander glanced at the older woman who stood silently watching them. Donald had not mentioned his wife. "It will be a difficult trip even for one as young as you," he tried to explain to the younger woman.

"I am up to it," Anne Campbell answered without hesitation, as she continued to stare at the dark stranger, thinking there was something familiar about his voice.

Knowing he didn't have time to argue, Alexander headed for the door and placed his dirk in the latch to make it harder for anyone on the other side to raise the bolt. It wouldn't hold indefinitely, but it would give them a little time. When he turned back he noticed the frightened servant girl in the shadows.

"Can ye trust her?"

"Aye. Elspeth will tell no one what has happened here," Maura said, squeezing the young girl's hand, "but perhaps it would be better if we took her with us."

"No. 'Tis impossible. We only have two horses," he said as he turned back and gracefully leaped upon the window ledge, holding out his hand to Maura Campbell.

She stared at him as if he were deranged, her violet eyes dark in her pale face. "I canna go like this. I must change," she protested.

"There isn't time."

"You expect me to climb down the castle wall in this wedding gown?"

" 'Tis exactly what I expect you to do, lass. I have no desire to carry you kicking and screaming from this place, but if I have to, I will."

11

"Maura, I agree with the gentleman. We must go now," her mother encouraged. "It will not be long before the servants return. Come now, we will be safe."

"Blow out the candle," Alexander instructed the servant girl. For a moment they stood in darkness until their eyes became accustomed to it. The sky was overcast and the dreariness oppressive.

"Good-bye, Elspeth," Maura said, hugging the young servant girl. "I will send for you as soon as things are settled. Take care of yourself."

Alexander turned his attention to the rope. When Maura moved beside him he placed her hand on the hemp. "It is knotted at intervals to give you a better hold. Use your feet against the wall for balance."

"My feet?"

"Aye, as you hold onto the rope walk yourself down the wall with your feet. One of my men waits below. Once you start down, dinna hesitate, and dinna look down. The rope is strong so dinna be afraid, lass."

Maura glanced over the edge of the wall. It was an incredible distance to the ground. No matter how reassuring this stranger's voice sounded, she had never climbed a rope or anything else for that matter, and the thought of falling to her death made her shiver.

"Take a deep breath, lass. Your mother and I will be right behind you."

She struggled momentarily as panic threatened to take her breath away, but she grabbed the rope with her sweating hands. She pushed away from the wall with her feet as instructed, and for one terrifying moment dangled in midair, unable to move in either direction as the velvet wedding gown hung like a weight around her legs.

"Move your hand to the next knot, lass," his voice

12

whispered from above her. "You are doing fine."

She loosened one hand experimentally and felt for the knot below her. She discovered with relief it was of sufficient size to afford a good grip. After that she moved slowly, but efficiently down the rope, sliding her feet against the wall for balance. Suddenly she ran out of knots and her heart stopped beating for a long agonizing moment. She was out of rope and there was still nothing below her but space.

"Let go, lass," a voice came softly from below. "I'll catch you."

Maura closed her eyes and dropped into the waiting arms of the man below her.

"Ah, a gift from heaven," the man laughed softly before placing her on her feet.

Moments later the figure in black appeared at the foot of the rope with her mother clinging to his back. "We have to move fast," he said, moving off towards the woods.

Maura took her mother's hand and followed the dark figure while the other man followed close behind. She kept tripping over the gown, and silently cursed the figure ahead for not letting her change into traveling clothes. As they tramped farther and farther into the woods, Maura began to wonder if they were going to be traveling by foot. She picked up the hem of her gown and attempted to keep it clear of the brambles and sticks that kept snagging her, but to no avail.

"Here, maybe I can help that," the young man said from behind her. He unsheathed his knife and knelt in front of her, quickly and efficiently cutting the gown so it hung just to her ankles. "Sorry to ruin your dress, lass, but we need to move as quickly as possible before your

English friends are breathing down our necks."

"Do not worry about the dress." She smiled at the young man, trying to place him among her Campbell relatives. "Thank you for your help."

After a few more minutes of thrashing through the woods, they came upon two horses tethered to a tree. "Thank God," Maura murmured to her mother. "I was beginning to fear we were going to walk to Scotland."

"Already complaining, lass?" the dark figure asked as he led his horse towards her. "I fear by the time we reach our destination you will think even less of us."

Maura tried to see his face, sure that she had heard amusement in his voice, but the dark hood kept his features in the shadows. "I'm sorry." She had the decency to look embarrassed. "It has been a trying day."

"Aye, and will get even more trying I assure you," he said as he lifted her in the saddle, then mounted behind her. Without another moment's hesitation, he urged the great black beast into a full gallop. There didn't seem to be an immediate pursuit from the castle, yet they rode as if the devil were on their heels.

Maura could do nothing but lean back against the broad chest of the stranger who held her so closely, enjoying the warmth emanating from his body. Even though she was now held in the cocoon of his black cape, her velvet gown was already soaked from their trek through the deep forest and she had begun to think it had penetrated to her bones.

Several hours later it began to rain, a cold biting rain which added to her discomfort. She felt stiff and ached in every bone. She glanced towards her mother who rode in front of the other stranger, and hoped the cold and dampness did not prove too much for her. She knew her

14

mother felt as she did, that a little hardship was nothing compared to the fate they would have suffered if she had been forced to marry Randolph.

All night long they rode. She still had not gotten a good look at the man who held her so intimately, yet she had a feeling she was safe with this silent Scot. Maura tried to shift her position, but riding sidesaddle with a heavy, wet velvet skirt flapping around her legs was not conducive to comfort.

"We'll stop soon, lass," her companion said, sensing her uneasiness.

True to his word, presently they came out of the woods into a clearing. Maura caught the scent of peat smoke and meat cooking. God, she'd forgotten how good food smelled cooked out in the open. She just hoped whoever was cooking it would be willing to share. She was starved.

A few moments later they came upon a crofter's cottage. Her companion slid from the saddle and held his arms out for her. As soon as she touched the ground her legs gave way beneath her and she stumbled against the hard chest of her companion. Again she tried to make out his features, but even though it was nearly dawn, there wasn't enough light.

"I am sorry to have had to push you so hard, lass, but it was necessary to put a lot of distance between us and your English friends."

"I understand. My mother and I are grateful for your assistance." Hesitantly she tested her strength before moving away on her own to where the other rider was helping her mother dismount. When she turned back to speak to her companion he had disappeared, leaving the other gentleman to lead them to the cottage.

"I apologize for the sparse arrangements," the young

15

man said, "but it was all that could be arranged on short notice. You will find a change of clothes and a hot meal inside."

Colin joined his brother in the small lean-to that served as a stable. "Seems your sacrifice to honor old Donald's request wasna so painful after all," Colin MacLaren said with a grin. "She's a comely lass."

"Aye, I suppose she is," Alex answered as he took the saddle from his horse, "but dinna forget she is a Campbell."

"Aye, when you put it that way I see your point. Look what handfasting with a Campbell did for Donald Gordon."

"Come along, brother. It smells like Simon has prepared rabbit stew, and I'm fair starved."

"Have you told the lass who we are yet?" Colin asked as they headed towards the cottage.

"No, but I think 'tis time."

"God's mercy, Alex, dinna announce it when she has a plate of stew before her."

Maura was standing behind a screen changing into the clothes the young man named Simon had given her, when she heard the other two men enter the cottage. The comradery between the three was cheerful, bringing a smile to Maura's face. It had been a long time since she had heard such lighthearted banter. She realized her mother was also enjoying it, as her laughter floated above the deep voices.

Maura hesitantly stepped from behind the screen. The

two younger men sat at the crude wooden table with her mother, but the man who had been her companion for the long ride stood by the fireplace, his profile to her.

"Come, sit down, lass," one of the men invited.

Maura glanced at the man standing at the fireplace. His raven black hair hung in wet ringlets around his tanned face. He was tall with powerful shoulders and chest, but then she had already known that, feeling an intimate knowledge of his hard body. He wore a leather jack, and boots trimmed with silver that reached above his knees. Still she couldn't see his eyes, and she wondered why he avoided looking at her.

"My mother and I wish to thank you for your help," she directed at him. "But I do not even know your name."

Alexander MacLaren finally turned to face her, preparing himself for that gasp that he knew would come. "Alexander MacLaren at your service, m'lady." He bowed gallantly before her, as if he hadn't noticed her reaction, "and the gentlemen with me are my brothers, Simon and Colin."

She heard her mother gasp, but she didn't react immediately to it. Instead, she continued to stare at him, unable to take her eyes from the ghastly scar that lined the right side of his face from the corner of his steel gray eyes to the corner of his mouth. He smiled at her, but there was pain in his eyes; a wariness of the reaction he must always receive—the reaction she had so cruelly provided.

A long moment of silence passed before Alexander spoke again. "I apologize if my face offends you, m'lady," he said coldly.

Finally what he had said moments before registered.

17

"MacLaren?" she repeated. Suddenly her violet eyes flamed to anger. "Sir, it is not your face that offends me, but your name."

He had the audacity to laugh deep in his throat. "No, I dinna suppose any Campbell relishes hearing the MacLaren name."

"The Campbells did not send you for me," she stated angrily. "Pray tell me, why did you scale that castle wall to rescue my mother and me?"

Alexander MacLaren smiled. "Have you not heard, lass, there are no dragons to slay. A man must now satisfy his primal instincts by rescuing fair maidens in distress."

"Even if the maiden does not need saving?"

His dark eyes flashed angrily again. "I dinna believe even you will claim that, lass. Your Lord Randolph had a firm hand in the death of your King, and who do you think led the massacre on the people of Kinross?"

Maura knew what he said was true. In all probability he had saved her from a fate worse than death, but just what did he have in store for her? The MacLarens' reputation was no better than Randolph's. She and her mother could suffer a brutal, unsuspecting fate at his hands. It was well known all over the Highlands that the Campbells were mortal enemies of the MacLarens.

"You told me the Campbells had sent you," she persisted angrily.

"I dinna believe I ever mentioned the Campbells, lass."

"Perhaps you did not," she reluctantly admitted, "but you led me to believe it."

"Did I?" he asked as he took a place at the table. "God's blood, but I'm starved, Simon. That stew smells

18

delicious," he said ignoring Maura.

"We are not through, sir!" Maura struggled to control her temper at his audacity to dismiss her so casually. "I want some answers. Why did you come for us? You are my family's enemy."

Alexander turned back to face her, his eyes sweeping over her boldly before coming back to her face. "Aye, I have no love for the Campbells, but your father is my friend. He heard of your impending marriage to his enemy and asked me to help."

"My father?" she whispered in disbelief. Maura glanced at her mother who sat silently, her face pale and ashen. "You are mistaken, sir," she said lifting her chin defiantly. "I have no father."

"Maura . . ." her mother moaned.

"I'm sorry, Mother, but I cannot believe after all these years Donald Gordon would care anything about my welfare. The man has never even attempted to see me," she said, trying to keep the hurt from her voice. "How do you expect me to believe that he cares what happens to me now?"

"You will have time to discuss that with him, lass," Alexander said. "All I can tell you is that your father is ill and he wishes to see you before it is too late."

"It is already too late," Maura retorted as she sank down onto the hard wooden bench.

"Donald is ill?" Anne Campbell asked, concern in her voice.

"Do not be taken in by their lies, Mother," Maura warned. "You should know you cannot trust a MacLaren. He is probably planning to hold us for ransom."

Alexander's gray eyes glittered dangerously as he

19

stared at Maura. "Dinna push me too far, lass. I have little patience for foolish women, particularly Campbell women."

"Foolish women," she sputtered angrily. "How dare you!" She raised her hand to slap his dark face, but he realized her intent and grasped her wrist painfully.

"I'd not advise it," he growled low. "You are not dealing with one of your English dandies now."

Her pride, more than his warning made her yank away and turn away from him. "You will regret abducting me," she warned beneath her breath.

"Aye, somehow I knew I would," he answered before digging into his bowl of stew. "I suggest you both eat. We ride again in a few hours."

Maura stabbed a piece of meat from her stew and angrily chewed it, while listening to her mother question Alexander MacLaren about Donald Gordon. She couldn't imagine why her mother should be interested after all this time. Donald Gordon should have attempted to see her when she was a child, when she needed a father. Now she would never forgive him—or this nasty arrogant man he had sent in his place.

She looked up to find his gray eyes on her. She felt like throwing her plate at him, but controlled her foolish urge. Instead she glared back at him. God, how was she going to bear traveling with this . . . this MacLaren? He was the scourge of Scotland, a barbarian.

What can we know? Or what can we discern,
When error chokes the windows of the mind?
                                Sir John Davies

Chapter Two

Night came early, and with it the incessant rain finally
ceased. In spite of her reluctance to once again ride with
the MacLaren, Maura now welcomed the warmth of his
arms and cape around her as they made their way along
the treacherous paths leading towards the rugged countryside where she had been born.

She had had a chance to talk with her mother about
what lay ahead of them, and had been shocked that Anne
had actually seemed excited about seeing Donald Gordon
again. If she were honest with herself she'd admit that
she had always been curious about her father, a man who
her mother claimed was kind and gentle, but she
certainly had no desire to meet him. Not when he had
ignored her all of her young life, when she and her
mother needed him. She thought of her mother's reason-
ing that they were far better off paying a visit to Donald
Gordon then they would have been if they had stayed in
England, but she wasn't so certain. The unknown always
seemed more frightening to her. From the pan into the
fire, she thought, sighing deeply. Nothing short of

drinking poison was going to help her now, and she certainly didn't intend to do that.

Maura shivered, remembering the man she was supposed to marry. He would not take her disappearance lightly, she knew. He could, at this very moment, be following them. She wondered if Alexander MacLaren had any idea how dangerous the man was from whom they were fleeing.

"Are you cold, lass?" Alexander asked, feeling her shiver.

"What could you possibly care?" she said with blazing animosity. "I'm a Campbell."

"Aye. Excuse my momentary lapse of memory," he growled. "For a moment I thought you were a maid in need of comfort."

"Certainly not comfort from you," she answered shrewishly.

"God's blood, but you are an ungrateful termagant. Even your mother had the decency to thank us for coming to your rescue. Why can you not be as gracious?"

"Gracious?" she laughed bitterly. "It remains to be seen what our fate will be, since we are now in the company of reivers and abductors."

"Aye," he said calmly. "We are reivers and abductors when it suits our purpose, but even at that, you are safer with us then with your English friends."

"And just what is your purpose? What is in this for you? Did Donald Gordon promise you a horse or two?"

Alexander laughed. "If I had known what I was getting into, lass, I would have requested a hundred fine horses. But if you must know, I owed him the favor. Donald has been like a father to me."

She laughed bitterly. "I'm glad he has been a father

22

to someone."

"Has Anne told you nothing about the man or why you were not raised under his roof?"

"We have never discussed it, but I do remember my Campbell relatives expressing their hate for him. They said he was an evil man."

"The Campbells shed Scottish blood across the countryside and have the nerve to call others evil?" He laughed bitterly. "They ravage their own land, these predatory Campbells. They betray their own, kill women and children—"

"That's not true," she quickly defended. "The Campbells were good to my mother and me."

"Really? And you have not wondered why? Dinna you ever consider that your association with the royal family gave them a voice at court? Tell me, lass, why did they not come for you when they knew you were being forced into a marriage you dinna want? I'll tell you why. Because their clan hoped for an advantage with your union with Cromwell's lackey, and the devil take you."

Maura swallowed, knowing what he said was true, but she would not admit it to him. "You don't know what you're talking about," she argued.

"Time will tell, lass. Someday you will learn the wisdom of my words. I just hope it willna be too late for you."

"Such words of wisdom from my enemy," she said sarcastically, trying to cover her confusion. "Do you think I would believe a MacLaren when he speaks ill of a Campbell?"

Alexander pulled the black stallion to a sudden halt while the other riders disappeared around a bend. "You can wait here for your Campbell relatives. I will tell your

23

father that he is better off not meeting his shrew of a daughter."

Maura twisted around to stare into his gray eyes, wondering if he truly meant to leave her alone in the middle of nowhere. "You would not leave me here alone!"

"I could and I will," he said, lifting her from the saddle and dropping her to her feet. "You've been too long among the English. In Scotland a woman knows her place, even if she is a Campbell."

Maura glared at him. "You are worse than a reiver and abductor! You are a . . . a MacLaren," she sputtered. "Go ahead and leave me, but be warned, when we meet again I will cut your heart out and feed it to the wolves."

Alexander walked the big black stallion towards her, forcing her to retreat step by step until she was at the edge of a loch. Maura glared up at him, her hands on her hips, determined not to show fear, but the black stallion with its black-cloaked rider seemed like an ominous apparition against the dark sky. They were so close she could feel the horse's warm breath.

"Another few steps and I willna have to worry about you," he warned. "Or perhaps that is your intent?"

Maura glanced behind her at the black water, then back at him, lifting her chin in defiance. "I'm not so fainthearted that I would let any man force me to end my life, particularly a MacLaren."

Suddenly Alexander laughed. "Then you must have more Gordon blood than Campbell." He reached down and lifted her back into the saddle before him. "See if you can keep that shrewish tongue quiet for awhile. With all your nagging I canna hear if your English friends are following."

On and on they rode, through the dripping trees, while the MacLaren held his arm before her face to protect her from the wet branches. She didn't understand the man, nor did she want to, she told herself. But still it surprised her that the man she had heard such dark tales about would be concerned for her comfort and safety.

After a few hours they stopped at an outcropping of stone boulders. "We are on Scottish soil now, so we'll rest for a few hours," the MacLaren announced.

In a few minutes Simon had a blazing fire going while Alexander and Colin went off to hunt for food. Maura sat next to her mother on a blanket by the fire, stretching her borrowed boots towards the heat. "I have never been so cold," she commented. "Are you faring all right, Mother?"

"I'm just fine," Anne answered. "I wish we could just keep traveling and never stop."

Maura looked at her mother in surprise. "I thought you were looking forward to seeing Donald Gordon again."

"I have very mixed emotions about it, dear," she softly admitted. "I loved Donald very much at one time, but I betrayed him and I don't know how he will react to my presence."

Maura shrugged her shoulders. "Don't worry about it, Mother. We won't be there that long. As soon as the Campbells learn we are being held by the MacLaren, they will come for us."

"Yes, that is something else that concerns me," Anne sighed. "I cannot stand the thought of blood being shed over us—not again."

"What do you mean, not again?"

Anne shook her head. "'Tis nothing, dear. I am just an

25

old woman voicing my rambling thoughts," she sighed. "Do you know, I am thoroughly enjoying myself. The MacLarens are good company, don't you think?"

Maura laughed bitterly. "You are not riding with Alexander MacLaren. He is an obnoxious, arrogant outlaw."

"But he is all man," Anne pointed out. "The Scots are so very different from the pompous gentlemen at court."

"I already know your weakness for Highlanders, Mother, but I prefer a man with manners who knows how to treat a lady."

"You do not have to pretend with me, Maura. I know how you felt about the dandies at court."

Maura sighed. "I am a Scotswoman, Mother, I've never denied that. And while I found most of the Englishmen at court boring, I certainly prefer them over the obnoxious, overbearing, rude manner of the MacLaren."

Anne laughed softly, thinking her daughter was objecting excessively. "He would be a handsome man if not for the scar," Anne mused. "I wonder when it happened."

Maura pushed a stick into the fire, stirring the embers. "He is still a handsome man," she reluctantly admitted. "I think the scar adds character to his face. He was probably too handsome before."

Anne Campbell smiled, but said nothing as Alexander and Colin returned with two fat partridges.

"I hope you have a good appetite, ladies," Alexander said as he tossed the birds to his brother. "You'll not find anyone who can roast a bird to the proper turn as Simon can."

"I am ravenous," Anne Campbell said enthusiastically. "But I insist on helping. I've been known to clean a bird or two."

Maura was starving too, but she said nothing as her mother joined Simon in cleaning the birds. The fire was slowly driving the chill from her bones and she felt content and relaxed. She hadn't slept since the night before the MacLaren appeared in her life. Even when she had had the chance, sleep wouldn't come. Taking the opportunity while everything was quiet, she lay back and closed her eyes, giving into the exhaustion that had threatened to overwhelm her since their flight from Cromwell's clutches.

Alexander glanced towards Maura and noticed she had fallen to sleep. He tossed a few more logs on the fire before placing his cloak over her. She opened her eyes as he leaned over her and stared at him for a long moment before burying deep into his heavy cloak.

She had stubborn, unyielding pride, he thought with a smile. He liked that. Since his face had been slashed most women were either afraid of him, or drawn to him for the violence they sought in their bed, but not this one. She wasn't even afraid of the MacLaren name or the fear it usually caused in people. He had heard rumors that mothers frightened their bairns with the threat of the black MacLaren if they did not behave themselves, yet this woman stood her ground and dared him to do his worst.

"We've driven them hard," Colin said at his shoulder. "Poor lass must be exhausted."

"Aye. I must admit, they have done better than I imagined they would."

Colin laughed. "I have a feeling the lass would die before letting you get the best of her."

"It must be her Gordon blood," Alexander commented

as he continued to stare at the beauty in sleep.

"Donald will be wanting a husband for her," Colin said gravely.

Alexander looked at his brother. "Are you thinking of offering for her, lad?"

"I may be. She is lovely to look at."

Alexander laughed. "It takes more than beauty to make a good wife, my brother. Remember, she is a Campbell. Besides that, I am not sure this lass would settle for our rude Highland ways after being at court all her life."

"Her mother tells me she hated being at court and has always longed to be back in Scotland."

"Really?" Alexander said, surprise in his voice. Suddenly he stood up. "She must have forgotten the hardships we face everyday."

"She is strong, Alex."

"Aye, she is, but she is also headstrong and stubborn. Think carefully before you make a decision, Colin. I dinna envy any man trying to tame this one."

There's a magical tie to the land
  of our home,
Which the heart cannot break,
  though the footsteps may roam.
                    Eliza Cook

Chapter Three

Never before had she sat by a campfire with no roof but the sky, yet feel so content and at one with the world. With her legs crossed beneath her and her face smeared with the delectable juices of the roasted bird, she felt like a sprite of nature, and at the moment could care less about her appearance.

She reached eagerly for another piece of meat that Simon offered on the end of his dirk. It was oddly exciting to be there with three fierce Highlanders, sharing their food and drink like the closest friends.

"You look like you have been doing this all your life, lass," Simon commented.

Maura smiled at him. "No, this is my first time, but it will not be my last. I've never tasted anything so delicious. My compliments to the chef."

"Thank you, m'lady," Simon bowed.

Alexander found he was unable to keep his eyes off the girl. She looked like a wild creature, her black hair tumbling about her shoulders and her violet eyes alive with the adventure of the moment. She would make some

29

man a good wife, he thought. She was spirited, and there was passion hidden in those eyes.

"Some more wine?" Colin offered Maura.

"Yes, please," she said, holding out her cup.

She glanced across the fire and met Alexander's dark eyes. He kept staring at her, an unreadable expression on his face. She watched the muscle twitch in his jaw and wondered why he seemed annoyed with her. They hadn't spoken two words since they had started eating.

Forcing her attention back to the two attentive brothers, she asked, "How is it that you look so different from your brothers, Colin?"

"My yellow hair comes from Father's side of the family," he answered, "and Alexander and Simon have our mother's dark looks. I suppose it keeps their memories alive when we look at each other."

"They are both dead?" Maura asked, surprise in her voice.

"Aye, our father died from the fever, and our mother was killed in a raid by the—" Suddenly he looked embarrassed. "She was killed in a raid," he finished abruptly.

Maura saw the dark expression on Alexander's face, and knew without a doubt what Colin had been about to say. "She was killed by Campbells." She finished his sentence for him.

"Aye," Alexander said coldly. "Our mother and sister were killed by Campbells."

"I am sorry, but many Campbells have lost their lives to MacLarens in senseless feuds also," she defended.

"Let us not speak of feuds," Anne Campbell quickly broke in. "Why not just remember that we are all Scots, and at the moment have one common enemy: Cromwell."

Maura nodded her head, not wanting to ruin the beautiful peace she was feeling. At the moment feuds and Cromwell seemed to be figments of another time. Here at this moment the sky was blue and she could hear water trickling over the rocks of a stream. No, this was a place of peace, not feuds, she thought with a sigh.

She was aware that Alexander was still staring at her, but she turned her attention to Colin. "How much farther to Rockhenge?"

"Are you so anxious to be done with the company of MacLarens?" he asked with a charming grin.

"I did not say that."

"Well, dinna worry, lass, it's no more than another day's ride. Isn't that right, Alex?"

"Aye. You should have your reunion with your father by nightfall tomorrow, but it will not be at Rockhenge. Your father and cousin are staying at Dunraven. I thought it would be safer to have them there where my men can protect them. Cromwell will be certain to send his men to Rockhenge to look for you."

Maura paled, remembering how much danger they were all in if Cromwell did find them. "I do not look forward to meeting this stranger who calls himself my father, but I look forward even less to being held prisoner at the MacLaren stronghold."

"Has Donald ever remarried?" Anne asked before Maura could say more to aggravate the already ill-humored MacLaren.

"No," Alexander answered. "His sister Mary and her daughter Glenna have lived with him for the past ten years. Mary died last year, but the girl stayed on. She has been a help to Donald since he has been sick."

"I am glad he has had someone," Anne said softly.

"Glenna sounds like she was a Godsend to Donald."

"Aye, she was," Simon answered. "She is a bonny lass, and I hope to convince her to marry me."

"Dinna believe a word he says," Colin laughed, giving his brother an affectionate jab. "Alexander has promised him Fraoch Donaoch as a wedding present when he does get married, so he is looking for anyone that will have him."

Maura sat silently, thinking about her own future. She knew she would have been miserable if she'd married Lord Randolph, but would she ever marry now? She wouldn't even have to love the man, but he would have to be good to her, and give her children to love.

Simon's deep voice interrupted her musings. "Tell me, lass, did you see the King before he was executed?"

"The last time I saw him was in June when I accompanied his younger children to Hampton Court to visit him. We were staying at St. James Palace with the earl of Northumberland, so we were allowed to visit him often. He seemed in good spirits at that time, but I do not think anyone ever believed he would be executed. He was even allowed to hunt and play tennis while at Hampton Court. It was all very civilized, and he seemed in good spirits. Later, of course, his treatment worsened, but at the time I think he believed he would be back on the throne soon."

"Is Hampton Court where you first met Cromwell?" Alexander asked.

"No. I met him earlier at Maidenhead when the King was being held there. At that time he seemed polite enough, but so tense and nervous."

"Huh," Alexander snorted, "if you had the devil on your back you'd be tense too."

"It was strange," Maura mused. "Cromwell seemed to know all about my family and connections in Scotland."

"Why is that strange?" the MacLaren asked. "'Tis how the man has gotten where he is. He arranged your marriage to Randolph, knowing full well who your father was and that he was on his deathbed. If you were married to Randolph, whom do you think would take over Gordon lands when your father dies?"

"God's blood, I never considered that," Maura said in amazement.

"Your Lord Randolph did," he said caustically.

"You said the King's treatment deteriorated," Simon interrupted. "What do you know of that?"

It was cathartic to finally talk about it, and Maura willingly spoke. "At first I was kept well informed by the earl of Northumberland. The King was certain things would right themselves if he were patient, but it was not to be. When he realized this, he also realized his life was in danger. That was when he escaped to the Isle of Wight. A few days later Cromwell sent for me and informed me I was going to be given the honor of marrying Lord Randolph. I was removed from St. James Palace and taken to Buckwell Castle where Cromwell was staying with his aides. After that my only news of the King came from the servants. I heard he was taken by the army to Hurst Castle. Rumor was that it was a terrible, forbidding place with cold damp rooms and noxious marsh air seeping in everywhere." Maura sighed deeply. "They say he was resigned to his fate, poor man, but I doubt it."

"That is more than I can say for Maura," Anne Campbell interrupted. "We tried three times to escape."

For some strange reason Alex was relieved to hear that Maura had not willingly gone to slaughter like a lamb.

"How did you try to escape, lass?" Colin asked.

"Twice under cover of darkness we tried to flee, but there were always too many guards on the grounds. I befriended one of them and thought he would help, but at the last minute he changed his mind. We nearly made it several days before the wedding was to take place. The earl of Northumberland sent over two of his finest race horses as a wedding gift, knowing what I planned. Cromwell knew that I liked to ride everyday and fortunately did not bother to inspect the horses that were sent. We would have made it to freedom if Lord Randolph had not decided that he would join us on the day we had planned to flee. I knew then escape was not to be."

"That is until you arrived," Anne Campbell said with admiration in her voice. "Maura and I are so grateful to be away from England."

"Glad to be of service, m'lady," Colin said, bowing before Anne Campbell.

Maura tossed a stick into the fire. "Yes, I suppose we are better off with a rabble of thieving MacLarens than with murderous Englishmen."

"Maura!" her mother gasped.

"Your gratitude is overwhelming, m'lady," Alexander sneered, "but keep in mind 'tis not too late to leave you in these rugged mountains."

Maura glared at the MacLaren, her violet eyes sparkling. "Why not just take us to our Campbell relatives. I will see that you are well rewarded."

"With a knife across our throats." He laughed bitterly. "Besides, there is nothing a Campbell has that a MacLaren would want," he growled as he began to kick dirt onto the fire. "We need to be on our way. We have wasted enough time."

Maura stood up and brushed the dirt from her skirt. "I will ride with Colin now," she announced defiantly.

"You will ride with me," Alexander said coldly.

Maura stared at him, her hands on her hips. "I am sure my mother would enjoy a change of company as much as I would."

"This is not a social event, m'lady," he said sarcastically. "We are trying to save your worthless neck."

"I do not see what difference it makes if we change—"

Before she finished her sentence, Alexander picked her up and placed her firmly in the saddle before mounting behind her. "I warn you, m'lady, dinna push me too far," he growled, seeing the obstinate look on her face. "I want nothing but silence from you."

"Believe me, you will get nothing but silence from me," she spat, each word ringing with bitter fury. "Until I can think of another way to make your life miserable."

His mouth curved in a mocking smile. "You are doing a fine job of that without trying."

"You have seen nothing yet," she retorted. "When my Campbell relatives learn of my treatment at your hands, you will regret your rudeness."

"I am quaking in my boots," he said as he spurred his horse forward into the forest.

Maura turned swiftly around, hearing the amusement in his voice. "'Tis glad I am that you find this amusing. It does not surprise me since I find you totally lacking in manners and intelligence."

Alex only smiled and pulled her back closer to his hard body, his hand resting just below her breast. Maura gasped and tried to jerk forward. "Unhand me," she whispered, trying not to draw the attention of the others to her predicament.

Alex made no effort to move his hand, immensely enjoying teasing her. "Be careful, lass, 'tis a long way down if you fall. If that lovely neck is going to be broken, I would want the honors myself."

"Anything would be preferable to being pawed by you," she hissed.

"There are a lot of women who wouldna agree with you, lass," he said so closely his warm breath tickled her ear. "Most women beg for my favors. Perhaps you do too, but are afraid to admit it. Is that why you are trembling?"

She was infuriated at his smugness, his self-assurance that his touch had any effect on her. The trembling she was feeling was from anger and nothing else. "You are conceited and arrogant beyond belief," she said, giving him a look of disgust.

"Arrogant?" He laughed. "Lass, I dinna know the meaning of the word until I met you."

She lifted her chin defiantly, deciding it did her no good to have a war of words with this uneducated, uncouth barbarian. She would bide her time and bring him to task.

They rode hard all day, the way becoming steeper, choked with boulders and rock slides. The Scottish horses seemed not to mind and made their way without trouble.

Maura tried not to lean against her companion, but it could not be helped. She was tired and cold and her mood was bleak at the prospect of what faced her.

Presently the horses began to descend into a wooded glen. "We will stop for the night," the MacLaren announced, bringing his horse to a stop at the edge of a loch. He dismounted and held his hands up for Maura. "Can you come unstuck from the saddle, lass?"

Maura stretched her cramped legs and slid from the horse, reluctantly grasping his shoulders as her legs gave way.

"It was a hard ride," he said, offering her an excuse for her weakness. "I am sorry it has to be this way."

Suddenly she felt tears threaten and it puzzled her. Why should a word of comfort from this man affect her this way? Shrugging it off, she said, "I may never ride a horse again."

Alex offered a silver flask to her. "Take a good draught. It will ease the aches."

"What is it?"

"Usquabae," he answered. "In England you know it as whiskey."

"I know it as usquabae," she answered irritably. "You forget I am a Scotswoman." The fiery liquid burned her mouth and choked her. "Faith, what eases the pain of that?" she gasped.

Alex laughed as he led her towards a group of rocks. "I am glad to see you still have life in you. You have been so quiet for the past several hours that I thought your spirit had taken flight."

"Never, sir," she said scornfully, yet her heart wasn't into warring with him just now. She was cold, tired, and hungry.

As if reading her thoughts, Alex placed his cape around her shoulders and led her towards the fire Simon already had blazing. "I've never seen a lass so forlorn," he said amused. She glared at him, but said nothing. "Sit down, lass. We'll have some food soon. Lady Campbell," he nodded to her mother. "I trust Colin has seen to your needs."

Anne smiled, wrapping Colin's blanket around her shoulders. "He has been most considerate."

"Perhaps you and your daughter would like to take a brief walk to the edge of the woods," he said, knowing by now both women must be in need of some privacy. "Do not wander too far from the campsite."

"Will this trip ever be over?" Maura sighed as they walked towards the stand of trees.

"Colin said we will sleep here and travel on to Dunraven in the morning."

"Thank heavens for small favors," Maura mumbled. "I know you must be exhausted. I certainly am."

"Perhaps if you would stop expending all your energy fighting the MacLaren, you would not be exhausted."

"Not you too, Mother?"

"I do not understand why you act like you hate the man. He has done nothing to harm us. Quite the contrary, if it was not for him you would already be wed and have shared the marriage bed with that beastly man, Lord Randolph."

Maura stared after her mother as she walked farther into the woods, but she said nothing. She shivered as she imagined her wedding night with James Randolph.

Her mother's sobering words left Maura in a pensive mood the rest of the evening. After eating her fill of trout and barley bread, Maura sat close to the fire, wrapped in Alex's warm cape. It was difficult to feel anger with anyone, she decided, when she felt much like a contented cat. The wind had blown the fog away and the stars now shone bright in the night sky. It was a beautiful sight, one she had missed living in London for so long.

She glanced over at her mother, already asleep next to the fire. Colin and Simon were lying across the fire from her, both apparently already asleep. She watched Alex stack more wood, finding it difficult to take her eyes off the hard muscles that bulged in his thighs as he bent to place a log on the fire. He was certainly a fine specimen of manhood, she thought, feeling the heat rise to her face.

"Your mother is a remarkable woman," Alex said as he sat down beside her. "She adapts very well to hardship."

"Aye." Maura had to smile. "I believe she has actually enjoyed this odyssey."

"And you, lass?" he asked as he leaned back against a rock, propping his arm on one raised knee.

Maura met his gaze, prepared to give him a cutting retort, but then she saw the laughter in the depths of his dark eyes—those hypnotic, probing eyes framed by the longest black lashes she had ever seen on a man. "You know how I feel about the company I am in," she sighed.

"How could I not? You have certainly told me often enough how you feel about the MacLarens."

"Particularly one MacLaren," she pointed out.

"Ah, so now I am to be singled out. Tell me, lass, what have I done to make you hate me so? Have I harmed you in any way?"

"You know very well why I dislike you. You are the enemy to my clan."

He smiled at her. "'Tis strange. I thought since you had spent so much time in England that your clan loyalty would have diminished."

Maura traced a pattern in the dirt. If truth be known,

she had never felt any loyalty to the Campbells, but she would not tell the proud MacLaren that. "Your reputation is enough to make any woman quake," she said trying to think of some reason for her dislike of the man.

"Really, lass," he said, plainly amused. "Tell me what you have heard."

Maura settled back against the rock next to him. "For years I have heard stories of your evil ways. They say Dunraven is a vile place of carousing and wild orgies."

"Is that right?" he asked, a grin on his handsome face. "God's blood, dinna let my men hear you say that. They will think I am keeping the maids to myself."

"Is it only gossip then?"

"You will have to judge that for yourself, lass. We will be at Dunraven by sunset tomorrow. Is there anything else you have heard?"

"Aye . . ." she stared into the fire. "I have heard you force yourself on women, seducing them from all virtue and reason."

His laughter surprised her. "Give me time, lass. I will try my best to uphold my reputation."

Maura's cheeks flamed. "I have no desire to see you uphold your reputation. I was just telling you what I have heard about the black MacLaren."

"And informative it is. 'Tis no wonder you are afraid of me."

"I am not afraid of you," she quickly denied.

"I am glad to hear that. I hope never to bring you grief, lass. Now lie down beside me and sleep. We ride at dawn."

"Lie beside you?" she repeated, her eyes wide with disbelief.

"Aye." He had a devilish grin on his face. "Is it asking

too much to expect you to share my cape with me. You did say you were not afraid of me."

"Aye, I did say that," she answered, her heart hammering in her chest at the thought of lying beside this man. Slowly she moved to lie flat, offering him part of his heavy cape for a blanket.

"Sleep well, lass," he said, lying beside her.

Even though she was bone weary, she knew sleep would be impossible. She could feel his hard thighs touching her leg and his warm breath close to her temple. She held herself rigid, afraid to move or even breathe. The nearness of the man was wreaking havoc on her already shattered nerves.

"Relax, lass. I have no intention of ravishing you with your mother so near."

Maura swallowed. Did he mean he would ravish her if her mother were not near? With that troubling thought running through her mind, she finally gave into a troubled sleep.

The Prince of Darkness is a gentleman.
Shakespeare

Chapter Four

When the horses paused Maura stirred from her slumber against the MacLaren's chest. Her breath caught in her throat as she stared at the black stone castle across a deep gorge.

"Is that Dunraven?" she asked breathlessly.

"Aye. 'Tis not as foreboding as it looks."

"You read my thoughts," she whispered as she continued to stare at her surroundings, wondering if what she had heard about the place was true.

Castle Dunraven sat on a rocky precipice above the sea, its towering bulk rising sheer from the edge of the crags. The gorge before them circled the gray walls to join with the sea according the castle a battlemented island unto itself. The tide was high and the turbulent water surged and boiled through the jagged gorge. The castle towered against the sky like a vast thundercloud, bleak and stark, and the arched entrance seemed to scowl in defiance against anyone who would dare approach.

The drawbridge creaked in protest as it was lowered to cross the gorge like a splinter across a river. Maura stiffened as the stallion's hoofs struck each wooden plank with a heavy clatter.

"You tremble, lass. Dinna tell me the brave Lady Campbell is afraid of something."

"Please, just pay attention to where we are going. One false step from this black beast and we could plunge to our death."

Alexander threw back his dark head and laughed. "Dubh Sith has crossed this drawbridge a million times, lass. Have no fear of his surefootedness."

"Dubh Sith," she repeated. "Doesn't that mean 'black fairy' in Gaelic?"

"Aye, 'tis true, so you see we could fly if we had to," he teased.

The stallion entered the courtyard with a last spirited dance to prove his mettle.

Maura looked about curiously. They were in a large cobblestone area surrounded by an assortment of stables, kitchens, and various household buildings. Now that they were inside the compound, it looked much like any other Scottish fortress. The only difference she noticed was the men in the courtyard; they all diligently worked at some chore. How strange, she thought, that no one gave into curiosity to stop and stare at them. The MacLaren probably has them all beaten daily, she thought in disgust.

Alexander lifted her unceremoniously from the saddle. A wave of intense weariness swept over her, momentarily making her dizzy. She breathed deeply, forcing herself not to give into the weakness.

"My mother will need my help," she said weakly, hoping the MacLaren did not notice her hesitation or her exhaustion.

"Colin will see to your mother. Come along, lass, we'll not eat you alive," he said as he stuffed his gloves into the wide cuff of his boots.

Maura lifted her chin, determined that he would not see her fearful anticipation. She was going to meet her father—to open old wounds. "I would think common courtesy would allow my mother and me a chance to clean up and rest before meeting anyone."

She saw the white flash of his grin before he pulled a fine linen square from inside his jacket. He grasped her chin and began to wipe her face as if she were a child.

"You do resemble a street urchin," he said cheerfully, "but I dinna think Donald will hold it against you."

She raised her arm and shoved aside his hand, but he only laughed as he pushed the huge, carved door open. Alexander took her by the hand and led her into the crowded great hall as Colin followed with her mother. Candles guttered fitfully in sconces along the wall as the chilly draft followed them into the great room. Maura glanced around at the men who all silently studied her.

"Lads, this is Donald's daughter, Lady Maura Campbell, and her mother, Lady Anne Campbell."

With as much gallantry as she'd experienced at court, they all stood and bowed in unison, punctilious to a fault.

She felt like a waif, her clothes torn and muddy, and her hair wet and tangled. Ignoring her disheveled state, she placed her hand on Alexander's proffered arm and gave the room a deep curtsy, determined the MacLaren's men would not see her exhaustion or fear.

"Donald has been in his room most of the day," one of the MacLaren's men informed him.

"'Tis just as well. I believe the ladies would like a chance to clean up and rest before visiting him."

Maura breathed a sigh of relief. At least she would not have to face Donald Gordon until she had a good night's sleep.

"Come ladies," Alexander said, leading them to the large table set on a dais. "I am sure you must be starved."

Servants rushed to set plates before them. Maura had thought she was too tired to eat, but the aroma of the food quickly changed her mind. They partook of smoked salmon and roasted venison. When she had eaten all she could and drank all the wine offered, she turned tired eyes up to the MacLaren. "Now if you would be so kind, sir, my mother and I would appreciate hot water and a bed on which to sleep."

Alexander motioned for a servant to come forward. "Mary, see that the ladies have everything they need. Are you finished preparing Lady Honora's room for Lady Campbell?"

"Yes, m'lord," the girl curtsied.

"Fine. You may put Lady Campbell's mother in the guest room near the tower."

"I do not wish to put anyone out of their room," Maura protested. "My mother and I would be happy to share a room."

"Dinna concern yourself, m'lady, we have an abundance of room at Dunraven."

They were led down a long corridor to another door before climbing a narrow winding staircase. They didn't stop until they were nearly as high as the battlements.

"Watch the last step there," Mary pointed out. " 'Tis higher than the others to trip you up if you are not welcome upstairs."

"I beg your pardon?" Maura said.

" 'Tis called the tripping step," Mary explained. "It

46

puts an attacker at a disadvantage, because he cannot run up these steps without tripping on the last one. It breaks your stride, you see."

"How very clever," Maura said, carefully stepping up the last step.

Finally the servant led them down another corridor that was lit by wall sconces. She opened the first door.

"This will be your room, m'lady," she said to Anne Campbell. "Rose will assist you with whatever you need," she said of the young woman who stood before the blazing fire in the room. "M'lady, if you will follow me your room is not far from here."

"Rest well, Mother," Maura kissed her cheek. "I'll see you in the morning."

Maura followed the young servant down the corridor. "Have you been with the MacLarens long, Mary?"

"Aye. My mother was servant to the late MacLaren, and Rose and I have trained all our lives to take her place."

"Is Rose your sister?"

"Aye, m'lady. She is a few years older than I, but not as bright so I was put in charge of the household."

"It must be a lot of work."

"Aye, it is. The MacLaren is admired and respected by all the Highlanders so there are always guests."

Maura forgot what she was about to say when Mary opened the door of her room. Someone had gone to a great deal of trouble to make the room warm and comfortable. The walls were covered with Flemish tapestries and the floor was covered with Turkish rugs. A fire blazed in the huge fireplace and before it a great wooden tub waited with steaming water.

"Whose room is this?" Maura asked, running her

hand over the gold velvet covering on the huge bed.

"It was Lady Honora MacLaren's room. She was mother to the laird and his brothers. The MacLaren does not usually allow it to be used, even though it is always kept cleaned and prepared at all times. When you arrived this evening he informed me that you were to be given this room since your mother would need the quarters we had prepared for you."

Why would he have done that? Maura wondered, as she ran her hand over the ornately carved chest at the foot of the bed. "'Tis a beautiful room."

"Aye, the finest in the castle," Mary agreed. "Come, m'lady, you must hurry before your water cools. Even the tapestries cannot keep the chill from penetrating these walls."

Maura quickly stripped out of her clothes and stepped into the steaming water. "Oh, this is heaven. I feel as if I am caked with dirt."

"Was it a difficult trip, m'lady?"

Maura sighed. "I suppose it could have been worse. At least the English soldiers did not catch up to us."

"The MacLaren's men feared he could not rescue you. There were many wagers made as to the outcome."

Maura smiled, doubting the MacLaren failed at anything he set his mind to.

"Would you like me to assist you, m'lady?"

"No, I'll be fine, Mary. I'm just going to soak here for a little while to ease my aching muscles."

"Fine. I'll go prepare you a cup of warm mead to help you sleep. I'll be back in a few minutes."

"Mary, there is one thing. My mother and I have only the clothes with which we arrived. Do you think anyone in the household would loan us a few items?"

48

"That is being taken care of while we speak, m'lady. A seamstress and her two assistants are working on dresses for you both and by morning should have something for you to wear. In the meantime there is a night smock for you to sleep in on the bed."

A little later, dressed in the soft wool sleeping gown, Maura slipped beneath the covers and stretched her feet into the depths of the enormous feather mattress that had been heated with warming pans. She wondered what Honora MacLaren had been like. Thank God the woman enjoyed a few luxuries unlike the usual spartan Scottish life. Even in the Campbell household the rooms were not as pleasant or luxurious as this one, expelling the rumors she had always heard about the MacLarens being uncivilized.

There was a soft knock at the door, startling Maura from her reverie. "Enter," she called.

"Mistress Campbell?" a young lady Maura had not seen before entered. "I am your cousin, Glenna Gordon. I am sorry I was not able to greet you earlier, but Donald has had a bad day and I have been constantly with him."

"I am sorry to hear that."

"I see Mary has taken care of all your needs."

"Aye, she has been very kind," Maura answered as she studied the young woman. She had red hair and blue eyes and was very lovely, she thought silently.

"You must have made quite an impression on Alexander. Guests are not usually allowed to use this room."

"I really don't know why I was given the honor, but it is a beautiful room, and I appreciate the MacLaren's hospitality while I am here."

"I understand your mother accompanied you."

49

"Aye, she did."

"I hope it willna overly upset Donald when he learns she is here."

"If it does than he should not have forced us to come here," Maura said shortly.

Glenna's blue eyes registered surprise before she spoke again. "I should let you sleep now. I know you must be exhausted."

"Aye, I am."

Glenna headed for the door, then turned back. "Your father is anxious to see you in the morning."

"Is he?"

"I hope all this excitement is not too much for him. Well, I will see you in the morning, Mistress Campbell. Sleep well under the MacLaren's protection."

Maura stared at the closed door. Why did she have the feeling they were adversaries? She sighed and blew out the candles. The firelight shadowed the room and flickered against the ceiling. She rubbed her hand over the throw, enjoying the luxurious feel of velvet after her rugged existence for the past several nights. Then she remembered why she was there. What would she say to her father? she wondered before drifting off to sleep.

Alexander paused outside of Donald Gordon's room, hesitant to bother him this late, but he had promised he would let him know as soon as they had arrived. Slowly he opened the door and found Donald sitting up in bed waiting for him.

"Come in, lad, come in. I heard horses in the courtyard a while back and knew you must have returned. What took you so long to come to me?"

Alexander laughed. " 'Tis sorry I am, my friend, but I had to see to our guests' comfort."

"What is she like, Alex?" he asked with excitement.

"She is a comely lass," Alex grinned, "but she is stubborn and has a temper to boot."

"Like her mother," Donald said as he reached beneath his pillow and brought out a flask. " 'Tis a sorry thing when a man has to hide his spirits. Would you join me in a drink?" When Alex shook his head no, Donald took a long drink. "Now tell me, what does she look like? Describe her to me."

Alex grinned. "She has hair black as a raven's wing, and eyes the color of the heather."

Donald's rugged face broke into a grin. "Sounds to me like she made quite an impression on you."

"I have to admit she has spirit. The trip was hard even for a man, but she stood up to it without complaint. She possesses a strength of will few men have."

" 'Tis her Gordon blood," Donald said proudly.

"Aye. I told her that a time or two."

Suddenly Donald became serious. "Do ye think they will come for her?"

"I am sure of it. I left a couple of men behind to report to me if they should make a move towards Scotland."

"Guard your back well, my friend. I would hate to be responsible for any more harm coming to the MacLarens."

"Dinna worry. It will take more than Cromwell or Randolph to bring down a MacLaren."

Donald knew the MacLaren too well not to perceive the serious resolve underlying his arrogant manner. Alexander was as hotheaded and impetuous as any Scot, but he was wise enough to temper it with iron nerves and a cool wit that had no equal in the Highlands.

"There is something else, Donald," Alex said hesitantly, not knowing how his friend would react.

"What is it, lad? Is something wrong with Maura?"

"Your daughter was not brought here alone. Her mother is with her."

"Anne is here?" he asked in disbelief. Slowly a smile spread over his face. "Anne is really here at Dunraven?"

"Aye. She is in the tower guest room. She was with the lass when I found her. Your daughter refused to accompany me without her."

"I dinna realize Anne would be with her," Donald said, staring into space.

"Is it a problem her being here?" Alex asked.

"No. As a matter of fact I am pleased. Very pleased. Tell me, Alex, did they come willingly?"

Alex threw back his head and laughed. "If you mean did I have to tie them in the saddle, no. To be honest, your daughter was the only one who objected to coming here, and I am not sure if her objection was to being escorted by a MacLaren, or having to face her father."

"Perhaps she had heard of your black reputation," Donald suggested with a twinkle in his eyes.

"Aye, that she had, and then some," Alex said, coming to his feet. "You are going to have a big day tomorrow, my friend, so I will let you get some rest now."

"Thank you, Alex. Thank you for everything."

Alex grinned. "You best hold off on your thanks, my friend. I fear by this time tomorrow you may be cursing me."

If you want to understand others,
Look into your own heart.
J. Christoph Friedrich von Schiller

Chapter Five

Maura stood before the fire in the great hall, thinking of the meeting she would have with her father within the hour. She had hoped for her mother's company, but Anne had not felt well and was going to stay in bed until later.

At least she had something to wear besides the bedraggled clothes she'd arrived in, Maura thought, running her hand over the gray velvet of her morning dress. When she had awakened, Mary had arrived with two beautiful dresses for her to choose from, both made by the talented seamstress and her helpers while she slept. She certainly couldn't fault the MacLaren's generosity or hospitality. The treatment of her mother and herself was impeccable.

She picked up one of the many books lining the wall. Was it possible she had been wrong about the MacLaren being uneducated? she wondered. Maura jumped as Alexander spoke behind her.

"Is this the same lass who only yesterday looked as if she'd bathed in mud?"

"Please do not remind me," she said feeling her cheeks grow warm from the way his gray eyes were openly appraising her. "I thank you for your hospitality."

He smiled lazily at her. "I expected to find you abed for a week after our ride."

"Then you have learned nothing about me," she said defensively.

He laughed at that, in high good humor. "Sheath your claws, lass. 'Tis true we got off to a bad start and we have years of hatred bred between us, but since you are going to be my guest for awhile, why don't we try to get along."

When he laughed the terrible scar on his face was no longer villainous. As a matter of fact, it had a devastating effect on her and she had to turn back to the fire to cover her confusion. "I canna imagine a MacLaren offering a Campbell peace."

"I said nothing of peace. Only a temporary truce."

"Either way, I find it difficult. I dislike being held against my will."

"There are no bars or chains keeping you here, lass. Why not enjoy my hospitality. It has to be better than what you had in England. If in a few weeks you are still unhappy, I'll see that you are taken to your Campbell relatives. Is that fair enough?"

Maura turned around to face him, unable to hide the surprise in her eyes. "Do I have your word?" she asked hopefully.

"Aye, you have my word."

"Good morning," Colin greeted as he entered the room. He bowed gallantly before Maura. "May I say you look lovely this morning, Mistress Campbell."

She gave him a small curtsy. "Thank you, kind sir."

Alexander listened to the easy banter between them and silently cursed his brother for his poor timing. They had been on the brink of a new relationship.

"Have you seen Donald yet?" Colin asked.

"I was about to take her to his room," Alexander said before Maura could answer.

Maura glanced around her as fear suddenly seized her. She had the urge to run, but she could not make her feet move.

Alexander took her by the arm. "Shall we, lass?"

"I . . . I need to freshen up." She cursed her voice for giving away her apprehension.

"You could not look lovelier," he said as he led her towards the door.

Maura had been prepared to hate her father, but when she saw the frail man lying in bed, his eyes filled with tears as he stared at her, she could not be cruel.

"You must not tire Donald," Glenna said as she closed the book she had been reading.

"Nonsense," her father exclaimed. "There is no way my daughter could do anything but improve my condition."

"Glenna, let us leave them alone to get acquainted," Alexander suggested.

The young woman looked about to protest, but she passed through the door Alexander held open.

"You have your mother's eyes," Donald said in a broken voice when they were alone. She could only nod, her emotions so close to the surface. "But your dark hair comes from the Gordon side of the family."

"So my mother has told me," she said, finally finding

her voice.

"I had always hoped when we met it would be on different terms. That I would be strong and well, but it is not to be," he said, tears brimming in his eyes. "You are most kind to come to a sick old man's bedside."

"You do not look that old to me."

He forced a smile. "Aye, maybe not in years, but sickness has a way of making the body old."

Maura sat in the chair next to the bed. "What is this illness that incapacitates you?"

"It is in my bones. There are days I am in fair shape, but then other days I cannot even walk and I just lie here and waste away. The men of medicine who have come say they know of no cure," he said, his face lined with pain.

Maura felt tears come to her own eyes, realizing how much her father must be suffering. "Mother has a way with medicines from the earth. Perhaps she can help you."

He smiled. "Aye, I remember your mother's gift. She is a remarkable woman and I have missed her."

Maura's eyes widened in surprise. "She was certain you would not want to see her."

"I am sorry she thought that. I knew your mother left me thinking it was to protect me. The Campbells had killed more than twenty of my men and a dozen of the MacLaren clan trying to get to you and your mother. Anne had a vision that the only way to stop the bloodshed was to return to her clan. We discussed it for days, and I thought I had convinced her not to leave me, that with the MacLaren help we could hold off the Campbells, but late the next night she bundled you up and left Rockhenge."

"I am so sorry," Maura whispered. "We should have

been together."

"Aye, lass, we should have been. In the beginning I tried to contact your mother, but it was useless. Years later when you went to court, I was able to keep track of what was happening to you, but by that time, I decided it was better for all concerned that I stay out of your life. I always feared your mother would marry, since we were only handfasted, but I understand she never did."

Maura took her father's hand. "I always wondered why my mother was never interested in the many suitors she had. She must still be in love with you."

"That is very kind of you to say, my dear, but when she sees what I have become, I fear she will only pity me."

"Mother is not like that. She is the most understanding, compassionate woman I have ever known." Maura sighed deeply. "I just wish she had not fled from you. All these years I thought you cared nothing for us. I swore I never wanted to see you."

"You had no way of knowing what had really happened, and I know your mother would never have let you know the sacrifice she made."

"But she seldom spoke of you—"

"She could hardly take the chance that you would want to come to me. It would have all started again—the fighting and bloodshed."

"Why is it different now?"

"There was no other choice. I couldna let you marry Cromwell's henchman. We can only hope they will not realize where you are until we have things settled here."

"What things do you speak of?"

"'Tis nothing for you to be concerned about, my dear. Now tell me, what did you think of Alexander?"

"Ha!" she snorted. "I will not forget the treatment I

received at his hands. He was rude, obstinate, and hard-headed from the first."

Donald laughed, the harsh lines of his face softening. "'Tis strange, I believe those were his exact words about you. Although he did say you were a comely lass."

"Did he?" Maura had to smile.

"Alexander may seem obstinate and hardheaded, but he is as fine a man as you could ever hope to meet. He has qualities which mark him off from other men."

"If you say so. Now tell me about my cousin Glenna," she said, changing the subject. "I met her only briefly last night. I understand she and Simon will marry."

A concerned look came over her father's face. "If she does not let her greed ruin her chances. I fear she has set her sights on bigger fish. Glenna has not had an easy life, and unfortunately it has made her very ambitious."

"Are you saying she has her sights set on Alexander?"

"Aye."

"But Simon said he hoped to marry her."

"It is Simon who is smitten by her, even when she gives all her attention to Alexander. I dinna know why the poor lad puts up with it."

Maura shook her head. "I cannot imagine why she would prefer Alexander over Simon. He is so . . . so intense and moody."

"Alexander needs a loving woman to soften his sharp edges," her father explained with a smile.

"Well, I do not envy that woman," Maura said lightly, but she felt an odd catch in her heart.

"There are a lot of them interested in taking on the job, but Alexander has spent a lifetime distancing himself from pain and loneliness. I am not sure he could ever become close enough to anyone to really love them, or to chance being hurt."

"Why is that?" Maura asked, suddenly interested in the MacLaren.

"His father died when he was fourteen, making him the laird of the clan. With it came the responsibility of a thousand or more people. He had been taught to fight before he could walk, as most Highlanders have, so he wasn't totally unprepared for the responsibility. His mother, Honora idolized Alexander, and she tried to keep things on an even keel for him, not wanting him to be just a warrior. She saw that all her sons were educated in France, and exposed to fine music and the arts."

"And then she was killed by the Campbells," Maura sighed, feeling her heart break as she thought of the pride Honora must have had in her sons.

"Aye, she and his only sister. It was a terrible thing. The fighting had stopped for awhile and we thought the Campbells had given up trying to get your mother and you back. We should have known better. I was hunting with the MacLarens, trying to restock the larders that had become bare from the seige. There were at least a dozen men left behind, but they did not stand a chance." Donald sighed before continuing. "All the men were killed, and then Honora and her daughter were tortured and raped before being thrown from the parapets."

"Oh God," Maura moaned, closing her eyes against the terrible scene her father described. "No wonder he hates the Campbells."

"He was barely seventeen when this tragedy happened. Hate kept him going until he finally had his chance for vengeance. The MacLaren killed Angus Campbell, the man who had led the murdering butchers to Dunraven, and twenty of his men. Alexander lost a half a dozen or

59

more of his own men, and suffered a near fatal knife wound to his side. That was also when his face was scarred."

"I believe the soul is scarred more than the face," Maura said softly.

"Aye, you are very perceptive."

"Has he never married?" Maura asked. "I always thought the laird of a clan felt heirs were so important."

"Alexander has always lived his life in peril and danger, and I fear he thinks falling in love would be a fatal emotion. Perhaps he believes if another person whom he loves depends on him, that he won't be able to keep them from harm. I just dinna know," he sighed.

"I am glad you told me this. It gives me a little insight into the man," she said sadly.

"All this talking has given me a terrible thirst," Donald said. "Would you pour us a cup of tea?"

"Of course," Maura agreed, moving to the table where the tea warmer sat. "I did not mean to wear you out with my questions."

"Nonsense. You dinna wear me out, lass. I ha' not felt this good in a long time. I believe I will join you for the evening meal later. That way I willna look like an invalid when I see your mother."

Maura smiled. "I know she was exhausted from the trip, but I really think she was afraid to face you today and that is why she has stayed in her room."

"Do you think she will take her meal with the MacLarens this evening?"

Maura smiled. "I will see to it that she does. Now I should leave you to rest so you will be up to tonight's excitement."

Her father laughed. "I am too excited to rest, but I

60

will try."

Donald Gordon leaned his head back against the pillow and smiled. It was a beginning, he thought, very pleased with himself. If she understood Alex, maybe, just maybe he would have a union between the two people he cared most about in the world—and if Maura were married to the MacLaren, Cromwell would not dare try to take her back to England.

Maura wandered down several corridors before finding the room her mother had been given. She tapped on the door, then entered to find Anne staring out the window.

"Are you feeling better, Mother?"

"Aye, much better, dear." Her mother came back to a chair before the fire. "Come, sit with me."

"Of course," Maura said taking the chair across from her mother. "The room is quite beautiful. The MacLaren clan must be very prosperous."

"Aye, it is very comfortable," her mother agreed, preoccupied. "Maura, have you seen your father yet?"

"Aye," she smiled. "And you can relax, Mother. He is looking forward to seeing you."

Anne's eyes widened in disbelief. "Did he actually say that?"

"Aye, that and much more," Maura assured. "He told me you left him to stop the bloodshed between the Gordon and Campbell clans."

Anne stared into the fire. "It was a painful sacrifice I am not sure I could make again. I loved your father very much."

Maura knelt in front of her mother and took her hand. "From what Father said, he loved you very much too. Do

61

you know he has kept track of us all these years?"

Tears came to Anne's eyes. "I had no idea. I was so sure he hated me for taking you away."

"He cannot wait to see you, Mother. As a matter of fact, he plans to leave his sickbed this evening so he can join us in the dining hall."

"Is he well enough to do that?" Anne asked with concern.

"I doubt it, but he insisted. Mother, maybe you can help him with some of your healing remedies. He said the pain was in the bones and ofttimes he cannot walk at all. It was a terrible thing to see, a man who must have been so strong now as weak as a kitten."

"Perhaps bracken root and fever moss would help, but it would have to be given with great care. Some people have been known to have a violent reaction to it. Donald would have to decide if he wanted to chance it. It could make him worse."

"If he would agree, would you try it, Mother? It is so sad to see him in pain and bedridden."

Anne patted Maura's hand. "Do not get your hopes up, my dear. As Alexander told us, the men of medicine do not give your father long to live."

"Perhaps he has not had anything to live for."

"Now you're letting your imagination run away with you. I am glad your father holds no hatred for me, but do not dream the impossible, Maura. Now tell me, did you meet your cousin Glenna?"

"Aye, for a few minutes last night."

"What did you think of her?"

Maura shrugged her shoulders. "She seemed nice enough, but I had the distinct feeling she resented me."

"I would not be surprised. Her mother never approved

of my relationship with Donald. She enjoyed making my life miserable the whole time I was at Rockhenge."

"Mother, there is something I wondered about. Why did you settle for handfasting instead of marriage?"

"It is as legal as marriage," Anne answered.

"Aye, I know, but is that why you never married? Because you had—"

"I never married because I always loved your father," Anne cut off Maura's thoughts.

"He will be pleased to hear that." Maura smiled mischievously. "Oh, I see our seamstress has been busy for you also," she exclaimed, picking up one of the velvet gowns lying across Anne's bed. "I discovered two gowns in my room this morning when I woke."

"The MacLarens have always been known for their capable staff."

"Tell me, Mother, did you ever meet Alexander's mother?"

Anne was silent for a long moment. "Aye, I met her several times. She was a very beautiful, intelligent woman. Alexander and Simon get their striking good looks from her."

"Do you know how she died?"

"Maura, I'd rather not talk about this—"

"I already know most of it, Mother. I know it was Campbells who killed her and her daughter."

Anne sighed deeply. "Did your father also tell you why it happened?"

Maura shrugged. "I assumed it was because the Campbells and MacLarens have always feuded."

"It is true, their clans have always feuded, but this time it was because the MacLaren clan stood with the Gordon clan when the Campbells came to get us."

"Oh, Mother, I did not know. My God, how he must hate us, yet still he came to our rescue."

Her mother paced before the fireplace. "Now you know why I had to leave Donald. I had to try to stop the bloodshed, but I should have known it would continue. The MacLarens had to have their vengeance. Apparently that is when Alexander's face was scarred. I knew they had sought vengeance, but I never knew the outcome other than Angus Campbell was killed."

"Aye, Father told me Alexander was nearly killed."

"Angus Campbell was a butcher and a disgrace to the human race. He got what he deserved. If only I had been able to stop them. If I had seen it before time . . . ."

"Do you mean a premonition?"

Anne turned to face her daughter, tears in her eyes. "Yes, I had one, but not until it was already happening," she admitted softly. "I could hear their screams, Maura. It was terrible," she said rubbing her temples. "Donald was hunting with the MacLarens. The few clansmen that were left behind rode with me when I told them I knew Honora MacLaren was in trouble." Anne twisted her hands, the scene playing vividly over in her mind. "It was too late. We found their terribly mutilated bodies."

"Oh, Mother, that had to be so terrible for you," Maura exclaimed, holding her mother in her arms.

"It was terrible, but the real horror was when Alexander returned. He nearly went mad with his grief."

"Did he blame you?"

"No. I wish he had, because I blamed myself. Honora and her daughter would not have been killed if I had not defied my family by handfasting with Donald. Instead Alexander blamed himself for leaving them, and he still carries that guilt with him. That is why I did not feel it

64

wise to return here, even though we needed help." Anne choked back a sob. "If the bloodshed starts again . . ."

Maura led her mother to a chair. "It won't. We won't let it happen. If the English or Campbells come here I'll go with them. There does not need to be bloodshed this time."

"I hope you are right, Maura, but I pray they do not come."

The light that lies in woman's eyes,
Has been my heart's undoing.
                              Thomas Moore

Chapter Six

Anne and Donald had a tearful reunion, then sat at the table talking quietly to each other, leaving Maura to be entertained by Colin and Simon. Alexander sat across from her at the center of the trestle table, with Glenna on his left.

Maura tried to keep her eyes off the MacLarens, but she ruminated over her father's information about Glenna having set her sights on Alexander instead of on Simon. She couldn't help notice that Alexander did not seem overly interested in the young woman, even though she fawned all over him. Maura noticed the bleak expression on Simon's face, and she felt a great sympathy for him. Even though he pretended to be deeply engrossed in their conversation, his dark eyes kept going to Alexander and Glenna.

Maura met Alexander's gray eyes and his inscrutable expression. She glared at him, letting him know just how she felt about his dalliance with his brother's intended, then turned her back to him to speak more intimately with Colin.

"I thought Glenna was Simon's intended," she said softly.

"Aye. Glenna is a fool if she thinks Alexander is interested in her. Alexander will never marry her or anyone else. He is married to his clan. She is going to make a fool of Simon once too often and he will finally realize she is not worth his time."

"You do not care for Glenna?"

"She is too greedy."

"But I thought you were all excited about Simon getting married."

"Aye, but not necessarily to Glenna."

Maura glanced back at Alexander and found his eyes still on her. He looked about to speak when one of his men slapped him on the back and loudly began a story that had everyone's attention.

Maura rested her head against the velvet headrest of her chair and toyed with her goblet of wine. It was good to be among the proud Gaels again, she reflected. There was no formality among men here. A man's pride in his race stood him in the most noble company and gave him the air of a gentleman, no matter what his rank of birth. Even the groom called the laird Alexander, apparently considering him a father figure, as did most of his clan. Respect was given him, but love as well, she thought. She had to admit, she was glad to be away from England where pride of name and self-respect were matters reserved for only a few.

She hadn't realized she was staring at Alexander until he spoke directly to her, breaking into her thoughts.

"I imagine you find us a barbaric people after your years in London."

"No, not at all," she said sincerely. "I was rather

enjoying the atmosphere."

"She is a Campbell," Glenna chimed in. "She has to be used to barbaric people."

Alexander glared at the young woman at his side. "She is also my guest and should be treated with respect."

Glenna laughed. "Surely you jest."

Maura stared at the young girl, surprised by her outburst. "I am no threat to you, Glenna. As a matter of fact, I am grateful to you for being kind to my father. So you see, there is no need for your rudeness. My mother and I will be out of your life as soon as it is safe to do so."

"That cannot be too soon," she mumbled. Seeing the dark look in Alexander's eyes, she decided not to pursue the subject. "I believe I'll check on Donald. I dinna want him tiring himself."

"I canna understand her," Maura commented when Glenna left them.

"She is dependent on Donald's kindness for her every need," he said bluntly.

"Are you saying she is only kind to him because he provides for her?"

"You are quick, lass."

"Yet you approve of a marriage between her and Simon?"

Alexander turned the silver goblet in his hand thoughtfully, making small circles on the linen cloths. "Sometimes the best way to dissuade a person from what he has set his mind to is to let him see first hand what that person is really like."

Maura smiled. "In other words, you are giving Glenna enough rope to hang herself."

Alexander returned her smile. "In a manner of speaking. Everyone but Simon sees Glenna for what she is: a calculating, deceiving slut who would share any man's bed that would have her."

Maura felt her face grow heated and she turned her gaze away from the MacLaren.

"Have I shocked you, lass?"

"I do not shock easily, m'lord," Maura said defensively. "But I wonder if you speak from experience with Glenna."

A slow grin spread over his handsome face. "There is only so much enticing a man can withstand, lass. Scottish lads are weaned to the sword and given the taste of battle before they can reach the stirrups, yet we are never taught how to resist a beautiful woman's seductive ways."

"Oh," Maura said, unable to cover her embarrassment. Because his steady gray eyes had not left her face, she said the first thing that came to mind. "I shall try to remember that when I am ready to take a man."

Alexander threw back his head and laughed. "Here I thought to shock you, and instead you are taking lessons from my words."

"Have you been teasing me then?"

"Would I do that?" He flashed her a smile that completely charmed her.

"I believe you would do anything that suits you," she said staring into his eyes.

"Aye, you are very perceptive, lass. I have never liked the confinement of rules or decrees."

Before Maura could reply, Colin interrupted. "Would you like to get a breath of fresh air, Maura?"

She was about to decline, but noticed Glenna heading back towards them. "Yes, I'd like that."

She did not miss the scowl on Alexander's face, but she

couldn't imagine why he would care if she went with Colin. Thinking he was worried about his youngest brother, she leaned towards him and whispered. "Do not worry, m'lord, I will not use my seductive wiles on Colin."

Before he had a chance to retort, she turned her back to him and accepted Colin's arm.

Alexander stared after them, a smile on his face, yet at the same time he had the urge to throttle his brother. The girl had the strangest effect on him, he thought silently before refilling his goblet.

They moved down the stairs to the courtyard. "We have an excellent stock of horseflesh if you would like to see them," Colin suggested.

"Yes . . . yes, that would be fine," she said, her thoughts still on her conversation with Alexander.

"You and Alex seemed to be enjoying yourselves. What were you talking about?"

"The evils of women," she said with a secret smile on her face.

"Well, I know Alex is an expert on that subject."

"Is he?" Maura asked, not sure she wanted to hear more about the MacLaren's virility.

"Aye. Whenever we go to France the ladies keep him occupied for days on end." He laughed. "And when we are here, all the well-meaning parents parade their daughters before him, each one thinking their lass will be the one to change Alex's mind about marriage."

So her father was right, she thought silently. What was it about the man? "Do you get to France often?" she asked.

A strange expression came over Colin's face, as if he had said something he shouldn't. "Occasionally. Have you been there?"

"Aye, with the Queen on one of her trips. It was very exciting."

"Here we are," Colin said, leading her into the stable.

The building smelled of horses, hay, and oiled leather, a smell that Maura had always loved. She had few fond memories growing up, but her experience with horses had been one of them. She passed a dozen or more fine horses, touching noses and speaking softly. "Where is Dubh Sith?" she asked Colin.

"He's kept in the back. He doesna take to strangers."

"I only want to see him," she said, heading towards the rear of the large stable. "He's such a splendid animal."

"Alex was the only one who could train him—or even wanted to after a couple of us were thrown. He was such a wild brute when we got him."

As they neared the great black stallion, he raised his head and moved uneasily. Colin spoke softly in Gaelic, stroking the velvet black nose. Maura lifted her skirt and climbed up on the crossbar of the stall to get closer.

"He is the most magnificent animal I've ever seen," she exclaimed softly. "All you have to do is look at him to know his ancestry and breeding."

"Aye, he is proud and scornful, as if he has never known the humiliating mastery of the bit and reins," Colin mused. "But then he doesna let anyone master him but Alex, and I think that is only because they are very much alike."

Maura leaned over the stall and gently touched Dubh Sith's nose. The horse nuzzled her hand. "He is not so fierce. I have been on some of the best horseflesh in

England, and I would wager even I could handle him. I believe your brother tells everyone this magnificent animal is too much for anyone else to handle just to make himself look good."

"Aye, I spend my waking hours training him to be more fierce and ill-bred than myself." Alexander's voice came from behind her, lazy and amused.

Maura didn't move. She wondered how long he had been standing behind her.

"I was just showing Lady Campbell our fine stock of horses," Colin explained, as he continued to stroke Dubh Sith's neck.

"Ah, yes, but you must be careful what you show Lady Campbell, lad. She may recognize some of our contraband."

Maura jumped from her perch and brushed her skirt off. "A horse thief," she said with distaste. "I should have known."

"But a discriminating one, would you not admit?" he said waving his hand to encompass the excellent stock. "We only steal the finest horseflesh."

"How discerning of you."

Alexander laughed. "I would love to stand here and bandy words with you all evening, lass, but your father is about to retire and wishes to say good night."

"Thank you." She curtsied. "I shall return then. Thank you for the tour, Colin. Perhaps we can continue it another time."

"It will be a pleasure, m'lady."

After saying good night to her mother and father, Maura decided she was too keyed up to retire, yet she did

73

not want to return to the great hall and chance running into the MacLaren again. She decided to do some exploring on her own, taking the tower stairs past her room up to the parapets. Even in the dark it was a breathtaking sight. She stared out across the moonlit mountains, the cold wind gusting her hair about her shoulders. Taking a deep breath, she tried to ease the tension she felt. What was it about Alexander MacLaren that kept her in a turmoil, she wondered. He hated her, yet he had a way of looking at her that made her blood turn to fire in her veins. Perhaps that was the way he affected all women, and why so many panted after him.

Suddenly she heard a woman's voice. Maura moved slowly towards the stairway she had come up, hoping to escape, but there were two people blocking her way. She froze when she heard part of the conversation.

"Come to me tonight, Alexander," Glenna was pleading. "I have missed you. I was bored to distraction while you were away."

"Were you," he said flatly.

Maura stood in the shadows and watched as Glenna wrapped her arms around Alexander's neck. She wanted to move away, yet she could not make her feet move. Besides, they stood just a few feet from the stairway.

"Why not find Simon, lass? You know how he feels about you."

"You are most ungallant, Alexander, to mention him when you know it is you that I want."

"I am flattered, but not interested," he said, removing her arms from around his neck.

"'Tis that Campbell woman!" Glenna said in disgust. "You have been cold to me since your return."

Alex stiffened when he heard a gasp from the shadows.

Then a smile came over his face. "She is a fair lass to look at, but not my type. She is a she-wolf with a temper to match."

Maura clenched her fist. The nerve of the man! If she dared show herself she'd give him a piece of her mind.

Glenna was not to be put off. Again she wrapped her arms about Alexander's neck and kissed him. "Leave me to some peace," he said in exasperation. He turned his back to her and looked out into the blackness. "I came up here to think."

"Will you come to me later, Alexander?"

"Perhaps."

"You willna regret it. I will take your mind off your troubles."

"I fear it will take more than a tumble with you to do that," he said coldly.

When Glenna finally disappeared down the tower stairs, Maura moved silently from her hiding place and headed for the stairway.

"'Tis very poor manners to hide in the shadows and eavesdrop on private conversations," he said without turning around.

Maura froze. He had known all along she was there. "Do not flatter yourself. Your conversation with your lover was certainly of no interest to me. I was already up here getting a breath of fresh air when you arrived. I wanted to leave you to your privacy, but you were blocking the staircase."

He turned around and smiled at her. "A likely story, lass."

She pulled her black cape around her with a haughty air. "You should be ashamed of yourself carrying on like that with the woman your brother is so fond of."

"I thought I had made myself clear on that matter, lass. Glenna will never marry a MacLaren."

"Ha," Maura snorted, unladylike. "So you think she is not fit to marry into your family because she is a Gordon."

MacLaren had to smile. "Her name has nothing to do with it. Glenna is not to be trusted, as you just saw. Honor and trust are important, particularly in a wife."

"Then you use her only for your . . . your unsavory lusts!" she stammered.

Alexander moved towards her. "Aye, I suppose you could say that, but I would not mind you taking her place if you'd like to volunteer. A woman to warm my bed is all I care about. It doesna matter her name."

"God's blood, but you are unbelievable," she gasped.

"Surely you must be accomplished at pleasing a man since you have been at Court for so long."

Maura knew she was in over her head with this conversation. No matter what he thought, she was not experienced at bantering with men about anything so intimate. "Do you delight in insulting me, m'lord?"

He bowed gallantly. "I find 'tis the only way I can meet you on even terms."

Maura turned from him and stared out into the darkness. It had begun to snow and her hair and cape were quickly covered with immense white flakes.

"I have a blazing fire in my quarters, and a fine French brandy. Would you not prefer that to the cold out here?"

"I fear you would find it even colder in your quarters, m'lord," she said sarcastically. "For you see, I am nothing like Glenna or your other bedwarmers."

He smiled as he brushed a snowflake from her eyelash. "I am pleased to hear that, lass."

Maura didn't know what to say to his confession, said in such a soft, caressing tone.

"Why should that please you?"

He shrugged his wide shoulders. "'Tis something I'm not sure of myself."

She turned from his probing look and stared out over the sea. "What lies beyond here?" she asked, hoping to change to safer ground.

"A million miles of cold water," he answered, as he leaned against the wall to stare at her.

She could hear the surf hammering at the rocky cliffs as the wind picked up. "In the darkness it seems like we are in a world separated from everything else."

"All is not as it seems. If you delved into the darkness you would find a break in the cliff to the south a short distance from here where there is a narrow cove. The only way to enter is to sail in at ebb tide."

"Why would anyone want to enter such a place?"

Alexander laughed. "'Tis a safe harbor if someone wanted to keep a ship there."

"Would that someone be you?"

"Are you asking for yourself, lass, or for your Campbell relatives?"

Maura gave him a level stare. "I am not a spy, if that is what you are implying."

"I will take your word for it," he said smiling. "My mother enjoyed delicacies only France could provide, so years ago Father started smuggling them in. My brothers and I have continued the tradition. More importantly, it gives us a means of escape if we should ever need it."

Maura noticed he hadn't said anything about being educated in France, but she didn't comment on the omission. "So you have a secret harbor," she said, staring into the darkness. "After seeing the terrain of Dunraven, I should not care to navigate a ship in so precarious a spot."

Alexander laughed. "That very reason keeps our enemies from discovering it."

Maura looked up into his eyes. "You live a very dangerous life, Alexander MacLaren: a smuggler, a horse thief, an enemy to Cromwell . . ."

"Dinna forget kidnapper of virtuous maidens," he added.

"Aye, that too. Are you not afraid of being hanged?"

"I do not fear death, lass. Besides, 'tis best to be hanged for a reason than for none at all."

Maura shivered, remembering the gibbets that had become a daily sight in England, with their pitiful burdens swaying grotesquely in the wind, a mute warning to all who would cross Oliver Cromwell.

"Why so silent, lass? Does the thought of my hanging appeal to you?" he asked lightly.

Maura met his dark eyes. "There is naught about hanging to jest about."

"Even if it is a MacLaren who hangs?"

"You are the one who hates with such a passion, Alexander MacLaren. I feel no hatred towards you or your clan."

"You did not give me that impression, lass. There were times I feared turning my back to you," he said with a glint of humor in his eyes.

Maura smiled. "'Tis a wise man who fears his enemies."

"Aye, I have been told that, but did we not just resolve that we are not enemies?" he said, wrapping a strand of her hair around his fingers.

The simple gesture made Maura tremble. "I should get

back inside and leave you to your rendezvous with Glenna. It would not be polite to keep her waiting."

Alexander laughed deep in his throat, then before she could guess his intentions, he pulled her towards him, his cape enclosing her in a warm cocoon against his body.

"You are wrong about me hating you, lass," he whispered before his lips descended on hers, warm against her cool skin. He brushed them lightly across her closed mouth, forcing her lips apart.

Alexander was aware of her lips softening involuntarily, and of the wild pounding of her heart—or was it his heart? His tongue plunged into the sweetness, exploring, savoring.

Innocent of the heated passion he was so skillfully arousing in her, she leaned into him. When he raised his head and smiled down at her, she felt completely confused. Her pulse was throbbing with an unsteady, erratic pace and she found it difficult to breathe properly.

"I had not intended that, even though I have wanted to since first seeing you."

Maura took a deep breath. "Do not ever try it again," she said, fighting for composure. "I am no strumpet for you to paw," she snapped before hurrying towards the staircase.

"Coward," he called after her with laughter in his voice.

Maura entered her room and slammed the door behind her. Why had she let him kiss her? she chastised herself as she threw her cape on the bed. My God, she had acted like a harlot. The man didn't have a shred of decency. One minute he was kissing his . . . his whore, or mistress, whatever Glenna was, and the next he thought he

79

could treat her the same way. She should have slapped him.

She touched her lips, still warm and tingling from his kiss. It wasn't the first time she had been kissed, but it was the first time a kiss had affected her that way. She still felt weak in the knees, and her hands trembled.

Moving to the bed, Maura undressed and slipped into the sleeping gown laid out for her. She snuggled down into the warm feather mattress, still thinking of Alexander MacLaren. Why couldn't she have met a man in England who made her feel weak in the knees with no more than a look?

She sighed softly and fell asleep, but it was a sleep disturbed by dreams. He was there with her, his warm, hard body covering hers, his gray eyes delving into her soul. The rumors she had heard about him were true; he could seduce innocent women of their virtue. He was a devil with strong powers, and if she were not careful he would possess her.

Alexander stretched out his long legs as he reclined in a chair before the fire sipping a brandy. He thought of the girl in the room next to his and felt a tightening in his loins. This is not smart, he silently warned himself. It would never work, no matter how desirable he found the girl. She was a Campbell and his many memories of the atrocities that the Campbells had committed against his family were all too vivid. He thought of his beautiful mother and sister.

Suddenly he came to his feet, throwing the glass into the fireplace. "Campbells! Gutless, bloodthirsty Campbells!" He could not let this Campbell with the guileless smile and violet eyes possess him. It would surely be his downfall.

The web of our life is of a mingled yarn,
Good and ill together.

                                    Shakespeare

Chapter Seven

Maura was still lying in bed when she heard a great clatter of horses in the courtyard. She jumped up and rushed to the narrow window. Leaning forward, she could see that it was Alexander and Simon and several of their men preparing to leave. Suddenly Alexander looked up towards her, and at the same time his stallion reared his forelegs dramatically in the air.

"What an arrogant man," she whispered in the silence of her room, yet still she had to smile. She had never met anyone quite like him.

"M'lady, you will catch your death there without a robe on," Mary exclaimed as she entered the room.

"I know," Maura said, rushing back to the bed, "but I was curious about the riders in the courtyard."

"'Twas the MacLaren and his men leaving for Ardven to see if there is any word from his messenger from England. 'Tis only a two-hour ride from here so they will return soon."

"Why didn't his messenger just come here?"

Mary looked at Maura, a puzzled expression on her

face. "I imagine 'tis to protect you, m'lady. I heard him say the longer the English are in the dark about your whereabouts, the safer you will be."

"Of course. I should have realized that," Maura sighed, feeling guilty again that her presence put everyone in danger.

"Your mother would like you to meet her in her room. I will serve you tea and scones there if 'tis agreeable with you," Mary said as she laid clothes on the bed for Maura.

"Thank you. That will be very agreeable," Maura said, picking up the beautiful blue gown lying on the bed. "Mary, could you tell me who has been making these beautiful clothes for me?" she asked as she slipped into the gown. "I would like to thank her personally. She is a jewel."

"Her name is Grizel, m'lady, and she and her helpers do most of their work in the tower room late at night when everyone is asleep."

"If you should see her would you tell her I would like to speak to her?"

"Of course, m'lady."

Maura found her mother agitated and nervously pacing her room. "When I left you last night you seemed so happy. What has upset you this morning?"

"Shortly after I was up Glenna stopped by to tell me she did not think I should see Donald today, that he was exhausted from yesterday. And here I had hoped to talk to him about trying some of my remedies."

"That woman has a lot of nerve," Maura fumed. "Come along with me, Mother. We'll talk to Father this morning. If he wants you to attend to him, then I'll go about the hillside and find whatever you need."

Maura tapped on her father's door, then entered. She

was ready to do battle with Glenna, but her cousin was nowhere in sight.

"I was hoping you'd come," Donald greeted. "I fear I was too active yesterday and now I am far too stiff to do much else but lie here."

Anne sat on the side of the bed. "I tried to see you earlier, but Glenna said you were too exhausted to have company today."

"I will have a talk with Glenna. You and Maura are family, and I will always see you."

"Thank you, Donald. I wanted to talk with you this morning about using some of my potions to help ease your pain."

"I'll try anything you suggest, Anne."

Anne smiled, pleased that he trusted her. "I need to explain the dangers. Some of these things are very strong and often have harsh side effects."

"Anne, look at me. Dinna you think I would take any chance to be able to live again?"

"Then we will start the treatment tomorrow. Maura will find me the bracken root and fever moss today, and I will prepare it this evening."

Donald took Anne's hand. "And perhaps by spring, I will be able to walk in the heather with you."

Maura smiled as she watched the tender scene between her parents. At least something good came of their flight from England, she thought.

"What are you doing in here? I told you Donald could not have company today," Glenna raged as she stormed into the room.

"Glenna, I appreciate your concern, but I want Anne and Maura to visit me anytime they wish."

"Do not be fooled by their false concern. They care

nothing for you, and are only here because they need your protection."

"Just a moment." Maura faced her cousin. "You are obviously not aware of all the circumstances that separated my family."

"I know your mother chose her Campbell relatives over Donald."

"Enough," Donald ordered. "Anne and Maura are my family and they are entitled to respect."

"But Donald, they are Campbells," Glenna continued to protest.

"No more, Glenna," he warned. "I willna have you speak to my family this way."

"I canna believe this," she spat as she headed for the door. "I hope you dinna regret this. For all you say they mean to you, they are still Campbells, and that means trouble for all of us."

"She is right, you know," Maura said sadly when Glenna left. "It would be better for all concerned if Mother and I went to the Campbells and begged for their protection. At least then you and the MacLarens would not be in danger because of us."

"I willna listen to such nonsense. You are my family. I have neglected my duties to you long enough. 'Tis time I am the one who protects you."

Maura kissed him on the cheek. "I hope we do not live to regret it, as Glenna warned."

Maura went in search of Colin, deciding it would probably be best if someone accompanied her to collect what her mother needed, but she was told Colin had been called to one of the crofter's cottages to settle a dispute. Instead of waiting for his return, she decided she had already wasted enough time, and headed for the drawbridge that would put her on the other side of the gorge.

When she came upon the clansman guarding the drawbridge, she smiled charmingly. "Would you lower the drawbridge for me. I must get to the other side."

"'Tis sorry I am, mistress, but I've orders not to lower the bridge until the MacLaren returns," he said apologetically.

"But I only want to collect herbs and roots for my mother to treat Donald Gordon. It is imperative that I pick them while the sun is high."

"I dinna know . . . The Chief gave me orders."

Maura batted her eyelashes. "Oh my, I shall just weep if I don't get those plants today. It will mean my father has to suffer even longer."

"Well now, I've no wish to make a pretty lass weep." He began to turn the great wheel that let the drawbridge down.

"I will not be long," she shouted over her shoulder as she hurried across the wooden bridge.

It was a beautiful day, a hint of spring in the air. Maura followed a foot trail up the hillside, enjoying the sunshine in her face. She could smell the sweet wind blowing off the sea, and she breathed deeply, glad to be outside for awhile. Near the top of the hill she found one of the plants her mother needed. From her view on the hilltop she could see a sparkling stream below, just the kind of place she would find fever moss. With basket in hand she began her descent.

Upon returning to Dunraven, Alexander was told by his guard that Maura had wandered off into the hills alone. He was furious, and charged off in the direction the guard pointed. The little fool, he fumed silently. Didn't she realize the danger in leaving the safety of Dunraven? And what was Colin thinking, letting her leave by herself? When he was finished dealing with the two of them . . .

Anger was replaced by panic after he had gone a half-mile from the stronghold and there was still no sign of the girl. He topped the rugged hillside and looked around. Then he heard a sound: a voice raised in song. He slid from his horse and walked along the top of the ridge towards the sound. When he finally saw her he froze. She was wading in the stream, her dress pulled between her legs and tucked into her belt.

His anger evaporated as he listened to the lilting melody drifting over the hillside. She looked like a kelpie, but sounded like an angel, he thought with a smile on his face. The water had to be freezing, but she didn't seem to notice as she kicked and splashed in the crystal-clear stream. He stood mesmerized for a few minutes before descending the hill. He was nearly to her before she saw him.

"God's love, you scare a person to death," she gasped when she looked up and saw him.

"You should be afraid," he scolded. "Have you any idea of the danger you're placing yourself in?"

"What is to harm me? The birds or fish?" she asked sarcastically.

"I was thinking more of the two-footed predator."

"But I am on MacLaren land and in sight of Dunraven."

"You could be in danger from my own men, lass. They have been known to be bedeviled by a beautiful lass."

"You are talking nonsense. I only came out here to

86

gather plants that my mother needs for her potion, not to bedevil anyone."

"Is that what you are doing?" He smiled. "Does the singing and dancing add to the powers of the potion?"

Maura could feel the heat rise to her cheeks. " 'Tis a beautiful place and I was just enjoying it."

" 'Tis a Spartan diversion wading in a frigid mountain stream, lass. It will undoubtedly strengthen your character."

"My character is quite strong enough," she retorted. "Perhaps you should try bathing in it."

Alexander laughed. "I believe I will just lie here and guard you," he said, sitting on the mossy grass. "Sing if you wish. I was enjoying your lovely voice."

"Thank you," she said as she stepped from the water and let her skirt drop back around her ankles. She was wondering how she was going to slip her stockings on without him noticing her predicament, but when she glanced his way he was lying on his back, his hands behind his head as he studied a hawk flying overhead.

"Did you learn anything from your messenger?" she asked as she pulled her stockings on.

"My messenger never showed up," he answered shortly.

"I am sorry. I hope he did not run into trouble."

"Aye, he would appreciate your concern. Now tell me," he said, leaning up on one elbow, "how did you convince my clansman to lower the drawbridge for you, and why did you not have Colin escort you?"

"Colin had gone to one of the crofter's huts, and I told the guard I needed to collect roots and herbs for Donald. He was very understanding."

"And you are not above flirting a bit to get your way,"

he smiled devilishly.

"Did your clansman say that?" she asked, her eyes wide with disbelief.

"He dinna have to. I could see the admiration in his eyes when he spoke of you."

"'Twas not his fault," she said contritely. "He tried to dissuade me, but I worked on his sympathy."

"I shall have to see that he is given a job where a fair lass canna tempt him."

"Please do not punish him," Maura pleaded. "I really was quite persuasive."

Alexander laughed. "I have no doubt of that, lass. I am sure you could make any man forget his job."

Maura sat on the grass beside him and slipped her shoes on. "My mother is going to treat Donald's illness."

"I assumed that was the case. I knew your mother had the gift of second sight, but I dinna know she was also a healer."

Maura glanced at him, wondering if he was remembering when her mother found Honora MacLaren. "Aye, she has had the gift ever since I can remember."

"Do you also have the gift?"

"Not of second sight, but I have learned a great deal from her about healing. I just pray she will be able to help Donald."

"Aye. He has suffered greatly. I would also hope she can ease his pain."

Maura leaned back on her elbow and studied the MacLaren as he continued to stare at the sky. "You and my father have been friends for a long time."

"Aye, our clans have been allies for centuries."

They were both silent for a lengthy interval before

Maura spoke again. "How long will we stay here, Alexander?"

"In this valley?"

She could see the teasing grin on his face. "You know I mean at Dunraven."

"For however long you want to stay."

Maura lay back in the grass, her hands behind her head. "I am constantly amazed that you would offer my mother and I your hospitality."

"Why not? You are certainly better company than most of my men."

"You tease me again, Alexander MacLaren."

"Do I, lass? Have you never had anyone tease you before?"

"No, I suppose I haven't. As a child I spent most of my time alone."

"Did you not have any relatives to play with when you were young?"

"Would it surprise you to know that my Campbell relatives never treated me like family? Even though they did not want my mother and I to live with Donald, they did not really want us. They made us feel that we should be grateful to have a roof over our heads and food in our stomachs."

"I am sorry, lass."

Maura laughed shortly. "I did not tell you that for your sympathy." She turned away, wondering why she had told him. She had never confessed to anyone how lonely her life had been, but there was something about this man that made her want to pour her heart out to him. "With two brothers, I am sure you have never known loneliness."

"You do not have to be alone to know loneliness, lass," he said softly.

His words were spoken with such feeling that she wanted to reach out to him, to offer words of comfort, but she didn't know how. "Colin tells me you were not happy with your life in London," he continued.

Maura shrugged her shoulders. "We lived much better there than with the Campbells. 'Tis strange, I have never felt like I belonged anyplace we've been."

"There is an old Gaelic saying, that once a man or woman has known Scotland, they will always be tempted back."

"Aye, I can believe that, particularly if you have a place like this in your memories."

Alexander turned over on his side and stared at her. "So you like my secret utopia. While you are staying at Dunraven you are welcome to come here anytime you wish, but only with me."

"I will keep that in mind," she smiled.

"Did you know that your eyes are the color of heather, lass?"

For a moment she could only stare back at him. He was looking at her as he had on the tower the night before—the hungry look of a cat about to pounce on its prey.

She reached out and gently touched the scar on his face. "Does it hurt you?" she said softly.

"Not anymore," he said, catching her hand and pressing a lingering kiss on her soft palm. Her touch had stunned him, leaving him with a curious, tingling feeling.

She sat there on the bank, her feet tucked beneath her skirt, and stared back at the man who was the black lord of Dunraven. She had heard he was dangerous and evil, but anyone who ever sat with him near a bubbling stream would know better. He was doubtless a rogue and a black-guard, but there was something about him that intrigued her. He was definitely charming, but it seemed a charm that was calculated to a fine degree. He was very cautious about showing his true feelings, but every so often she could see the sadness in his gray eyes.

Finally forcing her eyes from his face, she picked a flower and began to pluck its petals. "What do you do to occupy your time when you are at Dunraven?" she asked, thinking she chose an innocent subject.

Alexander smiled. "We spend our time scheming of ways to save lovely maidens."

"And of course there are many of those."

"Hundreds," he agreed, "but my preference is for the violet-eyed ones."

Alexander also picked one of the blooming wildflowers. "Damn," he exclaimed, picking a sharp thorn from his finger.

"Wogan thistle has thorns on it, Alexander," she giggled.

"So I just found out."

"Here, let me see," she instructed, forcing the small puncture to bleed. "'Tis not poisonous, just an irritant."

"I am glad to hear that. It would be most embarrassing to fall over dead when all I'm trying to do is impress you."

"Impress me?"

"Aye, lass, why does that surprise you? Since we've put our petty differences aside I find I enjoy your company and your lovely face."

Maura picked another flower and pretended to study

91

it. "Well, at least we know now that you've red blood in your veins, Alexander—ordinary blood like any other man."

"What a disappointment for you, lass. I'm sure you thought it would be nothing but cold water."

Maura laughed as she lay back on the grass and closed her eyes, enjoying the beautiful day and Alexander's pleasant company. She was not aware that he had moved to lie above her until she opened her eyes. For a long moment they stared into each other's eyes, then he lowered his head slowly over hers, capturing her lips with his own. His hands, so brutally strong, so accustomed to violence, were oddly gentle as he caressed her neck and shoulders.

Alex had meant only to kiss her lightly, but the fresh scent of roses engulfed him from her hair and body, and he tightened his arms around her, bringing her closer to his body. Again he found his senses reeling from her response to his kiss. She had such fire, such passion.

His mouth moved gently against her lips, teasing, nibbling. Maura slipped her arms around his neck, clinging to him. He was experienced, persuasive, making her feel things she never imagined feeling.

He kissed her until he felt her tremble with the same burning desire that he felt—until he knew if he didn't stop then, he wouldn't be able to stop.

Drawing a steadying breath, he lifted his head from her, and stared down into her passion-filled eyes.

Struggling to find her voice, Maura finally said, "Please let me up. My indiscretions have gone far enough. I must return to Dunraven."

He lifted a dark brow. "Do you feel your virtue threatened by an innocent kiss, lass?"

"Was that what you call an innocent kiss?" she asked in disbelief.

A wicked grin came over his handsome face. "Perhaps you would like me to demonstrate the difference . . ."

Before she could object, his lips touched her again. This time he wasn't as gentle. He parted her lips, kissing her deeply and passionately, consuming her in his heat. His tongue thrust into the soft recesses of her mouth, then retreated, again and again, until she whimpered with unknown desire.

Suddenly she shoved at him, rolling to her feet before he could move. "My mother will be needing these plants," she said breathlessly.

Alexander laughed as he got to his feet. "All right, lass, come along then. Dubh Sith is waiting at the top of the hill. You can at least ride back with me."

"No thank you. I will walk," she said, fearing what would happen if she were held in his arms again.

"Maura, you said Anne needed the plants. The quickest way back is to ride with me. Besides, I have changed guards, and you may not be able to charm your way back inside."

Maura faced him, her hands on her hips. "I will ride with you, but I will not allow you to paw me again, Alexander MacLaren," she said with tears in her eyes. "I am not a strumpet. Someday I will marry and my husband will expect me to be pure."

Her words bothered him more than he wanted to admit. He stared at her, sadness in his eyes. "I apologize, lass."

Tomorrow will be a new day.
Miguel de Cervantes

Chapter Eight

For two days Maura helped her mother administer the remedies to Donald, staying by his side night and day. As Anne had feared, he took a turn for the worse on the second day, becoming feverish and delirious. It was all they could do to restrain him. Then on the third day it was as if a miracle had taken place. Donald woke up without pain. He was much stronger and able to walk without his cane for the first time in years.

"This is not a cure, Donald," Anne warned. "You will have to continue taking small doses of these medicines at least once a week, and we need to change your diet. You should eat only vegetables for awhile. Then we will slowly reintroduce meat into your diet, and at least three times a week you should soak in hot water with pine needles and barley. That will open the pores and the poisons will be steamed out."

"Anything, Anne, anything," Donald exclaimed flexing his legs. "God's blood, I feel I could take on the world."

"There will be no talking like that, Father," Maura

scolded. "You are going to take it slow and easy so you do not find yourself flat on your back again."

"Of course, my darling daughter. But I understand Alex is expecting Angus MacPhee and his family today. Surely you will agree that I am up to joining in the banquet that is being prepared."

Maura glanced at her mother. "Do you think he is up to it?"

Anne smiled. "I think he is up to it. Besides, I hate to see a grown man beg."

"Ah, sweet Anne, 'tis begging I would do to get you to return to Rockhenge with me."

"Donald, please. I told you it is too soon to talk about that."

"All right, my sweet, but may I at least plead for your lovely company tonight?"

Maura smiled as her mother took Donald's hand. "If you two will excuse me I believe I will take a walk."

Maura stood on the parapets staring out at the sea below, its angry waves crashing against the rocky cliff. This place was like Alexander MacLaren—unapproachable and forbidding, she thought with a sigh. She had seen little of the man the past few days, except at the evening meal in the great hall, where he would sit staring at her, a brooding expression on his dark face. She had no idea what she had done to displease him. There had been the kiss the day he had joined her when she was collecting herbs, but since their silent ride back to Dunraven they hadn't spoken except to nod to each other. Perhaps he was angry that she had rejected his advances. He seemed to always have a tortured expression on his hand-

96

some face.

She sighed dispiritedly. What is wrong with you, Maura Campbell? What does it matter if he is displeased with you. He is an arrogant, overbearing, moody Scot. Even his brothers were having to suffer the brunt of his foul temper. They seemed to find it humorous, though she couldn't imagine why. She found it extremely unnerving.

She was lost in thought, staring at the strangely alluring sea that seemed to lull her with its steady rhythm. She didn't hear Colin come up behind her, and he startled her when he spoke.

" 'Tis beautiful, is it not?"

"Oh Colin," she gasped. "I did not hear you approach."

"I'll be sure to whistle as I approach you the next time." He grinned boyishly. "What are you doing up here? I thought you'd be preparing for the party this evening."

"I did not realize it was to be a party," she said, preoccupied with her thoughts of Alexander.

"Aye, Alex always entertains lavishly when the MacPhees visit. Angus has been a loyal friend since my father's days."

"Oh yes, Father did say something about that. I suppose I have been so wrapped up in his care that I have not paid much attention to what was going on here at Dunraven."

"Well, be prepared, lass. There will be dancing 'til the wee hours of the morning. Old Angus MacPhee has two beautiful daughters," he said, rubbing his hands together in anticipation.

Maura laughed. "Oh, so that's why you are so excited

about this evening."

Colin stepped back, putting his hand over his heart. "Lass, you hurt me to the quick. You know I only have eyes for you."

"Oh, stop!" She laughed at his dramatic antics.

"Why won't you take me seriously, Maura?" he asked, suddenly very solemn. "It may be better for us all in the end."

Maura stared at him dumbfounded. "I . . . If I had a brother, I'd want him to be just like you," she stuttered, adding insult to injury.

"Brother or brother-in-law?" he asked.

Maura felt the heat rise to her cheeks. "I don't know what you mean."

"Don't you? Well, no matter, lovely lass." The serious mood was gone and he grinned engagingly. "If 'tis a brother you want, then I shall do my best."

"That is very kind of you," she said, relieved. "I am in no position to make a commitment to anyone, Colin. I hope you understand that."

"Aye. By the way, MacPhee also has a son, Iain. Perhaps you met at court."

"No, I don't believe so," she mused, "but the name does sound familiar."

"Be cautious around him, lass. It would be wise if you dinna say anything about the MacLarens rescuing you from Cromwell's clutches. I dinna trust young Iain, and neither does Alex. Personally, I think he would sell his grandmother if the price were right, and knowing that the English have offered ten thousand pounds Scot for Alex's head in a noose concerns me."

"Oh my God," Maura gasped. "I did not know. Has this happened since he brought me here?"

Colin laughed. "No, lass. Alexander has always been a rebel. The English know the clans are loyal to him and they dinna care for that. The Highlands seeth with rebellion and Alex has always been the instigator and leader. Why I am concerned about Iain MacPhee is that he has no money of his own, and I understand his father's fortunes have dwindled considerably of late."

Maura looked concerned. "Why would you have someone here as your guest when you don't trust him?"

Colin smiled again. "I told you, he has two beautiful sisters."

Maura was too wrapped up in her worries to realize he was teasing her. "Faith, if the English find out the MacLaren rescued me they will surely increase the reward for him. Oh, Colin, I hate this. I have already caused your family so much pain."

"'Tis in the past, lass. Dinna dwell on it. These walls are haunted enough with memories of bygone days." Suddenly he smiled and tilted her chin up. "You best take special pains with your dress this evening, lass. I am sure the MacPhee ladies are coming to get a look at their competition. Leanne MacPhee has had her sights set on Alex for several years."

"My word," Maura forced her voice to sound unconcerned. "She has no reason to be curious about me. I am no threat to her. I must say though, I imagine you and Simon have a terrible time dealing with the fact that all the young women in Scotland seem to desire your moody, intense brother. Faith," Maura laughed, "here I remember feeling sorry for him with his scarred face."

"Dinna waste your pity on Alex, lass. I believe women are drawn to him because of the scar. They have delusions of wanting to ease his pain."

"Perhaps that is true," she said in deep thought.

"Anyway, since I am so mistreated and ignored, would you not take pity on me?"

Maura tried not to laugh at his pathetic expression. "I am not to waste my pity on your brother, but save it for you. Is that what you're saying?"

"Aye," he said sheepishly. "I thought perhaps you'd be my partner in the dancing tonight."

"And what about Simon. Shouldn't I show him pity also?"

"He will have to speak for himself. 'Tis the early bird who gets the—" Suddenly he hesitated. "I am sorry, mistress. 'Tis a poor choice of words."

Maura had to laugh. "I would be honored to be your partner tonight, Colin, but if Simon should ask me to dance I will have to take pity on him also."

"Of course, kind lass. And I am sure you will take pity on Alex too, particularly since he has been in such a black mood of late."

Maura moved away to look back at the sea. "Do you know why he has been in such a terrible mood the last few days?"

Colin smiled. "I fear Alex is facing a problem he has never faced before."

"Oh, a problem with the clan?"

"No, lass. Let me just say 'tis a complex personal problem. I'm not sure even Alex realizes what has him in a turmoil."

"You make no sense, Colin."

"Aye, you are probably right. Only time will tell."

Suddenly they could hear a clatter of horses arriving in the courtyard.

"It seems our company has arrived."

"I should go and rest before this evening then." She grinned at him mischievously. "I certainly don't wish to disgrace you this evening."

"You could not disgrace anyone, lovely Maura. Until this evening," he said, kissing her hand.

After bathing, Maura decided to try to rest before dressing for the evening. She hadn't gotten much sleep in the past few days and she certainly didn't want to look haggard around the MacPhee ladies.

Instead of falling to sleep, she started thinking about her conversation with Colin. What had he meant about Alexander having a personal problem of which even he wasn't aware? She sighed deeply. The man was definitely the moodiest individual she had ever met, yet at the same time he was an enigma. He seemed either on the brink of violence or merriment, his dark eyes springing to life with laughter.

Drawing a shattered breath, she remembered the emotions his kisses had provoked. She had been helpless under his tender onslaught. Yet what had it meant to him? "You are a fool, Maura Campbell," she said aloud. "Your kisses mean nothing to him if what Colin said was true. The man has women falling all over him."

Freshly bathed and dressed in a black velvet doublet and white linen shirt, Alex sat at the long table in the great hall with his men and guests. Lively conversation surrounded him, but his attention was on the doorway, as he struggled to control his impatience. Colin and Maura Campbell had still not appeared, and he knew his brother

101

had gone for her more than a half an hour ago. He wouldna put it past his brother to—

"The Campbell woman's manners are deplorable," Glenna interrupted his thoughts. "I canna believe she would make you look like a fool in front of your family and—"

Before Glenna had a chance to finish her sentence, Colin appeared in the doorway with Maura on his arm.

Alex's heart skipped a beat as he stared at the black-haired beauty. She was dressed in a lavender velvet gown that highlighted her eyes. It was the most daring gown she'd worn, the deep neckline nearly exposing her breasts. Desire tightened in his loins and he silently cursed himself for letting her have such a volatile effect on him. She was beautiful, but he had had many beautiful women. Why couldn't he put this one from his mind?

He gritted his teeth as Maura laughed seductively at something Colin whispered to her. He headed towards them, fighting to control his instinct to wipe the smug look off his brother's face. Before he reached them, Iain MacPhee stepped out in front of them and bowed over Maura's hand.

Even though he was annoyed, Alex had to smile at the expression on Colin's face. So there is retribution, he thought. Let my dear brother suffer the same fate he has forced me to suffer since bringing Maura Campbell to Dunraven.

"We never met in London," Iain MacPhee was saying, "but I've heard of you. There was a story making the rounds of court about how you dressed as a man and challenged one of the King's knights to a horse race."

Maura could not help laughing at the memory the handsome young man brought back. "I won too," she

102

said, pleased with herself.

"Did it become fashionable for ladies of court to race horses after that?" he asked, his blue eyes sparkling with laughter.

"No." Maura laughed. "I fear the King did not look kindly on my little escapade. I was kept extremely busy with his children after that."

"'Tis a shame," he said with a smile. "We needed more entertaining, unpredictable ladies like you at court. You were the talk of London, and I am delighted to finally have the chance to meet you."

"Fortunately, infamy was fleeting in my case." She laughed.

Suddenly she noticed Alexander standing just off to the side. He was listening to them and appraising her with his dark eyes. Automatically she curtsied.

"Your most humble servant, mistress," he said, bowing his dark head over her hand.

For a brief moment his warm lips were against her skin, sending shivers down her spine. When he released her hand she rubbed the back of it as if she'd been burned.

"I am pleased you could join us," he said, one dark eyebrow raised. "I was afraid you had been taken ill. Come, let me introduce you to our guests," he said, politely removing her from Iain MacPhee's company.

While introductions were being made to Angus and Briget MacPhee, Maura had the feeling the young woman on their left was staring holes through her.

"Lady Campbell, I would like to introduce you to my daughters, Leanne and Katherine. I see you have already met my son."

Maura smiled politely. The young lady introduced as Katherine seemed more interested in Colin than in her, but Leanne was a different story. Her green eyes hadn't left Maura's face since they had been introduced. The young lady was beautiful, she had to give her that. Her long auburn hair and green eyes were a striking combination, sure to turn any man's head. And she seemed very sure of her beauty, Maura thought, or else she would not look at Alexander MacLaren with such obvious intimacy. The man was beyond belief, she thought in disgust, noticing that Alexander was smiling at the girl. Had he no decency?

"I understand you and your mother are guests of Alexander's," Leanne finally spoke directly to her. "I am amazed the MacLaren has welcomed you into his home. We dinna care for Campbells in these parts."

Maura was surprised by the young woman's blunt attack, but she forced a smile. "If that is true, then Alexander has certainly covered his dislike of us. He has been most kind and generous with his hospitality." She smiled sweetly at Alex, placing her hand intimately on his arm. "He makes it very difficult to even think of leaving."

Leanne looked shocked. "How long do you plan on staying?"

"No longer than necessary," Maura smiled.

"Lady Campbell is Donald Gordon's daughter," Alex pointed out, "and she is welcome to stay as long as she likes."

"I see." Leanne looked flustered. "Is your dress the work of the MacLaren's seamstress?"

"Aye, it is. I believe Grizel could sew for the Queen, she is so talented. Your dress is also beautiful. White certainly suits your coloring. It makes you look like an angel, my dear," Maura said condescendingly.

Leanne's green eyes narrowed coldly, then she smiled at Alexander. "Looks can be deceiving."

"If you say so," Maura smiled. "Please excuse me. I wish to speak to my mother and father. It was very nice meeting you. I do hope we have a chance to talk again." She leaned over and picked up Leanne's pewter goblet. "Alexander, *our* guest's cup is empty. Why don't you get her some more wine," she said before walking away.

"Did you see the expression on Alex's face?" Donald whispered to Anne. "Whatever Maura did he found amusing. Aye, I believe the young man is smitten with our daughter . . ."

"Shh," Anne hushed him as Maura approached them.

"But we dinna have much time . . ."

"Not now, Donald."

"My, but I am a lucky man," Donald said as he stood up and kissed his daughter. "My wife and daughter are by far the most beautiful women here—maybe in all of Scotland."

Maura laughed. "Now I understand why Mother has never forgotten you. You are a charmer, Father," she said returning his kiss.

"You do look lovely, my dear," Anne agreed.

"Thank you, but I have to give the credit to Grizel. She outdid herself with this dress. If it weren't for her talent, I would look like a street urchin compared to the lovely MacPhee ladies."

"Speaking of the MacPhees," her father commented, "whatever did you say to Leanne to give her that look of outrage?"

"It was really nothing. I bested her evenly and fairly."

Donald winked at Anne. "Had you already met Iain in London?"

"No, but he is charming. He was reminding me of a few incidents that happened while I was in London," she explained, glancing towards Iain. "I am surprised I had never heard of him. His handsome face and courtly manners would certainly have made him popular with the ladies."

"Ha!" her father snorted. "He looks like a pretty boy among the rugged MacLarens."

"There is nothing wrong with having manners and being gentle," Maura defended. "I am fairly starved. Do you mind if I sit with you?"

"I believe Alexander planned for you to join him."

"I won't be missed," she said, noticing that Alexander was surrounded by Glenna and the MacPhee women.

The servants began to place great dishes of food on the table. They feasted on smoked salmon, fat roasted capons stuffed with mushroom dressing, and tiny peas with sweet butter.

"The MacLaren complains that the taxes he pays to the English have him poor," Maura commented, "but he must keep something aside to be able to entertain like this."

"He has his ways of making ends meet," Donald answered.

"By stealing horses and cattle," Maura said sarcastically.

"'Tis a way of dealing with Cromwell's harsh laws," her father was quick to point out. "He thinks to break the Scots, but 'tis English gold making a full circle, so they make a fool of him. A Scotsman, even if he admits defeat, does not conform. He is a rebel at heart and has never accepted a restraining hand, and never will."

A perfect description of Alexander MacLaren, Maura

thought, trying without success to keep her eyes from the dark head so close to the auburn one of Leanne MacPhee. She sighed, tapping her fingers against her silver goblet in agitation. Why did it bother her? she wondered. He certainly meant nothing to her.

Donald followed her gaze and smiled. "Leanne MacPhee fancies herself the next mistress of Dunraven, and her father would like nothing better. They are an old family and have always been loyal to the MacLarens."

Maura forced her eyes from the MacLaren's. "I thought Glenna was going to be the next mistress of Dunraven."

"Aye, the woman seems to find him irresistible. The ladies would like to think he takes them more seriously than he does."

"Well, I for one find him excessively arrogant and moody."

"He has a lot of responsibilities, Maura. That can take its toll on any man, but I've always thought Alex handled it well for one so young. He's fought in many bloody battles against other clans, and against England, yet somehow he's been able to keep his family and clan together. The man constantly lives with danger."

"I have no doubt he is a fierce warrior, Father, but the Scots have been fighting intrigues and politics until they've fair bled themselves to death. Perhaps it is time to try to bring peace to the land."

"Bonnie words, lass, but I fear it will never happen in our lifetime—perhaps not ever."

Maura raised her eyes and looked at Alexander MacLaren. She realized he must have been watching her for some time. His eyes were cool and measuring, even though the strong lines of his face were shadowed in the candlelight. There was something alert and provoking about him even as he relaxed. She drew a deep breath and forced her eyes away from him, but it did not serve to free her mind of his presence. She touched her lips, remembering his kiss, then her eyes went back to his face and she found him smiling at her, as if he knew what she was thinking. Damn the man! Of all the arrogance . . .

Suddenly Colin was beside her, his arm resting along the back of her chair. "You are far too serious over here. Dinna anyone ever teach the Gordons how to have a good time?"

"If you intend to ask me to dance, Colin MacLaren, you better think twice," Donald Gordon warned with a twinkle in his eyes.

"No offense, sir, but I believe I prefer the company of your daughter."

"Then take her and show her the way of it. She has been in England far too long. It has made her morose."

Colin stood up and offered Maura his hand.

Their dance was barely over before Iain MacPhee claimed her, his polished manners a change from the more rugged, outgoing MacLaren. While they were dancing she noticed Alexander watching her, his eyes dark and unfathomable. When the music ended, Simon was at her side.

"I believe you promised me this dance, mistress."

Maura curtsied, then a wide smile came over her face as she heard the music. "Did you ask them to play this, Simon?"

"Do you know the Volta?" Simon asked, a mischievous grin on his face as the fiddlers broke into the lively country dance that the clansmen loved and called their own.

"What kind of Scottish lass would I be if I did not?" she laughed.

Alex watched them, a smile on his face as Simon spun Maura around. They were now the only dancers on the floor and everyone stood around clapping in time to the music.

"'Tis a wanton dance," Leanne said in disgust, "scarcely the kind of dance one would learn at court."

"I agree," Alex said still smiling. "It takes more talent to be accomplished at the Volta than can be taught with a lesson. If you will excuse me, I believe I will show my brother how it should be done." Leanne stared after him, her mouth hanging open.

Simon saw his brother heading towards them. He bowed before Maura and placed her hand in Alex's before she had time to object.

When he placed his hand on her back it sent her blood racing. The candles along the wall reflected in his dark eyes, glittering mysteriously. While she was trying to understand the strange emotions he evoked, he swung her into a circle, lifting her in the air, taking her breath away. The fiddlers increased the tempo until it was as wild and boisterous as a reel.

Maura laughed aloud as Alex whirled her about, not giving her a chance to catch her breath. His large hands were warm on her waist, sending heat through her entire body.

Finally the music came to a final, wild crescendo and they spun in a continuous circle until she was sure she would lose her balance and fall to the floor. When it ended Alex held her in his arms to keep her from falling, laughing as she clutched the front of his jacket.

"I was once told by a very wise old sage, that a man had

only to watch a woman dance to know how skillful she would be at other pleasures."

Maura's eyes widened. "You delight in insulting me. If we weren't being watched, I'd slap your face."

Alex threw back his head and laughed. "Lass, if we weren't being watched, I'd kiss that frown off your lovely face. Come with me," he said, taking her by the arm. "I need some air."

"I do not," she protested, knowing all eyes were on them. "You are making a scene."

"Then come with me and give them something more to gossip about," he said, pulling her along.

Colin watched his brother leave with Maura. So, it was as he feared, he sighed. For years he had hoped his oldest brother would find someone special, but damn, did it have to be Maura, the woman who could so easily steal his own heart? Donald Gordon would like nothing better than to have his daughter marry a MacLaren, and he had hoped he would be the choice, but if Alexander was interested . . .

Colin glanced across the room and met the soft gray eyes of Katherine MacPhee. She was a lovely lass, he thought, pushing away from the wall, and she had always shown an interest in him—even when Alex was around.

"He thought to provoke her before all," Donald Gordon said with a smile on his face, "but she proved a match for him. It is going well, wouldn't you say, sweet Anne?"

"You have said Alex has sworn never to marry. What makes you think he will this time?" Anne asked.

"I can see it in his face everytime he looks at her. God's

110

blood, Anne, have you not seen the way they look at each other? The whole room seems charged."

"But Maura says she does not care for Alex," Anne persisted.

"It is all a sham, my dear, but it is what intrigues Alex the most. He is not use to women ignoring him."

"You sound like an expert on the MacLaren, but I still doubt he will be easily convinced to go through with your plan, and Maura! Faith, when she learns—"

"I have known Alexander a long time, Anne, and have always known it would take a special woman to win his heart. Our daughter is that woman, I am sure of it. Together they will produce the finest and fittest Scotland has ever seen. Where is your gift of sight, Anne? Tell me you see it."

Anne shook her head, deciding it best if she didn't tell him she saw a rocky future for Maura and Alexander—but they would be together.

"What is it, Anne? Have you seen something?"

"No. I was just thinking I hate to see Colin get hurt. I think he cares deeply for Maura."

"Look across the room, my dear. Young Colin has already found someone to help ease his miseries. Another reason I knew he was not the one for our Maura. He is a fine young man, but not mature enough. Maura needs a man who will give her his heart and soul for life. A man who has enough experience to keep her satisfied, and enough sense to know he has finally found the only woman he will ever need."

"Even if everything is against them?"

"Aye, even more so, love. They can overcome anything together. Mark my word."

"They will have to, I fear," Anne sighed.

There is something in the wind.
Shakespeare

Chapter Nine

"Where are we going?" Maura asked as Alex led her out a side door. "My mother and father will be concerned."

"They know you are with me."

"Even more reason for them to be concerned," she said caustically.

"Aye, you are probably right. Now stop scowling, lass," Alex teased as he pulled her along. "I hate to see a woman sulk."

"I am neither sulking nor scowling," she retorted. "You have a very high opinion of yourself if you believe my feelings so delicate they would be offended by anything you could say or do to me."

"'Tis glad I am to hear it. I also hate to see a woman humble herself to a man."

Maura finally pulled away, facing him with her hands on her hips. "I'm surprised you would want to leave all your admirers behind."

"Ah, there is that streak of jealousy again." He grinned at her.

"I don't understand you, Alexander MacLaren," she

laughed in exasperation. "It seems everytime we are together you try your best to make me angry."

"And I seem to succeed without much effort."

Maura grinned. "Aye, that you do."

"I've been wanting to tell you all evening how lovely you look tonight, lass," he said, touching a strand of her silky black hair. "You should always wear the color of heather."

"Are you saying I look terrible in any other color?" she asked breathlessly.

"'Tis a shabby way to beg a compliment, but I must admit you'd be lovely wearing rags."

Maura had to turn from his admiring gaze. "I think I prefer your insults. I do not know how to take Alexander MacLaren the gallant."

Alex took her hand again. "Then come, we will take a walk in the moonlight, and I will try to think of biting remarks to make."

"Are you sure 'tis not to shove me off a cliff?"

"That all depends on you, lass."

Maura stumbled on one of the rocks, but Alex's hand was under her arm instantly steadying her.

"Are we not about to walk off the cliff?" she asked, hearing the pounding of the sea on her right.

"Trust me. I know the path like the back of my hand, I have something to show you."

Suddenly they stopped. Maura glanced down and in the moonlight she could see the tall slender masts of a ship etched against the sky. "Your ship," she whispered, delighted. "I have never been on a ship."

"Come, there's a path over here," he said.

It was no more than a narrow foothold clinging to the side of the cliff, and only his guiding hand kept her moving downward towards a longboat that was beached on the sandy shore. Alex lifted her into the boat, then took the oars and rowed toward the ship.

Maura stared at the silhouette of the vessel. It had the bold reckless lines of a pirate ship, she imagined, suitable indeed for the MacLaren.

"Do you keep a crew aboard all the time?"

"No, only a few men when the ship is anchored in the cove. The rest of my crew spend the time ashore with their families. Can you manage a rope ladder in those skirts?" he asked as the longboat bumped against the hull of the ship.

"If I had known I would be climbing mountains and rope ladders, I would have worn breeches."

"But it would not be nearly as interesting." He grinned as he held the bottom of the ladder for her to begin the climb.

Maura glanced at him, shaking her head at the devilish smile on his face. She would not dwell on the immodest view she was surely giving him. Suddenly a lanthorn was held over the side and a pair of strong arms lifted her the last few rungs.

"Thank you," she said breathlessly.

"'Tis my pleasure, m'lady," the seaman answered with a smile.

"Good evening, Evan," Alex greeted. "Did we wake you?"

"No sir. I was expecting you."

Maura glanced at Alex, wondering why this seaman would have been expecting them, but she said nothing as he told the man they wouldn't be aboard long.

"Evan is my captain when I can't sail with them," he explained as he led her up narrow stairs to another deck.

115

"Do you sail the ship yourself when you are aboard?" she asked, not having thought of the MacLaren as a seafaring man.

"I certainly do. I prefer it to almost anything else."

"Does she have a name?"

He laughed. "Aye, her name is *Nightwind*."

"'Tis a lovely name."

"This is the quarterdeck," he said, leading her to the wheel.

Maura placed both hands on the spokes, rubbed to the feel of satin by countless rugged hands. Glancing up at the stars, she let the scent of the sea and the feel of the ship beneath her feet ignite her imagination.

As if realizing that, Alex placed his hands over hers and whispered closely to her ear, "Stand by to come about, lass. Follow the stars. It will take you to your destination."

"It sounds terribly exciting," she said, imagining the wind blowing in her face, and Alexander MacLaren by her side as they sailed across the sea to all the exciting places in the world. "We could chase the rainbow and always have good luck," she said with longing in her voice.

"Aye, we could," he agreed. "Perhaps someday we will do that, lass."

Maura glanced at him, but said nothing.

"Come, let me show you the captain's cabin."

They went through a swinging door and down a companionway. Maura was amazed when Alex opened the door. The cabin was beautiful, from the polished tables to the brass fittings on the lockers. She had not expected it to look so much like a room in his castle. There were cushioned seats beneath the window that stretched

116

across the stern of the ship, and a large bed that looked amazingly comfortable. A leather lanthorn hung above the table, casting a warm glow over the smooth planking.

Maura walked to the window and watched the gentle surge of the waves lapping against the hull. The moonlight reflected on the water, throwing rippling patterns against the ceiling. "I envy you," she said softly. "It is so peaceful here. I cannot imagine why you stay in troubled Scotland when you could sail in peace anywhere in the world."

"A man cannot always do as he pleases. My father's death gave me the responsibility of many people," he explained as he poured them both a goblet of wine. "Besides, if I was always off sailing the seas I would not have had the chance to be with a lass with lovely violet eyes, now would I?" His voice held a teasing tone, but his eyes did not.

Maura turned away, picking up a book that lay on the table. "I will think of you when next you sail, now that I know what your ship and cabin look like."

"That is nice to hear. The hours are often long and lonely aboard a ship, but I believe they will be easier now that you have been in my cabin."

Maura glanced at him, a puzzled expression on her face. "I don't know what you mean."

"You will possess this cabin, Maura Campbell, as you have come to possess Dunraven. I fear I'll never be done with thoughts of you."

She was finding it difficult to breathe. His eyes held hers as intimately as if he were touching her. Maura turned her back to him, pretending to be interested in the other books on the shelf. When she could finally find her voice, she said, "I am sure I will only haunt you for as long as it takes to find another woman who will listen to your flattery."

Alex laughed softly. "You make it very difficult to be gallant, lass."

"I would say you are being absurd, Alexander MacLaren. Have you forgotten that I am a Campbell? Surely your hatred for my clan has not suddenly vanished."

"No, but I see more Gordon than Campbell in you, lass."

"How convenient," she said as she sipped her wine.

"And I must admit, I have always liked the idea of toying with danger." He placed his goblet on the table and moved towards her. "When one walks along a cliff, sometimes it is a great temptation to see how close one can walk on the edge without falling."

He was so close his wide shoulders shut out the rest of the cabin. Removing the goblet from her hand, he placed it on the table beside his. "I believe 'tis time to throw caution to the wind, Maura Campbell. We will forget names and faces."

Maura stared up into his face, trying to find words. "I . . . I believe 'tis time to return to Dunraven," she said, still mesmerized by his piercing gray eyes.

He smiled down at her. "Are you always to be a coward, lass?"

"You talk in riddles."

"Do I?"

"We should get back to your guests."

"Not just yet, lass." He captured her face between his strong hands, for a long moment studying her face as if trying to memorize it. Then slowly his mouth descended on hers, sending a flame throughout her body that

118

burned sweetly and languorously, consuming in its blaze all protests, all fear. She gave herself up completely to his ardent kisses, moaning with pleasure as his hand caressed her back, forcing her closer to his hard body.

"Maura, Maura, you are a sorceress," he whispered against her mouth. "You weave a spell over me like a gossamer web—"

Suddenly there was a harsh knock at the cabin door. Alex cursed softly as he moved from her. "Yes. What is it?" he asked angrily.

"I am sorry to bother you, sir, but a message from your brother just came," Evan said.

Maura was trying to gain some semblance of poise as Alex talked with his man. Then she heard the door close and felt Alex's warm breath close behind her. "It seems my messenger has sent word he is in Inverness."

Maura spun around to face him. "Cromwell—does he know I am here?" she asked, fear in her voice.

"I dinna know yet, lass, but it seems we will soon find out. I will ride to Inverness at dawn."

"Oh God," she moaned. "When is this going to end? I am so sorry, Alex. I never meant to put your family in danger again."

Alex shrugged, dismissing the matter. "Danger is something all Scots learn to live with."

Maura turned swiftly to face him. "Alexander, let me go with you. I will go crazy if I have to stay behind and wait for word."

His voice, oddly gentle, yet firm, cut across hers. "No, lass."

"Please," she begged.

"'Tis too dangerous. I willna chance it. Someone in Inverness could recognize you."

"I could dress as a man," she persisted.

"Only a fool would not recognize you for a woman," he said, his grin deepening at her persistence.

Maura sighed, pretending to accept defeat. "I suppose I would only be a nuisance to you."

"More a distraction," he corrected.

"I hate being a woman."

" 'Tis grossly unfair," he agreed.

"We are not frail and weak as you would have us. I'd wager I can ride a horse better than most of your men."

"I dinna doubt it, lass," he said lazily, "but it does not change the fact that your safety is my concern."

Maura turned away and stared out the ship's window at the glittering water. She had always hated the staid womanly chains of convention that seemed to rule life. Why couldn't she go on raids and fight the English? She hated needlework and the other trite female pursuits she was supposed to enjoy.

Suddenly Alex's hands were on her shoulders, turning her to face him. "Why is it so important for you to ride with me?"

For a long moment she did not answer. Then she sighed. "What does one say to explain the maddening dullness of always being left behind while the men go off hunting and raiding? I am aware that no respectable woman is supposed to feel this way, and perhaps that is why I rebelled so often at court, dressing as a man and attempting to best the strutting peacocks at their own games." She shrugged her shoulders. "I don't know. Maybe it's just because you tell me I cannot do it, and I see no reason for such restrictions, simply because I am a woman. All I ask is to have some control over my own life," she explained, hoping he would understand her.

Alex smiled. "I think you've the heart of a rebel, Maura Campbell, and the misfortune of living in a world that despises all rebels and outlaws."

Maura looked up into his dark eyes. "Then you are familiar with this feeling?" she asked softly.

He was silent for a long moment. His hands were still on her shoulders and the warmth of his touch tingled through her blood. He knew his desire for her was clouding his thinking, yet he could not refuse so sincere a request. "Perhaps I will give you this chance to be a rebel, sweet Maura, but you must promise me two things. You will tell Donald what you plan, and you must follow my orders precisely, else you will endanger my men as well as yourself."

"I promise," she said, elated beyond measure. "Thank you, Alex, thank you."

She stood on tiptoe and briefly kissed him, but he wasn't willing to accept so small a kiss. He brushed his lips against hers, before his tongue slipped inside her sweet mouth. His large strong hands moved from her face, down her neck, his thumbs caressing the pulse that pounded in her throat. When he ended the kiss he smiled at her confused expression. "If you are to speak to your father tonight, we should return to the castle."

"Yes, of course," she answered, reluctant to leave the warmth and safety of his arms.

Maura sighed as he took her hand and led her from the beautiful ship, *Nightwind*. No matter what happened, she would never forget the brief minutes of harmony and friendship she had known there with the infamous black MacLaren, the outlawed highland chief, the smuggler, the seducer of her soul.

No matter how fair the sun shines,
Still it must set.

Ferdinand Raimund

Chapter Ten

She was too excited to sleep. Alex had given her a pair of leather breeks, a shirt, boots, and a plumed hat to wear, telling her as long as she was going to pretend to be a man, she may as well be a well-dressed one.

Long before dawn she got up and dressed in her borrowed clothes, then headed for the stables, determined not to be left behind. She found Simon and several other men already preparing the horses.

"God's blood," Simon exclaimed, seeing her. He circled her, whistling appreciatively. "I have never seen a more fetching lad."

Behind him Alex laughed. "Find your own company, Simon. This comely lad rides with me." He took Maura by the hand and led her to a fine mare. "Did Donald give his approval?" he asked.

"Well, maybe not wholeheartedly, but he said he knew 'twas a bit late to start telling me what I could and could not do."

"Your father is a wise man." He laughed.

"I knew you'd be the lass's downfall," Simon said, a

twinkle in his eyes. "And she was such an angel before meeting you."

Alex smiled down at Maura. "There is something far more intriguing about a fallen angel than a virtuous one."

Maura laughed. "Would you two stop?"

Alex gave her a hand up into the saddle, and she smiled down at him. "Thank you for allowing me to join you."

"We'll see how you feel about that later, lass."

They clattered across the drawbridge, Maura, Alex, Simon, and ten of his men. There had been some amusement among the men about her appearance, but now she was one of them.

As Alex had said, they rode hard, and within four hours they arrived in Inverness. When they slowed the pace, Alex instructed her to drop back. As she did, the ranks of MacLaren's men closed around her, and in a matter of seconds she was screened on either side, as well as the front and back.

"We're almost there," Alex said absently, his dark eyes searching each crossroad, each doorway.

"Do you want me to keep the lass outside while you meet with Gilmore?" Simon asked.

"No, I think it would only draw attention to her. Besides, she will probably need to quench her thirst and hunger like the rest of the men."

Simon grinned. "What should I do if she desires a quick tumble with one of the fetching barmaids?"

Alex laughed. "I dinna think you need worry about that."

Two men were left with the horses while the rest followed their leader into the dark tavern. Alex stood in the doorway, pausing a moment to get his bearing. It was surprisingly crowded for so early in the day, and the place already smelled like burnt meat and unwashed bodies. "A charming place," Alex commented. "I'll have to have a talk with Gilmore about his choice of meeting places."

A yellow-haired serving girl hurried across the room towards them. "Over here, sirs," she said, leading them to a large table at the back of the tavern.

Alex took a seat with his back to the wall, while his men settled around him. Maura sat next to Simon opposite Alex.

"We ha' a delicious lamb stew today, lads."

"Aye, that will do nicely," Alex said, dropping coins on the table, "and ale all around."

The girl smiled, tucking the coins between her ample breasts. "Right away, sir."

"Did not Gilmore say he'd meet us at this hour?" Simon asked, glancing around the crowded tavern.

"Aye. I am sure he'll be here."

Moments later the girl was back with a tray loaded with bowls of steaming stew and tankards of ale. Alex smiled as he watched Maura take a long drink, then wipe the back of her hand across her mouth like a man.

"Are you enjoying yourself, lad?" he asked softly.

"Immensely. I just pray the news you receive is good."

"Aye," Alex agreed, not telling her that he doubted it would be. "Eat now. We leave as soon as Gilmore relays his message."

Everyone had finished his food and was lingering over his ale before the messenger slipped into the empty chair beside Alex. Someone set a tankard of ale in front of him, and he drank it as he glanced around the table.

"I was expecting you several days ago," Alex commented.

"I am sorry, sir, but there was a complication we did not expect."

"What was that?"

"There was a young servant girl taken—"

Maura's gasp was audible. The courier glanced at her then back at Alex. "Is this a new man?"

"Aye, he is fine. Go on with your news."

"They questioned this girl, sir, then they killed her."

Simon's hand was on her knee, warning her to be silent. She felt as if the world was closing in on her. She needed air, she needed to scream, but she kept her silence, staring into the tankard of ale.

"Apparently she didn't tell them anything," the messenger was saying, "because they haven't made a move yet."

She didn't tell them anything because she didn't know anything, Maura wanted to scream.

"Is there anything else?" Alex asked his courier.

"No, sir. Graham stayed behind to report if they should start moving, but I would be surprised if they did. The rumors were that Cromwell has his hands full with his Parliamentarians, and has even sent Lord James Randolph to Ireland to take care of some problems. Maybe they will be kept too busy to bother us."

"Aye, maybe they will," Alex answered. He glanced at Maura, a concerned look on his face. God, if he had any idea the news would be of this nature he would never have let her come. He knew it was taking every ounce of will power she possessed to remain calm and quiet.

"Simon, you and the lad see to the horses," Alex instructed. "The rest of us will join you in a few minutes."

Maura shakily got to her feet, praying she would not do

126

something as stupid as fainting on the way out. Once outside she took several deep gulps of air.

"Be brave, lass," Simon whispered as they stood next to their horses. "Our safety depends on how good an actress you are." Maura shook her head, but said nothing.

Moments later the MacLaren and the rest of his men came out of the tavern. "Mount up," he said, still not speaking to her.

They rode, for what seemed like endless miles to Maura, before Alex dropped back beside her. "Are you all right, lass?" She nodded, fighting back the tears. "We will stop soon."

When they topped a hill and rode into a peaceful glen along the bank of a stream, Alex held his hand up for his men to halt. He dismounted, and before Maura could protest, lifted her from the saddle. "Sit down, lass," he said, leading her to the edge of the stream. "You dinna have to act brave here."

Maura dropped to the grass while Alex dipped a cloth into the cold water. He knelt on one knee before her, gently wiping her face. "If I had any idea what the news would be, I would never have put you through this."

She stared at him, her eyes bright with unshed tears. "Why, Alex? Why would they do such a thing. Elspeth knew nothing."

"Desperate people dinna need a reason for what they do, lass."

"She was only a child," she choked back a sob, "an innocent."

"I know, lass. I wish I could spare you this pain."

Maura suddenly lifted her chin and wiped her hand across her eyes. "I will not hamper our journey to

127

Dunraven. Shall we return to our horses?"

"Look at me, Maura." She raised her eyes to meet his steady gaze. "Do not feel guilty for what happened to your friend. It was my decision to leave her behind. The guilt is mine, and mine alone."

She knew he was trying to ease her pain, but somehow it did not help. Shaken, she got to her feet, holding fast to his hand. "Thank you, Alex. I know you must find it wearisome to continually play nursemaid to me. I will be fine now."

When they arrived back at Dunraven, everyone was in the great hall enjoying the evening meal. Alex and Simon went around to the side entrance so Maura could escape being seen. She stopped on the stairs and turned to Alex.

"Please join your company. I believe I will seek the peace and quiet of my room now."

Seeing Maura's pallor, Alex turned to Simon. "Give my regrets to our guests. I'm going to escort Lady Campbell to her room."

Maura said nothing as Alex led her down the long corridor. Her silence and ashen coloring frightened him. She was too distraught even to notice when he stopped at his room and returned with a bottle of brandy. Moments later he opened the door of her room and led her inside.

"I think you need a brandy."

She stood frozen where he left her until he led her into the room. "I just need to rest."

"Aye, I agree, rest will help. You did well today, lass. My men were proud to be with you," he said as he poured her a brandy. "Here, drink this."

Maura downed the brandy as if it were water, then gasped and choked as the liquid burned like fire.

"Brandy should be sipped, lass," he smiled sympa-

128

thetically. "Here, try again," he said, refilling her glass. "It will numb the pain."

After giving her the glass he led her to a chair before the fire. He knelt in front of her, encouraging her to sip the brandy. She stared at him as if she didn't know him, her eyes shadowed with pain and guilt.

"Talk to me, Maura. Tell me what you are feeling," he encouraged. He had seen grown men go mad after battles, and he feared the shock of hearing about her friend was too much for her.

"I should never have been born," she whispered, tears filling her eyes. "I have caused so many deaths, and I fear 'tis not over. I am so—Oh Alex . . ." She couldn't go on. The words froze in her throat as tears blinded her. She felt his arms go around her.

"Dinna be afraid to cry, lass. It will help," he said, caressing her silky hair.

The tears came spilling over her cheeks. She clung to him and his hold tightened around her. "It will be all right, Maura. Everything will be all right. I willna let anything happen to you."

"It is not myself I am worried about," she said in a broken sob. "I have brought you enough pain. There is no reason for you to be involved in this."

"Perhaps that was once true," he admitted softly.

"I must do something," she sobbed.

He slid his arms around her and lifted her to the bed. Then he sat with her, holding her in his arms. "Hush now. Try to get some rest."

She shuddered, turning her face into his shoulder. "Elspeth was so good, so sweet. How could they?"

"Take another sip, lass." He held her gaze with his hypnotic gray eyes as she sipped the amber liquid.

There was nothing about him that was not dark and hard, tempered with as ruthless and dangerous an edge as the sword he wore at his side, yet he showed her a side of himself that was gentle and compassionate. "You are not at all as you seem in the harsh light of day," she whispered softly, the brandy beginning to have an effect.

"Dinna be fooled by a sympathetic ear, lass. I am as I seem by day or night."

"But you feel my pain . . ."

"Aye, I feel it," he said, pulling her back into his arms. He placed a comforting light kiss on the pulse of her temple. "Do you want me to leave you alone so you can sleep?"

"No. Not yet," she pleaded, wrapping her arms about him.

The only light in the room came from the fireplace, and they silently listened to the crackle of the fire. He could feel her tense body began to relax against him, and he hoped she would fall asleep soon because he didn't think he could bear the torture of wanting to make love to her much longer. Her soft breasts were pressed against his arm as he held her, and he fought the urge to caress them. He smoothed back her silken hair with gentle fingers, forcing himself to be content with that.

Maura felt safe. She had never had a man comfort her, not a father or a grandfather. It was something she had missed terribly, particularly when she was young, and she wasn't anxious to let him leave her alone with her grisly thoughts. Reality would come flooding back all too soon as it was.

"Are you feeling better, lass?" Alex asked as he gently tilted her chin to look at her tear-streaked face.

"A little."

His hand moved from her chin to softly caress her neck. Her eyes were locked with his, innocent, yet inviting. Alex moaned before touching his lips to hers, gently at first, then demanding.

Maura melted against him, returning his drugging kisses, letting his tongue explore, teaching her the exquisite sensations it could evoke. She needed his warmth and nearness—she needed him.

He tried not to frighten her with his passion, yet he felt about to explode. It was the hardest thing he'd ever done, restraining himself when he couldn't remember ever desiring a woman as much as he desired this one. His hand slid possessively over the smooth skin of her throat, then down inside her shirt to caress her breast.

Helpless under his expertise, Maura was willing to let him do anything he desired. There was no thought in her mind but the moment. She wanted to savor the sensations he was evoking. Forgetting everything else, she urged him on with soft, breathless words.

When he finally dragged his mouth from hers, he held her firmly against his chest, his breathing ragged. "Not like this," he moaned. "We are going to make love, Maura, but not here where someone could walk in on us."

She stared at him dazed, unable to fathom his words as shame washed over her. My God, what powers did this man have over her?

Alex sighed, seeing the look of control come back over her face. "Maura . . ."

"You should go to your guests. I can sleep now," she lied.

Somehow Alex found that amusing. "I was thinking of a midnight swim in the icy waters of a loch. Would you

131

care to join me?" he asked as he stood up.

"No, thank you. I think I have done enough to make you think I am a . . . a harlot."

"If I thought you were a harlot there wouldn't be any need for me to leave to save your reputation," he said in a tone of calm finality. "I am certain Anne will be checking in on you when she learns we have returned. I dinna wish to shock her."

Maura watched him leave, wanting to call him back, but afraid she'd only make a bigger fool of herself. He had saved her from disgracing herself, yet she felt such pain, such loneliness.

Not wanting the company of the MacPhees, or anyone else for that matter, Alex decided to see if his horse had been properly stabled, if for no other reason than to take his mind off the violet-eyed, passionate woman he had reluctantly abandoned.

The cold night air had the needed effect on him as he stood staring up at the stars. God, what was he going to do about her? She was driving him insane. She was everything he ever wanted in a woman, yet he knew it would not be fair to expose her to the dangers he faced every day. What kind of a life could he offer her?

"You must have a lot on your mind," Colin said from behind him. "You just walked right past me in the hall without even seeing me."

"I'm sorry," Alex said shortly.

"Simon told me what happened to Maura's servant. I think I will return to the hall to check on her."

"She is fine. Leave her alone."

Colin raised a blond eyebrow. "You sound very possessive, big brother. Have you decided to court Lady Campbell?"

"If you are wise you will not bait me tonight, Colin. I am in no mood for it," he said with icy displeasure.

Colin laughed bitterly. "Why the hell don't you admit that you're in love with the lady. You're making life miserable for everyone with your stubbornness."

Alex grabbed Colin by the lapels of his jerkin, his eyes blazing angrily. Then just as suddenly he shoved him away and started back to the hall.

Colin laughed. "She has you, you bloody fool. You may as well surrender."

Glenna stood in the shadows listening to the two brothers. She had been looking for Alex, but seeing the black mood he was in, and hearing his angry words with Colin, she decided not to approach him. So he had been with the Campbell woman, she thought bitterly. Maybe she could use that to her advantage if what Colin said was true.

Circumstances rule men; men do not
rule circumstances.

Euripides

Chapter Eleven

Hazy mist drifted through her mind, and images of a dark-haired woman standing at the foot of her bed, telling her all would be well. Maura slowly opened her eyes and glanced around the room. It had seemed so real. She could actually remember what the woman said in her dream: Be patient; he is a good lad and he needs your love and understanding. She rubbed her temples. This whole affair was obviously affecting her. Anyone who imagines ghosts telling them to be patient . . .

She needed to get up, but the warmth of the bed felt so good, and she was so tired. The rain beating against the glass became louder, finally bringing her fully awake. She stared sleepily at the rivulets of water running down the panes of leaded glass. She sighed and closed her eyes again, wishing she could recapture the elusive dream, but only the harsh memories of the previous day would take form. She pulled the covers over her head, but it did nothing to black out the reality—Elspeth was dead. Killed because of her.

And then there was Alexander. He had been such a

comfort, until he had played her body like an instrument, then left her alone with her turmoil. She had nearly begged him to stay—to take her. Thank God he had the good sense not to have gone any further than he had. She closed her eyes, remembering how his lips and hands had felt on her. He had said they would make love. Would they? Would she be yet another conquest to him? Not if she could help it, she thought with a sigh.

Suddenly Maura heard the clicking of china. She shoved the covers down, expecting to find Mary there, but instead it was Glenna.

"Good morning, Lady Campbell," she greeted, as if they were best of friends. "Mary was so busy with our guests that I told her I'd bring your tea."

"That was very kind of you."

"Are you feeling better? Mary tells me you were quite under the weather yesterday."

"Yes, I am feeling somewhat better."

"You were missed by Iain MacPhee. I swear the lad paced the hall all day." She handed Maura the cup of tea, then asked, "Did you sleep well?"

"No, not really."

"I'm sorry to hear it. It doesn't seem like anyone got much sleep around here last night," she said with a laugh. "I was on my way to check on your father during the wee hours of the morning and ran into Alexander leaving Leanne's room. I suppose they will both be exhausted today."

The cup rattled on the delicate saucer Maura held. "That must have been very upsetting to you," she said, trying to keep her voice steady.

"To me?" Glenna looked surprised. "Faith, no. I have no interest in Alex. He is too much a womanizer for my

136

tastes. The man has left a brood of bastards scattered far and wide all over Scotland. 'Tis his brother Simon I will wed."

"Then perhaps you should start giving your attention to Simon. He's too fine a young man to be played the fool."

"I dinna know what you are talking about," Glenna said, pretending innocence.

Before Maura could explain, Anne entered the room.

"Are you all right, my dear?" her mother asked as she sat on the side of the bed. "I heard this morning about the dreadful news the messenger brought." Anne gently touched Maura's tear-swollen eyes. "You should have come to me last night."

Maura tried not to think about why she hadn't gone to her mother, but Alex's face came unbidden to her mind. "I was . . . I was better off alone."

"Since your mother is here I will go help Mary," Glenna said. "Have a pleasant day."

"I dinna care for that woman," Anne said when they were alone.

"I know. I pity Simon if he believes her lies."

"I will have to use some herbs on those eyes. You look terrible, dear."

"I am not surprised. I had a very strange night," she sighed. "Mother, I think we should leave here. We have imposed on the MacLarens' hospitality long enough."

Anne's face registered her surprise. "Maura, that would not be wise. We are safe here."

"Are we?" she asked, tears filling her eyes.

"Come now, dear, get dressed. You are just over-wrought about the news from England. Once you have time to think about it you will realize we are safer here than we would be anyplace else."

"Father is getting stronger. Couldn't we go home to Rockhenge?"

"Maura, we need Alexander MacLaren's protection."

And who protects me from Alexander MacLaren? she thought silently.

"I'm going to leave you to dress now. I want to check on your father. Shall I meet you downstairs?"

"Yes, of course," Maura sighed, knowing there wasn't any sense pursuing the matter with her mother. "I suppose the MacPhees are still here."

"They put off their trip today since Alex was called away yesterday, but I understand they are to leave sometime tomorrow."

"I'm glad to hear they haven't left. I look forward to spending some time with Iain," she lied, knowing her mother nor Alexander MacLaren would be pleased to hear that. "And look. It's stopped raining. Perhaps I will go riding with Iain."

"I don't think Alexander will approve of that, Maura," Anne warned.

"I know," Maura mused, thinking of getting even with Alexander for going to Leanne's room after leaving her. "It seems to me people go out of their way to please Alexander MacLaren. I think 'tis time someone stood up to him."

"Suit yourself, Maura. I know you will do what you want anyway. The MacPhees were told you were too ill to leave your room yesterday, but I want you to know that though your father encouraged you to take that trip with Alex, I did not approve. I dinna wish to see you ruin your reputation."

"I appreciate your concern, Mother," Maura said

staring out the window, "but I did nothing to ruin my reputation."

Alex spent the morning and part of the afternoon taking care of clan business. The sun finally appeared, and he found himself humming as he headed back to Dunraven. He thought about Maura and what had taken place between them the night before, remembering the look of passion in her eyes. He had been frustrated and angry when he left her, but after a sleepless night, he realized it was the only thing he could have done. Donald was his friend, and he had offered them his hospitality—and safety. He smiled to himself. One of these days he was going to find out just how much passion the lady had.

When Alex entered the great hall, he found Colin there with Katherine and Leanne MacPhee, but Maura was nowhere in sight.

"Do you know where Lady Campbell is?" he asked his brother.

"Aye, she and Iain decided to go riding since it cleared up."

"Riding!" Alex shouted. "You're a bloody fool, mon. Cromwell killed her servant trying to learn her whereabouts and you let her go off riding about the countryside with that young wimp."

"What was I supposed to do, Alex? She's not a prisoner here—at least you did not tell me she was. Besides, she told Donald and Anne where she was going."

"Ignorant fool!" Alex slammed his fist on the table. "What did she think she was doing? Saddle up, damnit, we have to go after them."

"Alex, I am sure Iain can take care of Lady Campbell,"

Leanne commented, perplexed that he should be so concerned.

"I canna take that chance. I am going after them."

As Colin got to his feet there was a clatter of horses entering the courtyard. "'Tis probably them now, Alex," he said, relieved that he didn't have to leave Katherine. He had been looking forward to enjoying the lovely day with her, but hadn't dare leave until his brother returned.

Alex stormed out to the courtyard in time to see young MacPhee lift Maura from the saddle. He knew she saw him standing there, yet she turned her back to him and laughed seductively at something MacPhee said.

He clenched his fist, fighting for control over his temper. He had never had a woman affect him the way this one did, he thought angrily. What the hell was she up to? Last night she had been so warm and willing. He had thought she was different, but she was like all the rest with their games and deceptions. He turned back to go inside, knowing if he didn't, he'd make a fool of himself. Damn her, he cursed silently. He should have taken what she offered last night and not given it a second thought.

That evening, Alex leaned back in his chair, his expression black as he watched Maura charm and flirt with Iain and his brothers. She looked absolutely ravishing in an ivory velvet gown trimmed with lavender satin. No doubt she had dressed for Iain MacPhee, he thought jealously.

He was forced to listen to them telling amusing tales about things that happened at court before the King had been taken prisoner. Glancing around the room, he noticed that everyone seemed to be enjoying the stories except for him. He stared at Maura with narrowed, suspicious eyes. She was too animated, too gay. It seemed very strange to him after her mood of last night. On top of that she hadn't spoken to him all evening. Damn Iain MacPhee! If the young fool did not take his eyes off her neckline he was going to strangle the bastard in front of everyone.

Maura glanced up and met Alex's black scowl. How dare he sit there and glare at her as if she were guilty of something, she fumed. How long would it be before he and Leanne slipped off to her room tonight? she wondered bitterly. She shook her head, trying to keep thoughts of last night from her mind. The man was beyond belief. He had women on both sides of him simpering over every word he uttered, yet he sat scowling at her.

"You made a remarkable recovery, Mistress Campbell," Leanne said. "Poor Iain worried over you all day yesterday when you took to your room."

Maura smiled at Iain. "I am sorry to have worried you, but as you can see, I am completely recovered."

"I fear you may still be feverish, mistress," Leanne persisted. "Your face is very flushed."

Maura knew the glow was from the sun and wind, but she only smiled. "Thank you for your concern, my dear, but I feel perfectly well today. I must say though," she couldn't help sniping, "you have dark circles under your eyes. Lack of sleep perhaps?"

She didn't miss the way Alexander looked at her, as if he thought she'd lost her mind. Well, let him. She wanted him to know she knew all about his late-night tryst with Leanne MacPhee. She turned her attention back to Iain and gave him a devastating smile. "Iain, be a dear and pour me some more wine. I am so thirsty this evening."

Iain couldn't take his eyes off her, even as he poured her wine. She was the most exquisite female he had ever seen, and Donald Gordon still had great holdings in Scotland. What a match she would make for him. God, why couldn't he have met her in London? He would have courted her properly there. Now she seemed to only have eyes for the MacLaren. He felt a surge of primitive jealousy towards the man. He would have to do something about that. She was too refined for him. Alexander MacLaren was an outlaw, reckless and arrogant, with a price on his head. Certainly not the type of man in whom a respectable, dignified lady of court would be interested. His ardent gaze lingered on the curve of her mouth, and the long sweeping lashes that veiled her violet eyes. He would write a poem to her beauty, he decided. That always impressed the ladies of court.

While Angus MacPhee turned the conversation to battles the Scots had fought, Iain jotted down his poem on a piece of paper, half listening to what was being said.

"And then there was the battle of Langside where Montrose was defeated by the Covenanters," Angus said.

"I believe that was the battle of Inverlochy, sir," Maura corrected.

"Aye, so it was, lass. In my old age I forget these things."

"How did you know that?" Iain asked, quite amazed that a woman would know such a thing.

"I am an intellect, I'm afraid. I enjoy reading everything I can get my hands on."

"Impossible," Iain exclaimed. "You are too beautiful

to be intelligent."

Alexander snorted, but Maura refused to look at him. "I found the time passed more swiftly as I was growing up when I read. I was able to escape whatever problems faced me that way," she patiently explained to Iain.

Donald Gordon watched his daughter, a worried expression on his face. "I see what you mean, Anne."

"I told you there was something going on between her and Iain MacPhee. I believe she and Alex may have had another argument. Maura actually wanted to leave here this morning."

"I will have a meeting with the MacLarens as soon as the MacPhees leave. There isn't any sense waiting until Cromwell is in Edinburgh."

"Alexander, would you accompany me for a breath of air," Leanne MacPhee asked, tired of being ignored. "It is suddenly so stuffy in here."

Alex dragged his gaze from Maura's face. "It would be my pleasure."

Maura watched them leave, her emotions in a turmoil. Why did she have the urge to scratch this woman's eyes out? She certainly didn't care who Alexander MacLaren chose as his bed partner—or did she? My God, what were these feelings she had for the man? She had never felt like this before.

Her agitation grew as his absence lengthened. She suddenly had a terrible headache from the wine she had drunk too freely and too fast. Colin and Katherine had also disappeared, leaving her to listen to Iain's voice drone on and on. Suddenly she could take no more.

"If you will excuse me, Iain, I am suddenly exhausted. I will see you in the morning before you leave."

"Let me walk you to your room," he insisted.

"That isn't necessary," Maura said, trying politely to discourage him.

"I know it isn't, but I insist. These halls are dark and unguarded. Why, last evening I actually got lost trying to find my room. Besides, I have something I want to give you in private."

What now? Maura thought, forcing a smile. She paused in the doorway and nodded to her mother and father before leaving the hall.

"I know why you are here, Maura," Iain said as they walked up the stairs. "I heard about your arranged marriage to Lord James Randolph. Beast of a man. I just wish I had been the one to help you get away from him."

"That is very kind of you, Iain. I am sorry anyone had to get involved in my problems. The only good thing that came out of it is the reunion with my father."

"Yes, I must admit I was surprised when I heard Donald was the one who arranged for your rescue. What do your Campbell relatives think of you being here with him and the MacLaren?"

"I have no idea, and no desire to know," she said sharply. "They were ready to sacrifice me to Cromwell."

"Ah, yes, I see your point. I just hate to think of you here with the MacLaren."

Maura glanced at him. "Why do you say that?"

"He is considered an outlaw, Maura. There is quite a reward on his head, and your presence here places you in danger as well."

"I fear 'tis the other way around, Iain. My being here

places Alexander and his family in danger, yet he offers my mother and I his hospitality without fear of repercussions."

"Well, if you tire of his dark stares and silent moods, come visit me in Edinburgh. I have a townhouse there now and I would love to have your company."

"Thank you, Iain. That is very kind of you, but 'tis safer for me to remain hidden. With all the English in Edinburgh, 'tis the last place I want to be right now."

"Aye, I see your point."

Maura stopped in front of her door. He was right, the corridor was dark, lit with only one candle on the wall. "Well, I will say good night now."

Iain pulled a piece of paper from his pocket. "I am not a poet," he said haltingly, "but when I looked at you these words just seemed to come to me."

Maura unfolded the paper and read the lines of poetry:

> Violet eyes that make my heart sing
> Soft, ivory skin that I desire to caress
> Black hair, beautiful as a raven's wing
> Pink soft lips that beg for my kiss

She looked at Iain, who anxiously awaited her reaction. She was touched by his words. "This is very lovely, Iain. I have never had anyone write me poetry before. I shall treasure it always."

She impulsively kissed his cheek, but before she could move away, he grasped her to his chest, kissing her deeply.

Maura closed her eyes, expecting her knees to go weak, but nothing happened. His kiss had no effect on her, no weak knees, no rapid pulse, nothing. She realized with disbelief that it was only Alex who affected her that way.

Finally Iain released her, feeling quite pleased with himself. "Please promise me you will be careful around Alexander MacLaren. He is a dangerous, ruthless man. I worry for my sister's safety and virtue whenever she is with him, but unfortunately my parents think he would make a good match for her."

"Is there talk of a wedding?"

"There has been talk of one for years, but nothing comes of it. I believe Leanne has had the good sense to put him off, knowing his reputation."

Maura had to smile at that, thinking of the way Iain's sister had clung to Alexander the entire evening. "Well, I must retire now."

"Please think about my invitation to visit me in Edinburgh," he said as he bowed over her hand.

"Yes, I will consider it. Good night Iain. I will see you in the morning."

Maura leaned against the door and closed her eyes. She didn't need this complication.

"What a touching scene," Alex said from the shadows.

"God's blood," she gasped. "Must you always sneak up on me?"

"I thought you more discriminating to whom you gave your kisses, lass. I had no idea your tastes ran to callow, unscrupulous youths."

"Have you been spying on me?" she asked, wishing she had made it to her room without seeing him. He wreaked havoc on the serenity she so desperately needed this night.

"I was just going to my room when I came upon your passionate rendezvous," he said sarcastically.

"I am surprised you're not staying in Leanne's room

146

again tonight."

He raised a quizzical eyebrow. "Are you jealous, lass?"

"Do not flatter yourself," she spat as she turned and entered her room. Before she could close the door Alex pushed his way inside and closed the door behind him.

"Just what do you think you're doing?"

"I want to know what happened between the time I left you last night and this morning. You've been treating me liko I had the plague."

"I'm surprised you had time to notice," she said, turning her back to him.

"I noticed."

"I'm tired, Alex, and I'm sure you have someone waiting for you."

"What the hell is that supposed to mean?"

"I'm not blind or deaf. I know where you went after leaving me last night. I was given quite a description of you leaving Leanne's room early this morning."

"Somebody has been lying to you," he said angrily.

"Aye, and we know who that is, don't we?" she said sarcastically.

Alex reached out and pulled her hard against him. "So that is why you've been giving all your attention to young Iain MacPhee. You've been trying to make me jealous."

She tore her gaze from his. "I'm sure I haven't the faintest idea what you're talking about."

"Don't you? Tell me, lass, did his kiss make you feel a fire in the blood? Did he make you feel breathless when he touched you? Like this." He traced her lips with his tongue, teasing and nibbling.

Maura knew exactly what he meant. Her knees had already gone weak when he parted her lips and kissed her deeply and passionately.

"Tell me, has any other man ever made you feel like this?"

She shivered as his hand caressed the nape of her neck. "You are arrogant and too sure of yourself," she said, struggling for an even tone.

He laughed deeply in his throat. "Perhaps I am sure of myself because everytime I kiss you, you melt in my arms. I can feel you trembling now, love."

God, he was so right, but suddenly she realized she could hear his heart beating rapidly, and his speech was rough with emotion. Her innocence gave her the nerve to point that fact out to him. "Are you not affected the same way when I kiss you? Does any other woman affect you the way I do?" His eyes suddenly had a vulnerable look, as if she had exposed his soul.

He realized she was right. She held as much power over him as he did over her—maybe even more. He was obsessed with her and had not even realized it.

"Damn you!" he swore before capturing her mouth in a punishing kiss, while his hands entwined roughly in her hair. "Damn you! You do possess me, and I never meant it to happen."

He suddenly released her and headed for the door.

"Where are you going?" she asked, reeling from his reaction.

"To find a dragon to slay. 'Tis much safer than rescuing fair maidens."

She would have laughed at his statement, but she knew it wasn't said in jest. The pain in his voice had been real—too real. Her father had said Alex had spent a lifetime distancing himself from feelings, and in one moment she had shattered his defenses, exposing him to the pain of caring, to the memories of his tragic losses.

She stumbled back towards the bed, grasping the post for support. She had worried about bringing pain to him and his family again, but she never imgagined that pain would be caused by love. This could not be. She would have to distance herself from him, for both their sakes.

All that we see or seem,
Is but a dream within a dream.
                    Edgar Allan Poe

Chapter Twelve

After another sleepless night with hazy images of a beautiful woman haunting her dreams, Maura sat numbly still as Mary brushed her hair.

"Mary, has anyone ever spoken of their sleep being disturbed by voices in this room?"

The brush froze in midstroke. "I dinna ken what you mean," she said, meeting Maura's eyes in the mirror.

Maura sighed. "For the last two nights I have dreamed that a woman, a very beautiful woman, is standing at the foot of my bed, telling me to be patient with Alexander, and not to do anything foolish, that he will come to his senses. "Oh, it's ridiculous, I know," she said laughing nervously. "I only mention it because I wake every morning totally exhausted."

"What does this image look like?" Mary asked as she resumed her brushing.

"As I said, she is very beautiful, with black hair and soft gray eyes that seem to hold so much pain in them."

"'Tis your imagination," Mary quickly said. "There," she continued tying a ribbon around Maura's long black tresses. "You best make haste or you'll be missing the MacPhees' departure."

"I certainly wouldn't want to do that," Maura mumbled to herself.

Everyone except Iain had mounted by the time Maura arrived in the courtyard. Seeing Alex standing beside Leanne's horse made her sick with despair. She forced her attention back to Iain.

"I hope you have a pleasant trip, Iain." She smiled at him.

"I was about to come looking for you," he exclaimed, as he kissed her hand in greeting. "I couldna leave without saying good-bye and arranging to see you again."

"I have enjoyed your visit," Maura forced a smile, "but I do not think I will be here much longer. I am hoping to return to Rockhenge very soon."

"Then I shall visit you at Rockhenge. I do wish you would reconsider visiting me in Edinburgh. We could have a grand time."

Out of the corner of her eye she noticed Alexander listening to them. "That would be very nice, but impossible I fear," she said, suddenly smiling sweetly at Iain. "I shall look forward to your visit at Rockhenge."

"Your family is impatient to be on their way, MacPhee," Alexander said restlessly.

"Until we meet again," Iain said, again kissing Maura's hand before mounting his horse. He thanked Alex for his hospitality, then waved to Maura before heading out of the courtyard.

"Young fool," Alexander mumbled as he headed up the steps.

Maura stared after him, wondering if the man was ever in a decent mood.

"You'll have to excuse Alex this morning," Simon said as he joined Maura. "He has a lot on his mind."

"What is his excuse the rest of the time?" she asked.

Simon laughed. "Is he too violent for your tastes, lass?"

"Fortunately I've seen little of his violent side, but I have certainly seen enough of his black moods."

"Like all Scots, I fear," Simon said ruefully. "Scotland is a quarrelsome place and a man must learn to be judicious to keep his head on his shoulders.".

"Do you often have to make excuses for him, Simon?"

"Only when I think it is important the offended person understand him. Besides," he laughed, "have not you already realized a Scot manages his affairs more by passion and fury than by logic."

"That seems to describe Alexander MacLaren perfectly," she said bitterly.

"Aye, we are a proud lot, Maura, but our hearts are in the right place. We are loyal to what we believe, and we protect our own with our lives."

Maura studied Simon for a long moment. "Why are you telling me this, Simon?"

He chuckled. "I think you should understand Alex. I know he gets under your skin, but I think he cares deeply for you, even if he has not admitted it to himself."

She shook her head. "If truth be known, he fairly drives me to distraction, but I have decided it would be better for all if I just try to avoid him."

Before Simon had a chance to ask her why, he was interrupted by Glenna. "Simon," Glenna called out from the top of the stairs. "Donald would like you to join him in the solar."

Simon held his arm out to Maura. "Will you join me, and we can talk some more?"

"Thank you, but I have not had anything to eat this morning. I think I will check with the cook and see if I can beg some food from her."

"Jane has a soft place in her heart for all bonnie lasses," he assured. "I am sure she will feed you."

Maura found the cook in the kitchen building, already starting her baking for the evening meal. "Good morning, Jane. I dinna wish to be troublesome, but I wondered if I could get a piece of bread and a cup of tea. I dinna get down in time this morning to have breakfast."

The big woman smiled at her. "I can do better than that, mistress. Do you like haggis?"

"Oh, yes, if you're sure it isn't too much trouble."

"No trouble, lass."

"Do you mind if I stay here to eat?" Maura asked, noticing the big wooden table in the corner. "No one seems to be around in the great hall."

"'Tis fine," Jane said as she dished out a bowl of the pudding. "Ha' the MacPhee left?"

"Aye, just minutes ago," Maura answered.

"I hear young Colin is smitten with the younger MacPhee. She is a sweet girl."

"Yes, she did seem sweet," Maura said, sipping her tea.

"Not like the other one," Jane said, a knowing smile on her face as she set the bowl of haggis in front of Maura. "Mistress Leanne fancies herself the Queen of Scotland."

Maura had to laugh. "How do you know so much when

154

you are out here cooking all day?"

"Gossip floats on the wind in Scotland, dinna you know? 'Tis part of our problem."

"Oh, this is wonderful, Jane," Maura exclaimed.

"'Tis glad I am that you are enjoying it. 'Tis one of the MacLaren's favorites."

"Have you been with the MacLarens long, Jane?"

"Aye, I was with his mother and father before him."

"It seems like everyone at Dunraven has been here forever," Maura commented as she ate.

"Aye, we Scots are a loyal lot, particularly when we respect the laird. He is a fine lad."

"So everyone tells me," Maura said, finishing off the haggis. "Thank you so much, Jane. I will leave you to your baking now."

Maura wandered back into the great hall. It was still empty and she was becoming increasingly curious about everyone's whereabouts. She headed for the solar, knowing at least Simon and her father would be there.

As she approached the room she heard male voices raised in anger. She froze, hearing Alex's voice above the others.

"I dinna like it, nor do I see how marrying one of us will help her situation. I am sure 'tis not what the lass wants, and I think she should have some say in the matter."

"It will mean James Randolph will have no claim on her," her father was saying. "That is most important now. You and I both know they will be in Edinburgh before too long."

Maura's throat tightened and she could scarcely swallow. Her father wanted one of the MacLarens to marry her to keep her safe from Lord Randolph. My God, she would not allow such a sacrifice.

She heard Colin's voice next. "You know how I feel. I would be honored to marry Maura."

Colin . . . Colin . . . Oh my God, it was Colin they wanted her to marry. No, no, it could not be.

Backing from the door, Maura ran to her room, the tears blurring her vision. They would not treat her like a piece of cattle or a lamb to be led to the slaughter. She wouldn't let any of the MacLarens be forced into marriage with her. She should have taken matters into her own hands long before this.

Maura quickly dressed in the breeches and warm shirt she had worn the day before. She desperately glanced around the room, trying to think of what else she should take. A weapon. Of course. She would need something to protect herself.

She slipped into the room she assumed was Alex's and as soon as she entered it, she had no doubt. It was furnished with massive furniture and on the bed was a fur throw. After searching his writing table, she found a dirk lying beneath some papers. She slipped it into her waistband, then started for the door. She hesitated, then grabbed the throw off the bed. The weather would still be harsh at night. There wasn't any sense freezing, she thought, throwing it over her shoulder.

Maura slipped down to the courtyard, trying to think of someway to get the guard at the gatehouse to let the drawbridge down without sounding an alarm to Alex. Then she saw a crofter's wagon filled with peat, and he was just about to leave.

Maura came to a decision. Whether it was a wise one, she wouldn't know until later.

* * *

"Has anyone seen Maura?" Anne asked after checking her room and the great hall.

"Maybe she is with Donald," Simon suggested as he looked up from polishing his sword.

"No, Donald said he hadn't seen her at all today, which is surprising."

"She was with me when the MacPhees left," Simon mused, "but I dinna see her after our meeting in the solar."

"Where is Alex?" Anne asked, wringing her hands.

"He said he was going to check the stock, and Colin went with him." Simon laughed. "I think he was still reeling from his announcement that he would be the one to marry Maura."

"Yes, that is what I want to talk to her about," Anne said, a worried expression on her face. "Is it possible that Maura went with them?"

"Aye, 'tis possible. If you're concerned I'll ride out and check."

"Thank you, Simon," Anne said, collapsing into a chair. She rubbed her temples in a circular pattern. "I know 'tis foolish, but I have this feeling—nothing definite—but I would feel better knowing where she is."

The wrong way always seems the
more reasonable.
George Moore

Chapter Thirteen

Maura stumbled over a loose rock and came sliding
down on her knees, tearing the breeches she wore. She
sat down among the rubble and touched her bleeding
knees. Tears came to her eyes, but it was more from anger
at herself, than hurt. She had been foolish to leave
Dunraven without a plan. She had no idea where she was
going, and dusk was already falling, with it a thin veil of
mist enshrouding everything in a swirl of gray.

Getting to her feet, she tried once again to follow
the rocky path. She should have stolen one of the
MacLaren's horses, she thought in frustration, and some
food. She'd probably end up starving to death wandering
aimlessly around in the rugged terrain.

The mountains around her rose up, primitive and forbidding as the shadows began to descend. The terrain was
littered with rocky crags and loose rocks, and every step
she took had to be a cautious one. She was quickly losing
daylight, and she was afraid she'd find herself sliding
uncontrollably down a gorge on the scree.

She sat for a moment and watched a golden eagle glide

on the air currents above her, graceful and free. "I wish I could trade places with you, Sir Eagle. It would make my journey so much easier."

After resting for a few minutes she continued on, hoping to find a stream or loch. She could do without food awhile longer, but it was difficult to quench her thirst with just the mist of rain falling.

She pulled her cloak over her head and continued on, having no idea where she was going, but knowing she had to keep moving. She had never imagined she would feel so lonely leaving Dunraven—or was it Alexander MacLaren? She thought of the way his touch affected her, then shook her head to dispel the memories. No matter what she did, his face kept appearing. She had to put him from her mind, she told herself. If he would allow Colin to marry her, he cared nothing for her. She brushed away a tear. At least now none of the MacLarens would be in danger because of her. She would find her Campbell relatives and stay with them until the danger from Cromwell and Randolph had passed. No one need know where she had spent the past couple of weeks.

Pangs of hunger gripped her and her throat felt dry and parched. She raised her face to the light mist, trying to get enough on her tongue to quench her thirst, if only for a little while.

She could barely see where she was going now. Everything seemed to be covered with thin gray gauze as darkness fell. Maura glanced around her as fear set in. God, she was hopelessly lost.

Suddenly she heard the sound of water. She rushed forward, looking down into the steep ravine. It was too dark to see the stream, but she could hear it, she could definitely hear it. She began walking the ridge, trying to find someplace to begin the decline. She paused, pressing her hand to her aching back. If she was going to get to flat land before it was totally dark she had to find a way down the cliff without wasting another minute.

Suddenly a terrifying shriek sounded from behind her. Maura spun around, coming face to face with a wildcat perched on a boulder, ready to pounce. Slowly she backed away, never taking her eyes from the hypnotic glowing eyes of the cat. The rocks she stood on began to move, and with a bloodcurdling scream, she began to fall. She tried to grab something—anything—as she tumbled down and down into nothingness.

Alex and Colin left the path, leaving Simon and the other men to continue following it. Alex knew Maura hadn't taken a horse, and he wondered how far she had gotten. Only the hardiest of men could survive in such a harsh environment, and only if they were well prepared.

Neither man spoke as their horses made their way over the treacherous landscape. Alex kept wondering what would have made Maura take such desperate flight. Would she have been fool enough to try to follow Iain MacPhee? he wondered. Surely not. He knew very well why she had led the man on. The only other possible reason was that she had overheard their meeting in the solar. That had to be it. He wouldn't blame her for being furious, but to run away into a wilderness she was not familiar with was suicide.

"Oh God," he moaned as he realized where his morbid thoughts were going.

"What is it, Alex?" Colin asked. "Do you see something?"

"No. No, damnit," he said, running his hand through his wet hair in frustration.

"We'll find her, Alex," Collin assured, his heart going out to his brother. He glanced at the pained expression on Alex's face. This was a side of Alex he had never seen. He had seen him cool and cunning in battle, wise and fair running his clan, but he had never seen him paralyzed by fear like this. Alex was definitely in love with Maura Campbell, and for some reason Colin felt sorry for him. It was the first time since their mother and sister died that Alex hadn't been able to control what he felt, and he had spent years building walls around his emotions. Now those walls were crumbling, his cool, dispassionate facade in ruins.

"We're going to have to leave the horses and go on foot from here," Alex said as they came to a gorge banked by high cliffs.

"'Tis going to be dark soon," Colin commented, glancing down at the dangerous terrain.

"Aye, I know. She must be frightened to death."

"Do you think she overheard our meeting, Alex?" Colin finally ventured to ask.

"'Tis the only reason I can think of for her to take flight."

"Poor lass. It must have been terrible for her." Suddenly Colin dropped to one knee. "Alex, look. 'Tis a piece of cloth . . . and a bit of blood on the rocks."

Alex inspected the cloth, then looked around. "It looks like there was a rock slide recently. At least if it was Maura she was able to continue."

"I suppose 'tis some sort of clue," Colin said with hope in his voice.

*　　　*　　　*

162

Maura slowly woke, the pain in her head and back unbearable. She shivered as the cold, damp night settled around her. She was freezing. Then she realized her lower body was lying in the cold mountain stream— ironically the same stream she had been so desperate to get to. She tried to move, but couldn't. The pain was excruciating. An overwhelming sense of despair flooded over her. She was going to die there alone, never to see her family or Alex MacLaren again.

Waves of pain washed over her again, and she tried to fight the blackness, but finally closed her eyes, giving in. It was easier, she thought. Then she heard the strangest thing—music, harp music drifting on the wind. Oh God, she was dying and already hearing heavenly music.

Colin had lit a torch as they continued to move over the rugged mountains, yet still it was difficult to see. They were both battered and bruised from the sharp crags and rock slides.

Finally after climbing down into one of the gorges, they slowed down long enough to drink from a stream. "Maybe we should stop for the night, Alex," Colin suggested. "We could go right past her this way and never know it."

"I canna stop, Colin," Alex said, pain and frustration in his voice. "I have to find her."

Colin put his hand on Alex's shoulder. "We will find—"

"Listen!" Alex silenced him.

Colin fell silent, wondering what it was his brother heard. "I dinna hear a thing."

"It is harp music, mon, canna you hear it?" Alex asked in frustration.

Colin stared at his brother, a concerned look on his

face. All he could hear was the croak of a frog and the hoot of an owl. His brother was strong. Surely he wouldn't let something like this send him over the edge. My God, he hadn't heard harp music since their mother died.

"Dinna you hear it? 'Tis coming from downstream," Alex exclaimed, already running in the direction of the sound only he was hearing.

Alex hesitated. The music had become louder then stopped. Slowly he moved along the water's edge, stumbling over something lying in the water. "God's blood . . ." His heart froze as he realized it was a body.

"What is it, Alex?" Colin asked, unable to see anything in the darkness.

"God, no. No, not again," he moaned in anguish as he cradled Maura's head in his lap. "Not everyone I love . . ."

"Sweet Jesus," Colin swore as he knelt on one knee next to his brother. "Is she . . . ?"

As Alex smoothed the wet hair from her face he noticed a flicker of pain across her features. "I think she lives. She is not dead," he exclaimed, finding a weak pulse in her throat. " 'Tis a feeble pulse, but 'tis there. We've got to find someplace nearby to take her where we can get her warm. We dinna dare move her too far before knowing the extent of her injuries."

"Old Sim MacLean's place hasn't been used the past few months. 'Tis not far from here," Colin said, picking up the fur throw Maura had lost in her fall.

Gently Alex lifted Maura in his arms. "Lead the way."

The hut had few luxuries, but there was a bed and

plenty of peat for a fire.

"I've got to get her out of these wet clothes," Alex said, trying to rub some circulation back into her hands. "Her skin feels like ice."

"I laid the fur throw on the foot of the bed," Colin pointed out as he busied himself with building a fire.

"She does not wince when I move her arms or legs," Alex said as he removed her wet clothes. "I fear 'tis this nasty knot on her temple that has done the damage."

"She must have taken a fall down that cliff, Alex. Why else would she have been in the water?"

"Aye, and if that is the case, we are lucky to have found her alive."

"I still dinna know how we found her at all," Colin said as the fire roared to a blaze. "We were about to cross the stream at that point. Whatever made you decide to look where you did?"

"I told you. I heard harp music. It led me to her."

"Alex, I dinna doubt there are spirits and witches, but harp music?"

"Not just harp music, Colin, but 'Coronach,' Mother's favorite song."

Colin had been keeping his eyes averted, but he quickly glanced up to see if his brother was serious. From the look on Alex's face he had no doubt.

"I wish she'd come around," Alex said, briskly rubbing her legs until the coldness disappeared. "I was hoping she'd wake up while I was undressing her and curse me for being so forward."

Colin watched as Alex pulled the fur throw up under her chin. "She is strong, Alex. She will come around."

Alex studied her beautiful face in repose. "Aye, she has to, Colin," he said in a choked voice. "I have to have

165

the chance to tell her I love her."

Colin put a comforting hand on his brother's shoulder. "You will have your chance, I am sure of it. By God, you had spirits leading you to her. How can you not have faith she will make it?"

Alex smiled. "Aye, I pray you are right."

"Do you want me to go back to Dunraven and get help?"

"No. 'Tis too dangerous in the blackness of night. In the morning see if you can find a way to bring my horse here before leaving to find the search party. Then return to Dunraven, and tell Donald and Anne that we found Maura, but it will be a few days before I attempt to move her. I have seen too many head injuries take a turn for the worse by moving the injured person around unnecessarily."

"Aye, you are probably right," Colin said, passing his brother a flask of whiskey. "Sim had to have another way into this place. I am sure he dinna climb that mountain everytime he came and went."

Alex took a long drink. "Why don't you bed down before the fire and I'll stay awake in case there is a change."

"You should lie down beside Maura and also rest. You willna do her any good if you are exhausted."

"I'll lie down later."

Alex sat there staring at her as she slept. She looked so beautiful, so vulnerable. He sighed deeply. Why had she felt it necessary to leave the safety of Dunraven? If she had overheard the conversation he had with her father, why hadn't she just come forward and told them all to go to hell. It wouldna have been the first time. She had more spirit and determination than any woman he'd ever met.

He smiled and gently touched her face. When had she come to possess him? Probably the day she had climbed down the tower of Beaumaris Castle, he thought. If he were honest with himself, he'd admit his vow to remain unmarried had been on shaky ground from the moment he looked into her violet eyes. He just prayed he would have a chance to correct the situation. He had always thought to let Simon and Colin produce heirs for the future security of the clan, but now he knew he wanted to marry Maura, to have children with her. God, grant him life with her, he prayed.

Music I heard with you was more
than music . . .
                              Conrad Aiken

Chapter Fourteen

Maura tried to open her eyes, but the effort was too great. Every bone in her body ached, but it was the pain in her head that threatened to send her back into the blackness of unconsciousness.

Slowly she realized she had nothing on beneath the fur pelt. What kind of person had brought her here and stripped her of her clothes? she wondered, afraid to open her eyes again. She could hear the crackle of a fire, but other than that all around her was quiet.

"Alex," she gasped in disbelief as she made out the sleeping form in the chair next to her bed.

Alex opened his eyes, relief flooding his features as he gently touched her face. "Welcome back, lass."

"How did you find me?" she winced in pain as she spoke. "I thought I had died. I even heard harp music."

Alex raised a dark eyebrow. "Aye, lass, so did I. 'Tis what led me to you. I think you should rest now and we'll speak of it again in the morning."

Maura smiled. "Alex, it is morning."

He glanced at the sunlight peeking in the window

beneath the wooden shutters. "Aye, so it is," he answered, realizing Colin had already left. Lying in front of the fireplace was his flacon of wine and his supplies.

"Where are we?" Maura asked.

"A deserted hut not far from where we found you. Would you like a drink of water?" She nodded her head. When he lifted her head, she gasped in pain. "Do you think something is broken, lass?"

"I don't know. I ache all over . . . and, Alex, my vision is blurred," she admitted, trying to keep the panic from her voice.

"'Tis no wonder. You apparently fell off a mountain."

"All I have to do is breathe to realize that." She smiled weakly. "I remember hearing a stream, and I was so thirsty. I was planning to climb down to it when a wildcat appeared out of nowhere. The next thing I knew, I was falling through the air."

"You are lucky to be alive," he said, touching a cool, wet cloth to her bruised head. "The blurred vision will disappear. Simon had the same thing once when he fell off Dubh Sith. After a few days' rest he was fine."

"Are we going to stay here?"

"Aye, you are going to have to put yourself in my hands for a few days. Colin returned to Dunraven to tell Donald and Anne that we found you."

A blush rose to her face as she remembered why she had taken flight. "Colin was here?" she asked hesitantly.

"Aye, I had all my men out looking for you. You gave us quite a scare, lass. Do you want to tell me why you left Dunraven?"

She closed her eyes, unable to discuss the marriage plans she had overheard. "I'm afraid I'm going to fall to sleep again. I am so tired."

"We will discuss it sooner or later, lass."

"Aye. Later then, please," she said with a yawn.

"All right, lass. I am going to catch us some breakfast. I willna be long."

When Maura woke next she could smell something delicious cooking, and it set her empty stomach to rumbling. Tentatively she sat up, pulling the fur throw up under her chin as she wrapped it around her. "Something smells wonderful."

Alex smiled at her. "Do not attempt any more than that, lass. 'Tis one thing to sit, but quite another to stand. Dizziness usually accompanies the blurred vision."

"Aye, I can attest to that."

"If you would like to try sitting in that chair before the fire to eat, I will carry you to it."

"I hate to put you to the trouble." Suddenly she laughed shortly. "That doesn't make a lot of sense, does it? I have been nothing but trouble to you since the day you rescued me from Deaumaris Castle in England."

Alex smiled at her. "I wouldna say that. Granted, they have been few, but I have had some pleasant moments with you."

"'Tis kind of you to say, but I realize that you would not be out here now, away from your clan, if I had not run off. It seems I am constantly placing you in danger."

Alex turned the fish over in the pan. "Do you want to tell me now why you ran away, lass?"

Maura closed her eyes and took a long breath. "I overheard Colin make the sacrifice of offering to marry me to protect me from Lord Randolph. I could not allow it."

"Why did you not just say so?"

Maura stared at the floor. "You make it sound so easy, but I knew if my mother and father were set on my marriage to a MacLaren, I would have no say in the matter, particularly if Colin was willing. Perhaps that does not make sense to you, but it did to me at the time. It is very difficult being a woman and having every decision concerning your life taken from you."

"Aye, I can see where it would be most vexing, but your decision to take flight almost cost you your life, lass."

Maura touched the bruise on her head. "Aye, I realize that. I fear I will have reminders of my folly for quite awhile. I should have been better prepared."

"Would you like me to move you to the chair?"

"I . . . I don't know." Maura clutched the fur to her naked body. "Alex, I have no clothes on," she stammered.

"Aye, I know." He smiled devilishly. "'Tis too late to be prudish, lass. You were soaked through to the skin when we found you." He leaned over, wrapping the fur tightly around her before picking her up. She looked lovely, he thought, with her midnight black hair tumbling around her bare shoulders, and her eyes wide with burning innocence.

"Then it was you who undressed me?"

"I could find no lady's maid, so 'twas that or leave you to take cold in your wet clothes."

Maura couldn't think of anything to say. She sat silently studying the scrapes and cuts on her hands where she had apparently tried to grab at rocks as she fell.

"Is your vision any better?" he asked.

"Aye, some."

"And the head?"

"Not so painful now, thank you."

Alex laughed. "Why so formal, lass?"

"This is all just a bit embarrassing. I know you must be angry with me, yet here you are waiting on me, and being so concerned."

"That doesna mean I am not angry with you," he said, taking one of her hands in his large one. "You gave me a terrible scare."

Maura met his steady gaze. "Did I?" A moment passed, and then another. He was staring at her, unnerving her. "I should not have caused you to leave Dunraven land," she said hastily. "If the English caught you here you would not stand a chance."

He shrugged. "These are hard times. All men must die sooner or later."

Maura shivered. "Please don't say that."

He gently kissed her sore hands. "Would it matter to you, lass?"

Maura lowered her gaze from his hypnotic gray eyes. "Aye. Particularly if it were my fault."

Alex laughed. "Ah, so 'tis only a clear conscience you care about."

"That's not what I mean," she quickly exclaimed.

"I know," he said as he stood up. "You must be starved. I did not notice any food on your person when I found you."

Maura looked embarrassed. "I fear I was in too much of a hurry to think of it. I did borrow a knife and the fur throw from your room though."

"That was very wise of you. I am sure you would have killed some game as you continued on your journey, and it is always important to be warm."

173

"You are making fun of me," Maura said.

"Not really, lass," he said good-naturedly. "I hope you are hungry. I caught a fine salmon, and Colin left us some bannock and a flacon of wine."

"It sounds wonderful. I am fair starved."

"A healthy appetite is a good sign," he said as he moved the small wooden table in front of her. "I apologize for the lack of eating utensils, but old Sim had only the barest necessities. I suppose we are fortunate to have plates to put our food on."

Maura broke a piece of the flaky fish off with her fingers and popped it into her mouth. "'Tis delicious just like this."

"I am glad you like it," Alex said, pulling a chair up to sit opposite her. "We may have to eat a lot of fish before we go back to Dunraven."

Maura's hand stopped midway to her mouth, and her violet eyes met his. "I am not going back to Dunraven."

He took a bite of fish before asking. "What do you plan to do, lass?"

"I will find my Campbell relatives and stay with them for awhile."

Alex took another bite of fish, considering what she was saying. "Why would you want to do that? You once said you cared nothing for your relatives."

Maura lowered her eyes to her plate. "Aye, 'tis true, but I will not force Colin to marry me."

"I dinna think Colin feels it would be such a sacrifice," he said with a shrug.

For some reason, his attitude angered her. "It does not matter. I cannot marry him."

Alex smiled, pleased with her answer. "Eat, lass. You need your strength for whatever you choose to do. We can discuss this later."

Maura took another bite. "I will not change my mind. You told me if I was not happy at Dunraven that you would allow me to go to my Campbell relatives."

"Aye, so I did. But for the next couple of days you willna be going anyplace."

"When will Colin return?" she asked.

"He will not. I told him when you were well enough to travel that we would return to Dunraven."

Maura thought it was strange that Alex was the one who had stayed with her, but then dismissed the thought, deciding it must be because he was the laird of his clan.

Alex poured wine in an earthen cup and handed it to her. "Thank you," she said softly. "I would appreciate it if when you return to Dunraven, you would explain to my mother and father why I could not return with you."

"Aye, when you make me see the wisdom in that choice, I will explain it to them."

"I told you why," she sighed in frustration. "You are in enough danger from the English without me adding to your problems. If I continue to depend on you I fear you will end up with no lands and no title."

"Look at me, Maura." When she did not look up, his hand gripped her chin firmly, forcing her to look at him. "I have killed many men, some in battle, some not, and I am sure I will kill many more. Nothing you do or have done will put me in any more danger than I have been in since I was born."

She stared at him, wanting to tell him that she would surely die if anything happened to him, whether she was the cause or not. But she could not. He was content to let his brother marry her, and that thought made her heart ache.

"What is it now, lass?"

She shook her head, and handed him the wine cup. "I am suddenly exhausted," she said, fighting back tears.

Alex removed the table from in front of her and easily picked her up. "Have I upset you?" he asked as he gently laid her on the bed.

She shook her head, but he could see the tears escape her closed eyes. He stood over her for a long time, considering telling her how he felt, but then he decided to wait until she was stronger, and perhaps more reasonable. He could not tell her he simply would not allow her to leave him. As stubborn as she was she'd take flight again.

Touching the soft skin of her jawline, he imagined her willing under his caresses. Faith, he ached to possess her, to awaken her inexperienced body. She was as ready as he was, of that he was sure. Just touching her sent a delightfully painful tingle through him.

Chapter Fifteen

Maura fell into a troubled sleep, beset by images of the English dragging Alex away from her. He was glaring at her, calling her a traitor, his face cold and angry. Soldiers surrounded them, with Oliver Cromwell barking out orders to kill the traitorous Scot, to hang the MacLaren and leave his carcass to hang in the streets of Edinburgh until the birds picked his bones clean.

"No!" Maura screamed. "Don't harm him." She pleaded with anyone who would listen, but everyone ignored her as if she weren't there. "Please, don't hang him. 'Tis my fault . . . 'tis my fault. He hates me—I am to blame for all his troubles."

"Maura, wake up," Alex gently shook her. "You're having a bad dream."

Maura reluctantly opened her eyes, afraid of what she would find, but Alex sat next to her on the bed, his hands on her shoulders, a concerned look on his face. She sat up and wrapped her arms around his neck, hugging him tightly to her trembling body. "I thought . . . Oh, God, I thought," she began to sob, but couldn't put her nightmare into words.

"'Tis all right, love. You were only having a bad dream," he comforted.

Maura raised her tear-stained face to his, her soft violet eyes full of anguish. "I pray I do not have my mother's gift of sight," she whispered on a sob.

"What did you see, lass?"

"I cannot . . ." She buried her face against his neck. "'Tis too terrible."

"I will not let anything happen to you, love."

"It is not myself I am concerned for."

"I told you to stop worrying about me," he said gently as he caressed her shoulder. "I can take care of myself."

Suddenly Maura realized the fur had dropped away and Alex held her nude body to his. The only indication she had that he was in any way affected by her was by the small muscle twitching in his jaw.

"I am sorry. You must think me a fool," she whispered, lowering her eyes.

"'Tis the furthest thing from my mind, lass," he answered, as his lips brushed gently against hers.

It was a soft caress, yet Maura shivered uncontrollably. He hesitated a moment before his kiss deepened, his tongue penetrating ever so softly the recesses of her sweet mouth. Her limbs seemed to liquify, and she felt as if he took every ounce of strength she possessed. His kiss was so intoxicating she wanted it to go on forever, to lose herself in the white-hot heat that spread through her body. Her senses throbbed as his lips moved from her mouth along the sensitive skin of her neck. She wrapped her hand in his thick, wavy hair, drawing him back to her mouth.

Alex stared into her passion-filled eyes. "I dinna want

to hurt you," he whispered huskily.

"The only way you can hurt me is to leave me again," she boldly admitted, surprising even herself.

His hand lingered just above the exposed ivory skin of her breasts. "Do you find it such a diverting game," he said quietly, "to court disaster?"

The look in his eyes set her pulse racing even more. "Would it be a disaster?"

He smiled down at her. "Speaking from conceit and pride, I wouldna deem it oo, but you are a chaste woman, and this moment of passion will change your life forever."

"My life was changed forever when I met you," she said softly.

"Oh, sweet Maura," he whispered, running his thumb along her jawline, "you give no quarter."

"Is it quarter you wish?"

His eyes were dark with passion as he took in the pale loveliness of her nude body. "'Tis the last thing I want," he admitted as he began to remove his linen shirt.

She watched him undress, holding her breath as she took in the hard rippling muscles, and the many scars along his golden skin. She had never seen a man this way. The secrets of the male body were now revealed to her, and she found them beautiful. "You have been hurt so many times," she whispered as she gently traced the jagged scar on his side.

"Does my scarred body offend your sensibilities?" he asked as he lay down beside her.

"Your body is beautiful. I only wish I had been there to help you fend off your enemies."

"Ah, little one, the last thing I would wish is for you to take up a sword to protect me."

His face was now above her, a mere breath away. She could feel his hard muscled legs burning her bare skin where he lay against her—and then his warm hand touched her breast. She gasped as his lips followed, blazing a fiery path to the hard peaks. When he sucked a nipple into the warm recesses of his mouth, she thought she would die. She felt it in every fiber of her being, igniting a fire that burned from her breasts to her loins. She arched her hips off the bed with an unnamed need.

Slowly, he told himself. She is an innocent—an innocent who was driving him over the edge. Her passionate response left him breathless, and rocked his lonely world. He knew in that moment of time his life would never be the same. He needed her as he needed air to breathe. Life would be meaningless without her.

His hands moved possessively up and down her back, pressing her lightly to his hard arousal. "You are so beautiful," he whispered hoarsely.

His kisses were intoxicating, making her crave his touch, his sweet words of seduction. Even though she trembled from fear of the unknown, she knew this was what she wanted. There was no turning back now. There was only the present—this moment. There would be time tomorrow to think of leaving him.

"Sweet, sweet Maura," he whispered, running his tongue along the outline of her parted mouth. "You are a seductress, a beautiful, desirable seductress. I am nearly crazy with wanting you, with wanting to possess you."

He wreaked havoc on her senses as his warm hand moved along the sensitive skin of her inner thigh, seeking her most intimate part. Despite her desperate need for him, she began to tremble violently, and closed her legs against him.

He instantly felt her fear, and moved his hand back up to softly caress her hip. "Dinna be afraid, lass. I will try to make it as painless as possible. Give me your sweetness. Open up for me and let me prepare the way."

Her reaction was to soar up against his hand, which allowed his fingers to press even deeper inside of her. She clung to him, mindless of anything except the exquisite sensations he was giving her.

"You are so hot, so wet," he whispered against her mouth. "Later I will savor your sweetness." When he heard Maura's catch of breath, he assured her, "Relax, love. You are going to love everything I do to you." He kissed her deeply one more time before kneeling between her legs. "I think you are ready now, love."

Bracing his weight on his arms, he held her face between his hands. " 'Tis going to hurt for a moment, my sweet, but know that 'tis done with love."

Maura stared at him, a confused look in her passion-filled eyes. " 'Tis done with love . . ." he had said. Before she had time to think on his words, he lifted her hips and slowly entered her moist softness. And she was ready for him. Her silken warmth embraced him, expanding to take him.

His groan mingled with hers as he forced himself to be gentle, delaying the inevitable, as he encountered the delicate barrier that he would have to break through. He withdrew by inches, trying to delay the pain he dreaded inflicting. When he could take the torture no longer, he drove full length into her. Her gasp of pain pierced him like a knife. "That is it, love. It will hurt no more," he whispered, holding her tightly against him.

For a long moment he lay perfectly still, and Maura found herself savoring the sensation of having him joined to her. Slowly he resumed his movement, Maura picking up the same tempo. She cried out, clinging to him as the pulsing deep inside her exploded, rocking her body with wave after wave of pleasure, and at the same moment Alex's whole body jerked as he poured his seed into her.

For a long time they clung to each other. Maura surfaced slowly, a riot of confused emotions railing within. How could he allow his brother to marry her after this? Surely what just happened between them was special. She gazed at his face, running her fingertip over the jagged scar. Maybe she was just fooling herself. He had had women all his life. Perhaps it was always like this for him.

Alex opened his eyes and smiled at her. "Are you angry with me, lass?"

Maura shook her head, surprised by his question. "Why should I be angry with you? You took nothing that I did not offer willingly."

He kissed her deeply, drawing the sweetness from her mouth into his own. "I can't look at you without wanting you again," he whispered against her parted lips. "Somehow I knew it would be like this with you."

Her fingers delved into his thick hair, marveling at the feelings he was able to evoke again so quickly. Driven by pure instinct, and following his lead, Maura ran her tongue over his skin, gently grasping his nipples between her teeth, as he had done to her. He moaned, and grasped her by the back of her hair. Beneath her mouth she could feel the rapid beating of his heart, and it pleased her that she held such power over him.

After experiencing all the exquisite torture he could stand, Alex rolled her under him and made love to her again, this time slowly, and with deliberate and consummate skill.

She was breathless and pleasurably exhausted when he finally held her in his arms and slept. She puzzled over his whispered words of love, hungering to believe the promises he had made during their lovemaking, words that had inflamed her senses, yet she was afraid to. He must have been born to the secrets of sorcery, she thought as she lovingly touched his face, because she had fallen under his spell as soon as he touched her. Would she ever be the same? One thing she knew for sure, leaving him would be the most difficult thing she had ever done in her life. She had never known such happiness, and mayhap it must last her for a lifetime.

Suddenly she thought of the irony of it all. Her mother had had to leave the only man she loved to keep him from harm. Life does repeat itself. Now she was faced with the same decision, the same sacrifice. The only way to keep Alexander safe from Cromwell and Lord Randolph was to leave him—no matter how hard it would be.

A moment lived in paradise
Is not atoned for too dearly by death.
J. Christoph Friedrich von Schiller

Chapter Sixteen

She must have dozed, because the next time she opened her eyes, Alex was staring down at her, his gray eyes amused. She could feel the heat rise to her face. He ran his thumb along her jawline, an affectionate gesture she was coming to enjoy immensely.

"I knew it would be incredible between us. You are a passionate wench, sweet Maura."

"You once said all you needed was a woman to warm your bed. You cared nothing about her name or her face."

"Aye, I did," he said, placing a light kiss on her nose, "but, sweet, you just proved me very wrong. I dinna realize I would find a lass who could set the bed ablaze."

She turned her face from his warm gaze. "Maura, love, what we did is quite natural. I shouldna tease you about it, but you pleased me greatly."

Drawing a steadying breath, she lovingly touched his cheek. "You pleased me greatly also. I never knew . . . I mean I had no idea it would be like this."

Alex smiled at her tenderly. "It is not always like this,

love. We just experienced something very special."

Something special, she thought silently, yet you would allow me to marry your brother.

"Is something wrong, love?" he asked, touching a curl of her black hair.

"No. What could be wrong?"

"Good," he said, quickly kissing her. "I better catch us some dinner. Maybe I can trap a rabbit."

"I'd rather have more of that wonderful fish." She smiled warmly.

"So be it, lass," he said, leaping from the bed. "Fish it shall be for my lady fair."

"Alex, where are my clothes?" Maura asked as she watched him dress.

"I burned them."

"Alex!"

He laughed at the shock on her face. "They are right there by the fire, but I like you much better just the way you are. As a matter of fact," he said, leaning over and kissing her leisurely, "If I had my way I would keep you like that all the time."

"Would you?" she forced a smile. Even if I were your brother's wife? she thought bleakly.

"I'll return soon, love. In the meantime, I want you to rest."

"I'm feeling better," she assured. "I think I'd like to move about."

Alex headed for the door. "Dinna overdo, lass."

"I won't."

When she was alone, she slowly tested her strength. She was still sore, but the blurred vision and dizziness had disappeared. There wasn't any sense in delaying the inevitable, she thought sadly. Tonight when Alex was asleep, she would leave. Today she would familiarize herself with the area, and with a little luck and discretion, she would learn where they were.

After dressing, Maura went outside to find Alex. She spotted him balancing on the rocks in the middle of the stream, a wooden spear in his hand. She glanced around at her surroundings. The cottage was a pretty little place, made of stone with a sod roof. Just a short distance from the house was a leanto where Dubh Sith stood chewing on hay.

She walked over to the horse and rubbed his velvet nose. "I may have to borrow you, my lovely friend. Would you allow that if I promised to have you returned to Alex? I wouldn't do this if I didn't have to. It is to keep him safe."

She sighed and turned back towards the stream. The sun was beginning to set and it was beautiful as a rainbow appeared in the sky, its colors bright and defined. Maura sat on the grass, imagining life here in their little utopia. It would be wonderful, she thought longingly. They would hunt and fish for their food, and have peace—peace to raise children.

Shaking her head, she gave her full attention to Alex, admiring his beautiful, graceful body. A body she now knew intimately. Just watching him made her tingle with excitement and desire.

He leaned over, jabbing the spear into the water and coming up with a flapping fish. He tossed it to the bank, then proceeded to do the same thing again.

Maura got to her feet and headed in his direction. "Bravo," she said, clapping her hands. "That looks like fun. May I try it?" she asked, thinking she may have need of such a skill in the next few days.

"Are you sure you are up to it, lass? I really dinna think you should even be out here."

"I am fine, Alex, and that looks easy enough," she said, examining the spear he had made.

"Easy?" he exclaimed. "Lass, I'll have you know this takes great skill."

"The only skill I see needed is the ability to stand on the rocks." She smiled smugly.

"Arrogant lass." He pretended to be offended. "Go right ahead. I'll eat the fish I have already caught, and let you eat what you catch."

"Fair enough," she agreed as Alex sat on the bank to watch her.

"Watch your step, lass, or I'll have to strip you from your wet clothes again," he warned, laughter in his voice.

"Would you please be quiet? You'll scare the fish away."

Maura paused over the water, her spear ready to strike. Catching the glint of silver heading her way, she jabbed her stick into the water and came up with nothing. She ignored Alex's laughter and tried again.

Despite the enormous effort she put into it, and after half an hour and a pair of wet boots, Maura finally gave up. "I don't understand it. Why is it you can catch fish so easily and I can't?" she asked in frustration as she dropped down beside him.

"I've been doing it since I could walk, lass. It takes years of practice and a quick eye. I tell you what," he said, tweaking her nose, "even though you made light of my skill, I will be generous and share my catch with you."

Maura smiled. "I'd rather you share your expertise with me. I really would like to be able to catch my own

188

fish, Alex. Who knows when it would come in handy."

"I think you've had enough excitement for one day," he said, getting to his feet. "Tomorrow I will teach you."

"Tomorrow? But . . ."

He pulled her to her feet. "Aye, we will have plenty of time tomorrow. I think you need to rest now," he said, placing his arm around her waist as they walked toward the cottage.

"I will rest, but I want to cook the fish this evening."

"Have you ever cooked before?" he asked.

"No, but it can't be too difficult."

Alex threw back his head and laughed. "You said that about catching fish, lass, and look what happened."

Maura stopped in her tracks, her hands on her hips. "Alexander MacLaren, I am not totally inept. I can ride a horse and use a dirk, and even though I hate it, I can sew and weave."

"Can you now?" He smiled. "Well, we will see if you can cook a fish, but only after you rest."

"Fair enough," she agreed, too tired to argue.

When she sat on the side of the bed, Alex shoved her backwards and began to remove her boots. "You look pale, love. I fear I let you overdo it."

"I'm tired, but I feel wonderful. You know, I would not mind living like this."

He leaned over and kissed her. "I wouldna either, lass," he said, thinking he had never been happier in his entire life. "Sleep now. I'll clean the fish and have them ready for you to cook when you wake up."

Maura was more successful with her cooking than she had been with fishing. She proudly offered Alex a piece of the flaky fish with her fingers.

"Excellent," he exclaimed, licking her fingers clean. "Faith, what a treasure you are. A cook, and a tiger in bed. What more could a man want?"

"Alex!" She laughed.

He pulled her onto his lap and nuzzled her neck. " 'Tis true, lass. If you were not recuperating from your fall, I'd forget that fish and just appease my hunger by loving you." He kissed her gently, tenderly, deliberately holding back, fearing their earlier lovemaking had been too much for her in her weakened condition.

Her taut nipples strained against the fabric of her linen shirt, reminding her of the ecstasy she had experienced in his arms only hours before. "I'm much better," she whispered against his mouth. "I believe after I have some sustenance I will be even stronger."

Alex caressed her cheek with his knuckles, his eyes soft with passion. "I suppose we will have to wait and see. I can barely keep my hands off you, but I certainly dinna wish to do anything to slow your recovery."

"I believe I have the good sense to know what would do me harm," she said, playfully kissing him all over his face, "and I firmly believe what we did earlier did me far more good than harm."

Alex groaned as her hand caressed his chest. "I am delighted to hear that, lass, but be warned, what you are doing to me is ruining my health, unless you plan to take that fish off the fire and make love to me this instant."

Maura laughed seductively and removed herself from his lap. "And ruin the beautiful fish you caught today?"

"You are a tease, lass," he moaned. "I will make you pay for that later," he warned, a twinkle in his eyes.

"Now watch yourself, Alexander MacLaren," she

waved the wooden utensil she had used on the fish at him, "or I'll not share this delicious fish with you."

"Then I will try to be on my best behavior," he assured, pulling her chair out with courtly grace. "Is this mannerly enough for you?"

Maura sat in the chair he offered and smiled. "I suppose when we are going to eat fish with our fingers, manners are of little consequence."

"Aye, 'tis all relevant, lass. I dinna believe I have ever seen you lovelier than when you were sitting at the campfire with pheasant juice dripping off your chin, and smudges of dirt on your nose."

"Oh, Alex." She laughed and nearly choked on a bite of fish. "That is terrible!"

"Why? 'Tis the truth."

Suddenly Maura became very quiet. "Did you really think I was lovely then?"

"Aye, lass. If truth be known, from the first moment I saw you in the tower I thought you were the loveliest, bonniest lass I had ever seen."

"But I thought you hated me."

"Your name, perhaps, but never you."

Maura fell silent. She sipped her wine, trying to think of some way of bringing up the subject of her marriage to Colin, but she couldn't. She couldn't bear the pain if he told her it would be best for all concerned, since he would never marry.

"What is troubling you, lass?" he asked softly.

She looked at him across the table, her eyes shining with love. She wanted to tell him, but the words froze in her throat. All she could get out was, "Alex . . . I need you to love me. . . ."

"Oh God, Maura," he moaned, coming to his feet so

fast he knocked his chair over. He picked her up effortlessly before she had a chance to move. His desire for her jolted through his system like a bolt of lightning. "I have found a violet-eyed angel who makes my life heaven and hell at the same time."

"Why hell?" she whispered.

"'Tis hell when I dinna have you in my arms," he said, his gray eyes turning a liquid silver. He placed her on the bed, kissing her with passion and fire, while his hands slipped beneath her shirt. As he caressed her hard nipples, an anguished sob escaped her lips beneath the sweet and possessive force of his kiss.

I love you . . . I love you, her mind cried out as he adeptly stripped her clothes and his. She could feel the urgent hunger in his body as he lay beside her. His hands were everywhere, stroking, caressing. She wanted to savor each feeling, each sensation. And more than anything, she wanted desperately to hold back the light of morning, to make these moments last her for a lifetime. In the darkness she could forget the harsh reality of having to leave him. There was only now, only this moment, and she would remember it, and rejoice in it for the rest of her life.

His kisses turned fierce, possessive, as if he meant to devour her. His warm hand parted her legs, caressing the curly black hair before plunging his finger inside of her. "You are ready for me, love, but this time I want to savor your sweetness."

Maura had no idea what he meant, then suddenly he was between her legs. The heat of his tongue plunged deeply into her softness, while at the same time his fingers moved inside her, giving her exquisite, torturing pleasure.

"Please, please, no . . ." she moaned, while her body writhed under his expertise. Unthinkingly, she held his dark head to her body, pulling him even closer, while she weakly objected to his onslaught. His mouth seared her, possessed her, causing her to cry out as she was caught up in a whirlwind of emotions and feelings. "Alex . . . oh God, Alex," she moaned, lifting her hips off the bed.

He moved up over her, kissing her deeply. "Put your arms around me, love," he commanded as he entered her, "Look at me."

She met his gray eyes as he filled her, stroked her. He whispered her name over and over before shuddering and releasing himself into her. They both lay gasping, clinging to each other.

"I am sure I just felt the earth move," she whispered breathless against his warm flesh.

"Aye, love, I believe we just moved heaven and hell." He lifted his weight from her and rolled onto his side, pulling her against him.

She swallowed a lump of painful emotion. Heaven was now, she thought as tears leaped to her eyes. Hell would come later.

There is a feeling of the heart
A dreary sense of coming evil
That bars all mirthful thoughts
And sends enjoyment to the devil.
                                    Greenhow

Chapter Seventeen

Maura gazed lovingly at Alex's face as she listened to his deep and steady breathing. She blinked back tears, knowing she had no other choice. She had to leave him, never to see him again.

A desolate feeling overwhelmed her. If only things had been different. If only there wasn't always war and hatred. She swallowed painfully as she touched his face. "I love you, Alex. Please forgive me, and understand. I cannot bring more pain to you and your family."

Slipping from the bed, she quietly dressed, all the while staring at Alex, trying to memorize every inch of his strong features. After gathering the rest of the bannock bread and one of the empty flacons she would use for water, she turned and tiptoed to the door. Silently opening it, she slipped out into the damp night air. Leaning against the door she waited to see if there was any movement from inside, but there was only silence.

She hurried across the darkened stretch towards Dubh Sith. As she reached the horse he whinnied loudly. "Quiet, boy," she exclaimed, glancing around at the hut.

She wasn't sure if it was her imagination, or if the sound had been as loud as she thought, but there was no time now to saddle the horse. If Alex had stirred from his sleep at the sound he would come looking for her. She untied the stallion and swung up on his back. She urged him slowly towards a worn path along the stream, hoping to keep the sound of his hooves down until she was far enough from the hut to urge him to a gallop.

She hadn't gone far when she heard a shrill whistle. She was stunned when the horse instantly stopped, rearing his front legs into the air. "No, no," she shouted as the horse turned around and galloped back towards the hut and Alex, who stood a few feet from the leanto, dressed only in his breeks. Even in the darkness she could see the anger in his eyes. "Stop, Dubh Sith. Halt!" She pulled sharply on the reins, but got no response. The horse was heading directly towards him.

"Damn you!" he shouted as he viciously dragged her from the back of his horse. "What the hell do you think you're doing?"

"Unhand me," she shouted back. "You have no cause to be violent with me."

"Unhand you?" he raged in disbelief. "I'm going to strangle you! You were going to steal my horse. You're a lying, cheating—"

"Let me explain."

"I dinna want to hear any of your lies, you little vixen!" He shook her so hard she thought her head would snap. His eyes blazed with his anger, and his hold on her wrist was crushing.

A chill of apprehension tingled down her spine, and she tried to back away from him. Suddenly all the stories she had heard about the black MacLaren came to her, stories of violence and death. His eyes were cold and icy, and she had no doubt he planned to crush the bones of her wrists, then strangle her.

"Please, let me go," she said, her eyes wide with fear. "I only meant to—"

"You meant to what? Make a fool of me again?" he asked coldly. "Where were you going this time, bitch? Were you running off to Iain MacPhee? God's blood, but I have been a fool! I thought I could trust you. I thought you were different."

"If you'd only—"

He nearly yanked her off her feet as he dragged her toward the cottage. The pain in her wrist was excruciating. She wanted to cry, but she wouldn't. She was afraid if she started she wouldn't be able to stop, and if she were hysterical, she wouldn't be able to explain, or defend herself against God knew what.

She fell to the floor as he shoved her inside the door, then he stood over her, clenching and unclenching his fists. She stared at him, stunned beyond words. This couldn't be the same man who had loved her so tenderly only hours before.

When he finally moved away from her she slowly got to her feet, rubbing her aching wrist. "I only meant to protect you, and I was going to see that Dubh Sith was returned."

He turned on her again, the rage in his eyes making her retreat a step. "Returned! Returned by whom?" he growled.

"By my relatives," she tried to explain.

He laughed bitterly. "Do you think the Campbells would have returned him to me? They would have butchered him to spite me, you conniving little bitch."

He walked to the fireplace, slamming his fist into the wooden wall above it, as he tried to vent his anger before doing something he would regret. He could not believe she would take flight again, and this time with his own horse. God's blood, his men would have laughed him to hell and back.

After a few moments he spoke again, his anger still very evident. "I canna believe after what we had here that you would take flight again."

"I cannot believe you would expect me to return to Dunraven and marry your brother!" she screamed.

Alex spun around and faced her. "You little fool! I had no intention of letting you marry my brother, or anyone else. You belong to me!"

Rage exploded in Maura's brain and she leaped at him, clawing his face and pummeling both fists against his chest. "Bastard," she screamed. "You let me think you wanted me to marry Colin! The torture I went through thinking that it didn't matter to you one way or the other."

"Be still, damnit!" he shouted, shocked by her reaction.

"Damn you to hell!" She continued to struggle. "You knew it was tearing me apart, yet you made me love you. You taught me to feel, to want, and then you casually mention that Colin did not think it a sacrifice to marry me. Is there no limit to your cruelty? I was willing to leave you, though it near broke my heart, to protect you and your family from Cromwell, while you were playing cruel games with me, using me."

Alex stilled her fists, pulling her hard against his body. His eyes blazed with silver flames as a trickle of blood ran down the side of his face from her nails. "I thought my

198

actions had shown you what I felt! I care for you too damned much."

"No!" She shoved away from him. "If you cared for me, why didn't you tell me? You call me a fool!" She laughed bitterly. "Well let me tell you, Alexander MacLaren, passion is not love. You've lain with Glenna and Leanne. Did you love them? Did they mean anything to you other than to satisfy your lust? How do I know it was any different with me, just because I satisfied your lust?"

"I was going to tell you how I felt," he said in exasperation. "How was I to know you planned to sneak away under cover of darkness. And don't tell me you were trying to protect me, damnit. That is the mistake your mother made years ago, and seeing that should have made you wiser. I can protect myself from my enemies—when I know who my enemy is," he said icily.

"Oh . . . oh!" she screamed in frustration. She picked up a plate off the table and threw it at his head, missing by inches. "Now I am your enemy again? How convenient that you were able to put your hatred aside long enough to bed me," she screeched, picking up a pan and throwing it at him.

Alex walked towards her menacingly while she looked for something else to throw. "You try my patience, Maura."

"The devil take your patience, and everything else you value! Particularly your manhood," she screamed as she threw the flacon of wine at him.

Alex fended off the flying objects and grabbed her around the waist. He stared down into her flushed face, then captured her mouth in a punishing kiss. She struggled against him, but he would not release her until he had subdued her. When she finally stopped fighting him, he raised his mouth from hers and whispered, "I am damned if I do, and damned if I dinna, but I love you, lass."

Maura stared at him, her eyes wide with disbelief. "Let me go," she whispered. When he released her she turned her back to him, gripping the table for support. "Is there no limit to your lies and deception?"

"I am not lying to you, Maura," he said close behind her. "I regret that I did not tell you sooner. It would have saved us both a lot of pain and misunderstanding, but I dinna know how you would react."

"You said you would never marry," she said softly, her back still to him.

"Aye, I said that. I once swore that I would never let anyone get close to me, but then I had not met you when I made that ludicrous oath."

Maura turned around and faced him, tears in her eyes. "Are you not just saying this because my father wishes me to marry into the MacLaren family for protection?"

"No, lass," he said, his voice choked with emotion. "I need no sword at my back to force me into marriage with you. I love you. I am sorry I dinna make you see that before you found it necessary to take flight from me."

Maura rubbed a tear away with the back of her hand. She felt humbled by his admission of love. "I am sorry I took Dubh Sith. But I swear to you," she said miserably, "I would never have let anything happen to him."

"I know you would have tried to protect him."

"What do we do now?" she asked, unconsciously rubbing her aching wrist. "Nothing changes the fact that my presence at Dunraven will bring Cromwell and Randolph down on your head."

"Here, let me see your wrist," he said, noticing the angry red welts. "I am so sorry, love," he said, kissing each of her wrists. "I never meant to hurt you."

"I know you did not. It will be fine with a little cold water," she assured. "I am sorry about this too," she said, gently touching the bloody gashes on his face. "I cannot believe I did that."

"You were a raving virago," he said with a tender smile. "I will know never to let you get too close again when you are angry."

"You are avoiding the subject, Alex. How do we avoid Cromwell's vengeance?"

"The English have been trying to capture me for a long time, lass. Why should my marrying you make their pursuit any more vigorous? Besides, I am willing to risk anything to spend whatever time I have left on this earth with you," he said, kissing her tenderly and lightly. "Do you dare risk the same?"

"I dare," she answered in a throaty whisper.

"Then we will return to Dunraven the day after tomorrow and plan our wedding."

"And tomorrow?"

"You will be too tired to travel tomorrow, lass, because I am going to make love to you until dawn."

"'Tis only a few hours away, my love," she smiled.

"Aye, but I want to see to your wrists first."

"I will forget them as soon as you start making love to me," she assured.

"Will you, lass? Will you ever be able to forget that I hurt you? I saw such fear in your eyes."

She lovingly touched his face. "Aye, I was afraid, but I now understand your reason."

"I swear to you, Maura, we will never let a misunderstanding do this to us again, and I swear on my mother's grave, I will never knowingly hurt you again. No matter what fear or apprehension either of us has, we will discuss it and deal with it together."

"Aye, together, Alexander MacLaren," she said, wrapping her arms around his neck as he picked her up. "Together we can face anything."

Come live with me and be my Love,
And we will all the pleasures prove . . .

Christopher Marlowe

Chapter Eighteen

"I did it! I did it," Maura shouted, holding up the spear with the wiggling fish on it as she balanced precariously on the rocks.

"So you did, lass," Alex said from his prone position on the bank.

"I caught dinner," she laughed delightedly, making her way towards him with her prize. "I shall cook for you again."

"To be honest with you, lass, I am tired of fish," he teased. "I was thinking of catching a fat partridge or two."

"Oh, you don't mean that," she exclaimed. "Faith, I have never seen such a beautiful fish. He will taste delicious, don't you think?"

"Aye, 'tis a grand creature," he agreed very seriously. "More the pity I cannot stomach the thought of another bite of fish. God's blood, but I'll be glad to have some of Jane's colcannon, or hotchpotch, or even a bowl of haggis."

Maura stared at him, trying to read his expression.

"Are you teasing me?" she asked.

He shrugged his shoulders. "I really think we should trap a bird or two to cook over the spit. I dinna believe that frying pan is any good since you hit me in the head with it."

"I missed you," she protested.

"Just barely." He laughed, pulling her down beside him. "I am sure your fish will taste delicious, lass."

"I have the distinct feeling that you wish to be back at Dunraven just so you can fill your stomach," she pushed against him playfully.

"Never, lass. If I had my way, I would stay here with you for the rest of my life," he said, nuzzling her neck.

"That is so sweet," Maura moaned, returning his kisses. "I am willing if you are."

"I am willing, but I would have to teach you to hunt for an occasional rabbit or partridge," he added. "A diet of fish can get very boring."

"Alex!" She pretended to be offended. "Is food all you can think about?"

Alex rolled on top of her, laughing. "Lass, by now you surely know what I think about when I am near you, but in all fairness, I canna keep you on your back twenty-four hours a day." He smiled down into her flushed face. "Or can I?"

"Not after we return to Dunraven," she whispered, pulling his mouth down to hers. "You best take advantage of me while we are alone. I fear my father and mother will not approve of you bedding me before our vows are spoken."

"Aye," he moaned, as she ran her hand inside his shirt. "It will be pure torture trying to keep my hands off you. That is why we will be married three days from tomorrow."

"Three days from tomorrow?" Maura exclaimed as she sat straight up. "Three days from tomorrow?" she repeated in disbelief. "How do you expect a lass to have time to prepare for her wedding in so short a time?"

"What is there to prepare for? Grizel will make you a gown, and Jane will cook a feast. So you see, there is no reason to delay. Three days should give us time to get the clergy to Dunraven. I assume you do want to be married by the clergy."

"If the other option is to be handfasted, you can be assured I want to be married by the clergy, Alexander MacLaren."

He pulled her back down into his arms. "Aye, somehow I thought that would be the case," he said, lightly kissing her. "Give a woman the option of putting chains of confinement on a man and she will take it every time."

"Are you getting cold feet, Alexander?" she asked as she nibbled on his ear."

"No, but I am getting . . ." A shudder racked his muscular body as her hand moved lower over his stomach. "Shall I just say, love, if you keep that up we will definitely try for twenty-four hours."

Her lips curved in a provocative smile. "I fear I am going to have to keep you very busy to keep your eyes from wandering to all the other women who desire you. Faith, but I never saw anything like the way Glenna and Leanne pant after you. 'Tis absolutely disgraceful."

"You have nothing to fear, lass," he assured, placing kisses on her face. "I have just been looking for the right woman to spend my life with, and 'tis you. You are my destiny, lass, dinna you know that? If I have you, I will never need anything else, unless it is a wee bairn or two."

"Aye, that would be nice," she sighed, sadly remembering her conversation with Glenna. "There is something that Glenna told me," she said, fidgeting with a piece of grass.

"What was that, lass?"

Suddenly she laughed. "It was nothing. Do you want to teach me to trap a bird? I really would be interested in knowing how."

"Maura," he said, "look at me." She raised her head, her eyes guarded. "Tell me what Glenna told you."

She looked back at the piece of grass in her hand. "She said you had wee bairns all over Scotland."

There was an almost imperceptive change in his face. "Did she? Glenna exaggerates my prowess, lass. Not that I can claim total innocence. I'll wager most men have fathered a bastard or two without knowing it, but that is the way of things. 'Tis a harsh world for a woman."

"Aye, and an even harsher one for the bairns," she sighed, leaning on one elbow.

"Is there anything else you want to know about my life, Maura. I want no secrets between us, so ask away."

"Maybe just one other question," she said as she snuggled against him. "How much do you love me, Alexander MacLaren?"

Alex laughed deep in his throat. "If you love me half as much as I love you, I'll be content the rest of my life. Does that answer your question, lass?"

Tears came to her eyes. "Oh, Alex, that is the most beautiful thing I have ever heard. You fair take my breath away."

He shrugged, trying to hide the smile on his face. "No accounting for tastes. Here I could have won you the day you climbed down from the tower at Beaumaris Castle if only I'd known all it took was a few sweet words."

"Aye, you are so right." She laughed. "Instead you taunted and insulted me until I thought I would go out of my mind with frustration."

"I was a villain indeed," he gave her a mock smile, "but to be honest, I enjoyed seeing your eyes flash with fire, and I particularly got pleasure knowing I could arouse you to anger so easily. You are a spitfire, my love, and I would have it no other way."

"Spitfire, indeed," she snorted.

"'Tis plain, if you are honest enough to admit it, that you enjoyed our battles. You could pretend to hate me, but I knew you felt just as I did."

"Aye," she smiled, knowing he was right. This thing between them had been there from the beginning. It could not be confined within the ordinary bounds of love or hate; it was too passionate, too contradictory. She would never relinquish the challenge, the aliveness of it for all the swooning, simpering Englishmen in the world.

"Once I saw your spirit, I was lost," he admitted. "I fear I have always been a fool when it comes to spirited women and spirited horses."

She glared at him, but could not help laughing. "Aye, so you may break them to your will, I imagine."

"I would never want to break you, lass. Perhaps just tame you a bit to my touch."

"You!" She laughed. "I believe there is an unwritten law in Scotland that says anything the MacLaren desires is his for the taking."

"Ah, now that is an interesting thought."

"Well I want you to know, Alexander MacLaren, that I am not one of your Highland wenches, eager to fall in your arms at your beck and call."

His grin deepened. "Really, lass? You had me fooled," he said, pulling her into his arms and placing kisses along her neck. "Umm, you smell delicious. Is it a Parisian scent?"

"No, kind sir," she giggled. "I believe they call it peat smoke and fish, a scent very popular in the Highlands. I am pleased you like it."

"I love it," he said, running his tongue over the pulse of her throat. "I hope you have it bottled."

Maura laughed, pushing away from him. "Speaking of Paris, do you mind telling me why you did not tell me you were educated there?"

"My, but you're an inquisitive piece of baggage," he said lightly. "If I remember correctly, my sweet, you called me an uneducated lout, or something to that effect, and I saw no reason to inform you otherwise."

She touched his face, running her fingertips over his lips. "I apologize," she said softly. "You are a man surrounded by mystery, and that always intrigues a woman."

"I wish someone had told me that years ago," he laughed. "Think of the women I would have had fighting over me."

"You had enough as it is," she said, playfully pushing against him. "Besides, it was not the mystery surrounding you that attracted me."

"Really, lass?" He smiled, raising one dark eyebrow. "Tell me more."

"It was devilishly unfair of you, Alexander. I never stood a chance once you turned your charm on me, showing me your tender, compassionate side as well."

Alex kissed the palm of her hand. "I fear you have seen

208

my best and my worst, lass."

"Mmm," she sighed, as he slipped his hand inside her loose-fitting shirt, sending a tremor through her body. "I suppose that means I should know what I'm getting into."

"You should, lass, but I doubt if you do," he smiled as he deftly removed her shirt.

"What are you doing?" she giggled.

"Please dinna laugh at my efforts, lass." He pretended to take offense. "I am seducing you and 'tis hard on a man's ego if the one being seduced finds it humorous."

Maura placed her arms out to her sides and lay very still, her eyes tightly closed. "Then seduce away, sir. I shall try my best to take you seriously."

Laughter rich and deep echoed from the recesses of Alex's chest. "What am I going to do with you, lass? You best me at every turn. Here I am trying to show you how I can master you with my touch, and you make fun of me."

Maura laughed with him. "If you think to master me, Alexander MacLaren, think again. No man will be my master."

"Is that the way of it?" he asked with a mischievous grin. "Shall I show you how wrong you are, my tempestuous young beauty?" Within seconds he had all of her clothes removed.

"I know you are stronger—"

"I am not speaking of strength, love. I will not lay my hands on you, but I will master your body."

"Impossible, unless you plan to use some other part of your body."

"No part of my body will touch yours," he said as he picked a long piece of grass with a feathery end. "They say pleasure is a sensation of the nerves and senses.

Visual pictures or descriptions can incite lusty thoughts.'

"I fear I am too new at this to know of what you speak," she said breathlessly as he ran the grass over her lips, across her jawline, and down her neck.

Maura stiffened, already feeling the tightening in the lower part of her stomach. "It tickles, nothing else," she lied.

"Is that right?" He flicked the grass over her breast, tickling and teasing. "At some other time I will pour wine here," he ran the grass over her navel, "and then I will drink it, lapping it with my tongue just where this grass is touching. And then here, even lower . . ."

The sensation was exquisite, tantalizing. She drew in her breath and fought against the urge to raise her hips, giving him access with his feathery light touches.

He trailed the grass along the tender inside of her thighs, down her long legs to her bare feet, then slowly and deliberately up again. With consummate skill he brought her near the point of pleasure, then backed off again by brushing the grass across her open lips and around the sensitive skin of her ears.

After a few minutes of this deliberate torture, she could hear herself panting. Her muscles tensed, waiting for the next touch, the touch that would bring her release. But nothing happened. Opening her eyes she stared at him, her eyes dark with passion. "Alex . . ."

"Have I done what I predicted, my love?" he asked, his own voice rough with emotion. "Have I mastered your body?"

"Aye, my body and my soul, I fear. Please, come to me, Alex, ease this ache. I cannot bear another minute of this torture."

He gathered her close, entering her softness with his

throbbing manhood. He pressed deep inside her as their breaths mingled in a deep and possessive kiss.

Maura clung to him, feeling as if she were drowning, spiraling, soaring. She gasped his name over and over as he spilled his life into her.

They lay clinging to each other, the sun overhead warming their naked bodies. Alex smiled tenderly at her. "I believe if truth were known, the mastery was the other way around."

Unless you can dream that his faith is fast,
Through behoving and unbehoving;
Unless you can die when the dream is past—
Oh, never call it loving!

Elizabeth Barrett Browning

Chapter Nineteen

They waited on the far side of the drawbridge, each lost in thought.

Maura knew the next few days would be hectic and she would have little opportunity to be alone with Alex until after the ceremony.

"Are you all right, love?" Alex asked softly.

"Aye. I was thinking of our little paradise in the mountains."

Alex smiled. "I too miss the peace and privacy we had there, but in a few days, it will always be like that for us."

"That sounds wonderful," she said, tenderly touching his face. "I dinna imagine we will be alone much in the coming days, so I will just have to keep that in mind."

Alex kissed the palm of her hand. "Do you have so little faith in me, lass?"

Maura looked up at him, seeing the devilment in his eyes. "You wouldn't . . ."

"Wouldn't I?" He grinned mischievously. "And here I thought you knew me by now. When I want something, lass, I will not let heaven nor hell stand in my way."

213

Maura giggled. "What about my mother?"

"Mothers are a different story." He laughed.

When the drawbridge was lowered, Dubh Sith pranced across the wooden planks to the cobblestone courtyard where Anne and Donald already waited.

Alex lifted her from the saddle, placing a quick kiss on her mouth before releasing her. The next moment she was being embraced by her mother and father, both talking so fast she couldn't understand a thing they said.

"I'm fine. I'm fine, really," she assured, tears in her eyes.

"We were so worried about you, my dear, but you look well," Anne said, examining her daughter. "Your skin is gold from the sun, and there is a rosy bloom to your cheeks."

"Well," Donald exclaimed. "'Tis an understatement, Anne. She has never looked better."

"Thank you, Father. I am sorry to have caused you both to worry."

"Have you been outside most of the time?" Anne persisted. "I had understood from Colin that you were being cared for at a deserted hut. How is it that you are tanned?"

Suddenly Maura was swept up in the arms of Colin, who swung her around, saving her from further explanation at the moment. "I knew you'd come through just fine. Faith, I've never seen such a capable lass. A man couldna have handled the rugged Highlands any better than you."

"Thank you, Colin." She smiled shyly, noticing many of Alex's men gathering around them.

"We canna begin to tell you how glad we are to see you looking so fit, lass," Simon said, giving her a kiss on the

214

cheek. Dunraven has been very dull without you."

"Don't you mean peaceful, Simon?" She laughed. Maura glanced around to find Alex, but her attention was drawn to Glenna who stood silently on the steps. She almost felt sorry for the girl. "Thank you all for such a warm welcome."

"All right, lads, give the lass room to breathe," Alex said coming to her side. "We have an announcement to make, and I want everyone to hear. Maura has agreed to become my wife."

The cheer that went up from Colin and Simon surprised Maura, and she had to laugh at their exuberance. "Were your brothers not allowed to marry until you did?" she asked Alex.

"You would think so." Alex laughed. "I believe their elation springs from the hope that my mood will improve now that we have settled things."

Settled things . . . Maura mused, remembering her father saying the same thing the first time they met. She smiled at Donald, knowing he had hoped for a match between her and Alex all along. "Are you happy, Father?" she asked as she hugged him.

"The only thing that could make me near as happy would be to see Cromwell in his grave."

"And you, Mother? Do you approve?"

"Aye, Maura. I am very fond of Alex, as you well know. I want nothing more than for you to be happy."

"I am happy, Mother. I love him very much."

"I thought that was the case." Her mother hugged her.

"There is something I have not told you," Alex said, drawing everyone's attention. "We want the wedding to be in three days."

"Three days!" Anne exclaimed. "That is so little time

215

to prepare."

"We care little about a fancy wedding, Mother. We just want to be together."

"God's blood, Alex," Simon exclaimed, "we better send word to the clans and the clergy this very afternoon."

"We just want family and a few friends," Maura tried to explain, but Simon was already naming off the clans that would have to be invited so as not to offend anyone. She looked at Alex, who smiled and shrugged his shoulders.

"Maura, come along." Her mother grabbed her by the hand. "We must find Grizel this very moment if you are to have a wedding gown. Three days! Faith, it will take a miracle."

Maura glanced back at Alex, a look of longing in her eyes. He winked at her as his brothers dragged him in the opposite direction. She could hear Colin promising a celebration they would be talking about in the Highlands for years to come.

God, what happened to our small intimate wedding? she wondered silently as she was swept up the steps by her mother. She had no idea they would insist on still giving them a large wedding with only three days to prepare, but she should have known better. In the Highlands, nothing was impossible when the Scots decided to celebrate, particularly the marriage of their laird.

When they reached Glenna, who still stood silently on the steps, Maura decided to be gracious. "Glenna, would you like to join us in the planning of my wedding? I could use your help."

"If you wish."

"Perhaps you could start by asking Jane to join us in

the solar," Anne suggested. "We need to discuss food for the wedding feast, and there will be guests."

Glenna headed down the stairs towards the kitchen buildings without further comments.

"She is such a bonny lass," Maura said sarcastically. "I am sure she will be a bright addition to the wedding party, if she doesn't poison us all."

"She sees Alex slipping away from her," Anne commented.

"She never had Alex," Maura said caustically.

"No, she did not, my dear," Anne said, putting her arm around Maura's shoulders. "Your father told me all along that you were the only woman who could win Alex, but I did not believe him. It always seemed to me you hated the man."

"I tried, Mother." Maura laughed. "I really did, but it is very difficult to hate Alexander MacLaren when he is charming."

"So you finally saw that," her mother said with a knowing smile. "I tried to tell you on the way from England that I found him so."

"I remember, Mother. You also told me you preferred the strong, forceful Highlanders to the pompous Englishmen."

"And now you agree with me." Anne grinned.

"Aye, I agreed with you then, Mother, but I would never have admitted it."

"I knew that, my dear. You couldn't take your eyes off the man," Anne said as they entered the solar. "Now sit down, dear, and tell me why you felt it necessary to leave here without telling anyone."

Maura was surprised by her mother's quick change of subject. "I should have known you'd get around to that,"

217

she sighed. "I left because I overheard a discussion. At least part of a discussion—about the only way to keep me safe from Lord Randolph was for me to marry a MacLaren. Unfortunately, what I heard led me to believe that Colin was the one I was to marry, and at that time I already realized I had very strong feelings for Alexander. I knew I could never marry his brother."

"Oh, Maura, I am so sorry. Then you did not hear Aléx say he planned to marry you?"

"No," Maura said as she stared out the window over the courtyard. "Actually, I heard him say that he didn't think my marrying a MacLaren would help my situation."

"'Tis a shame you did not stay long enough to hear the entire conversation. Alexander told your father that the reason he was marrying you was because he loved you."

"I know that now, Mother, but what's done is done. I cannot change the way things have happened, nor do I think I would want to. Alex and I needed the time we had together to get to know one another."

"I cannot say I approve of the two of you being alone, but at least the wedding is to take place immediately so there should be no scandal."

"We are not in England, Mother."

"No, but these Highland families have their own—"

"You sent for me, m'lady?" Grizel appeared in the doorway.

"Yes, yes, Grizel, please come in. I am afraid we must impose on your fine talents still further. My daughter and the MacLaren have just announced that they will marry in three days and Maura will need a wedding gown."

Maura felt embarrassed at being the cause once again

for the woman to have to work so hard. "I am sorry, Grizel. I know this makes it hard for everyone."

"'Tis no problem, m'lady," the old woman smiled. "I would have it for you by tomorrow if the MacLaren wished it."

Maura clasped Grizel's hands. "Thank you so much. Thank you for everything you have done for me. Your kindness will be rewarded, I promise you."

"'Tis reward enough to see the young MacLaren married to such a fine young lady. Now tell me what you have in mind for your gown."

"Something simple," Maura mused. "I do not wish to have lengths of material dragging behind me as is the fashion in England right now."

"Lady MacLaren had a bolt of white satin with a thread of silver running through it saved for her daughter's wedding. Perhaps this would be the time to use it."

"Oh, Grizel, I don't know. I don't know if Alexander would approve. It may bring back memories—"

"I approve, love," Alexander said from the doorway. "My mother would be more than pleased to have my wife use the material she chose."

Maura slowly walked towards him, taking his hand. "Are you certain? I want no dark memories to cloud our day."

Alex gave her a quick kiss. "Nothing will cloud our day, lass. It will give me great pleasure to know that my mother picked out the material."

"If you are certain," Maura said softly.

"Ladies, please forgive me for interrupting," Alex said, still holding Maura's hand, "but Simon plans to ride into Inveray this afternoon for some supplies, and he wants to know if there is anything you will be needing."

219

"I have not talked with Jane yet, but I will do so in just a few minutes," Anne answered. "If there is anything we decide on that she does not have, I will let Simon know within the hour."

"Thank you, Anne. I will tell him." Alex was reluctant to release Maura's hand. He pulled her with him towards the door. "Remind me to tell you something about my mother later," he whispered. "I think you will find it very interesting."

"You've piqued my curiosity, Alexander MacLaren," she said, refusing to release his hand. "Don't you dare leave without telling me what you are talking about."

"Later, lass."

"Alex . . ." she protested.

"My dear, Grizel needs more instructions about your gown if she is to have it made by the day after tomorrow," Anne gently advised.

"Yes, of course," Maura sighed, wondering if handfasting wasn't such a bad idea. She had a feeling the next few days were going to be pure torture.

That a lie which is all a lie may be
met and fought with outright.
But a lie which is part a truth is
a harder matter to fight.

Alfred, Lord Tennyson

Chapter Twenty

By that evening the festivities had already begun.
After an excellent dinner had been served, everyone
lingered around the great hall. Even though she was
exhausted, Maura enjoyed the toasts and good-natured
hazing Alexander's men directed at them. She knew these
were the people who were most important to him.

Colin stood up to make another toast as everyone
refilled their mugs. He winked at Maura before he spoke.
"You snatched her right out from under my nose, big
brother," he accused, "and even though I believe she
still prefers me to your blackness, I wish you both a world
of happiness and good fortune, and many wee bairns to
fill Dunraven."

Everyone laughed. "Perhaps you should ask her, little
brother," Alex encouraged. "I think you will find she
prefers a *man*."

Everyone in the room laughed at the tables turned on
Colin, including Colin himself.

"God's blood," Donald exclaimed, "but you've as
much vanity as Cromwell, Alex. But I suppose every

221

father wants a man who is sure of his prowess for his daughter."

Maura flushed. Things were getting a little boisterous for her tastes. She leaned over and whispered to Alex. "Would you be terribly offended if I said good night? I'm afraid the adventures of the past few days have finally caught up to me."

"No, lass, not at all," he said as he stood up and offered her his arm. "Gentlemen, will you excuse us. I fear the events of the past few days have worn out Lady Campbell and she is sorry to have to leave your fine company."

"I hope we said nothing to offend you." One of Alex's men bowed over her hand.

Maura smiled at all of them. "You did nothing but make me feel welcome, and I thank you. I shall look forward to your company tomorrow, and I will try to think of a few toasts to give back to you at that time."

They all laughed, cheering that their laird had met a woman to match his spirit.

"They love you," Alex said proudly when they reached the hallway. "And so do I," he said, pulling her into his arms.

"They are wonderful," Maura exclaimed. "I have never felt so welcome anywhere in my life."

"This is your home, lass. You should feel welcome in it. My clan will be as loyal to you as they are to me."

"I hope I am always worthy of their loyalty," she said, wrapping her arms about his neck. "I can only promise I will do everything in my power to make their laird happy."

"You have already done that by agreeing to be my wife," he said, smiling warmly at her. "Oh, love, how I would like to carry you up those stairs and make love

222

to you."

"Two more days, Alex, and we will never have to worry about what our family thinks. You and I will live and love under this roof, filling the halls of Dunraven with heirs."

"I feel like you are already my wife, love. The few words the clergy says over us will not change anything."

"I know, love, but everyone is going to so much trouble. I would hate to disappoint them."

"You have a heart as soft as melted butter, Maura Campbell," he said, kissing her nose.

"You have found me out." She laughed. "Now get back in there with your men. I will not have them accusing me of taking you from them."

"Are you sure you do not want me to walk you to your room?"

"I am sure. I know very well what would happen if you did."

Alex shook his head. "I should have known better than to have chosen an intelligent woman for a wife."

"Go!" She laughed.

Donald drew Alex aside when he entered the room. "I wanted to tell you how grateful I am, lad."

Alex shrugged. "There is no reason for you to be grateful, my friend. I love your daughter, and if anyone should be grateful, 'tis me. I should be thanking you for bringing us together."

Donald smiled. "I am pleased you feel that way. I know you will make her happy, my boy."

"You know I will die trying."

Tears brightened Donald's eyes. "Anne may be the one with the gift of second sight, but I have been the one who always knew you two were meant for each other, even before you met." He forced a laugh, not wanting anyone to see how emotional he was feeling. "God's blood, what children you and the lass will produce. Perhaps they will be able to save our Scotland."

" 'Tis not a birthright I wish to leave them," Alex said sadly. "England will never ease its tyranny and I fear our children and our grandchildren will be opressed even more than we are."

"Aye, but we can pray for honor and peace for our heirs, Alex. Perhaps someday it will come."

"Aye, perhaps someday."

Maura had just slipped into her bed when there was a knock at the door. She sat up, thinking it was Alex. "Enter," she called.

"May I speak with you for a few moments?" Glenna asked.

"Of course," Maura said pleasantly, thinking perhaps her cousin wanted peace between them.

Glenna stood at the foot of the bed, fingering one of the hanging rope cords. "There is something you should know."

"Yes, what is it, Glenna?"

"I am with child," Glenna said slowly.

Maura's heart began to beat unsteadily. Somehow she knew what was coming. She stared at Glenna, hoping for a moment to make her voice steady. "Will the man who fathered your child not marry you?"

"I dislike to tell you this, Maura," Glenna said softly, "but 'tis Alex."

"Alex," Maura repeated, keeping her voice calm as she struggled with her emotions. "Have you told him you are expecting his child?"

Glenna ran her hand over the velvet of the quilt. "I had planned to as soon as he returned, but then your marriage announcement was made. I know Alex is far too chivalrous to put me aside once he learns I carry his child," Glenna continued on deliberately, yet sweetly, "but I felt since we were cousins you should be made aware of what is to come so you can save face the best way you know how. I certainly dinna wish to see you hurt."

"I appreciate your concern, cousin, and I agree, Alex is far too chivalrous to turn away from the woman who carries his bairn."

"I know this is not something you want bleated about the countryside, Maura. I fear it would make you look the fool," she said, false concern in her voice. "Perhaps it would be best if you broke off your engagement to Alex and returned to London. Iain MacPhee should be arriving tomorrow and I am certain he would be honored to escort you."

Maura regarded her cousin deliberately, letting her eyes move from her face to her amazingly tiny waist beneath her gown. Glenna flushed and folded her hands in front of her stomach.

"How far along are you, Glenna?"

"Several months."

"Is Alex the only man you have bedded?"

"I am not a slut, Maura. This is Alex's child."

"You lie, Glenna," Maura said bluntly. "I do not believe you are with child, particularly Alex's child, and if you think this is a way to snare him, you are wrong," she said contemptuously.

"How dare you!" Glenna's pale face turned red.

"What will you do when he discovers you lie? I doubt

he would be amused by it. I have seen his anger and feared I would not live to tell about it, and I did nothing except try to escape his protection. What do you think he would do if you ruined his marriage plans with your lies? Are you so anxious to give up your life?"

"You do not scare me, Maura Campbell. I know what I want and I have the means of getting it."

"Then go tell Alex, Glenna, but be warned. He will not take kindly to your lies, neither will Donald."

"You will see, Maura. We both know he is a man who can easily be attracted to a pretty face. I realize he has had his dalliances with you and with Leanne, to mention only a few, but he has always come back to me."

"You are not exceedingly bright, Glenna," Maura observed flatly. "If Alex has bedded you so often, he should have the good sense to realize that others have also bedded you."

Glenna's face turned white with anger. "Take heed, cousin, I dislike your insults."

"Such a virtuous rage, Glenna. Think about it. Perhaps you were always there to warm his bed, but a man can scarce marry all the indiscreet women who would claim to carry his child."

Glenna's eyes blazed with fury as she clutched the rope cord, knotting and unknotting it nervously. "If you are wise, you will go back to London," she said between gritted teeth. "Alex will be mine."

"I pity you, Glenna. I know how it feels to love a man, but if you were the one for him, he would have wed you long ago. And since he did not, I feel no guilt that it will be me he marries the day after tomorrow."

"You are wrong!" Glenna screamed. "He has no

hoice but to wed me. He cannot prove whether I lie or not."

"'Tis unfitting for me to debate the subject, Glenna. Alex is in the great hall. I suggest you go talk to him. He is certainly a wise enough man to know if 'tis possible he is the father."

Glenna stared at her, her face crumpling. "I cannot believe you would want to stay here and face being ridiculed and mocked."

"If Alex chooses to marry you after you tell him what you have told me, I will step aside. Until then I will continue making my wedding plans."

The silence in the room was deafening. Glenna seemed held in a spell, frozen with some dark emotion within herself. A myriad of expressions crossed her face. "You're a fool," she finally said as she headed toward the door.

"Am I, Glenna? I do not think so. I believe you are the fool if you think you can lie to Alexander MacLaren and get away with it."

When she was alone, Maura sat staring at the door. Her heart was beating so loudly she could hear it echoing throughout the room. She climbed from her warm bed and wrapped her velvet robe around her shoulders. Sitting before the fire, she stared hypnotically at the flames. "Please God, don't let it be true," she whispered into the darkness.

"You must have faith," a female voice said from behind her.

Maura jumped up from her chair and glanced around the room. "Who is that? Who is there?"

"Do not be frightened, child."

In the flickering shadows thrown by the fire, Maura could make out a wispy, transparent figure. "Who are you?"

"You must be strong, child. Have faith in Alexander. He will never lie to you. He will need your strength and loyalty. He will need your love. . . ."

"How do you know this? Who are you?" Suddenly Maura knew she was alone again. "Are you Honora MacLaren?" she asked softly in the darkness. "Faith, I must be losing my mind," she said with a sigh. She had never thought much about spirits, but who else could it be? Why would this woman keep appearing to her on Alexander's behalf, if not the ghost of Honora MacLaren.

Maura paced the room, wondering if Glenna was at this very moment telling Alex her news. "God's mercy, I have to talk to him tonight," she said aloud as she wrapped her robe tightly around her. There would be no sleep until she knew the truth, and only Alexander could tell her that.

Maura slipped into Alex's dark room. The fire, which one of the servants had lit, was dying down and the room was cold. She knelt to add peat, wondering if she was doing the right thing by being there. Alexander was sure to be in a terrible mood no matter what the truth.

She glanced around the room, then decided to sit on the bed and use the fur throw for warmth. The words spoken to her in her room kept ringing in her brain. *Have faith in Alexander. He will never lie to you.* She closed her eyes and in a few moments had drifted off to sleep.

"What a pleasant surprise," Alex whispered as he kissed her gently on the lips.

Maura woke up, throwing her arms around his neck. "Oh, Alex, I am so glad you're finally here."

Alex smiled at her, thinking how lucky he was. She looked so beautiful and innocent with her black hair cascading around her shoulders, and her violet eyes wide and sleepy. "If I had had any idea what I'd find in my bed, I'd have been here hours ago."

"I dinna think I could sleep until we talked."

"Did you miss me, lass? I must admit I dinna relish sleeping without you by my side."

"Alex, please tell me, is the baby yours?"

"Lass," he said softly. "Are you saying what I think you're saying?"

Maura realized at once that Glenna had not spoken to him. "Alex, I did not mean myself," she said, her breath catching in her throat. "Oh God, Alex," she said clinging to him for dear life. "Glenna came to me tonight and said she was carrying your child."

His face was very grave as he stared at her. "So Glenna would have you believe she's carrying my bairn. Did you believe her, lass?"

"No, and I told her so."

Alex grinned at her honestly. "I will not lie to you, lass. I have bedded Glenna, but the last time was six months ago when I was visiting your father at Rockhenge. Glenna came to me and I did not turn her away. Could she be that far along and not be showing?"

"No," Maura exclaimed, feeling an unbidden happiness burn sweet and fierce inside of her. "She is as flat as a board."

"If she is with child, 'tis more likely Iain MacPhee's," he said as he caressed her jawline with his thumb. "They have been very close of late."

"Oh, Alex, I am so relieved. I was dreadfully jealous," she admitted. "But then I was told to have faith, and I do, love. I truly do."

Alex laughed. "What wise person advised you to have faith in me?"

Maura hesitated, staring at Alexander. "If I tell you, you may want to change your mind about marrying me."

"I canna imagine that, love," he assured.

"I have been listening to ghosts."

"Have you now?" He laughed, not the least unsettled by her statement. "Would it be a beautiful woman with long black hair?"

"You have seen her?" Maura asked in disbelief.

"No, I have not seen her, but I have heard her playing the harp. I believe 'tis my mother who counsels you, love. She is the one who led me to you in the mountains. That was what I was referring to today when I told you I had something to tell you about my mother," he explained. "Colin was with me, but even he couldna hear the music. Then when you mentioned hearing it, I knew I had not lost my mind. She was trying to help us. There was no way I would have found you in the darkness, lass. Colin and I were ready to cross the stream a long way from you when I heard the music."

"She has come to me often, Alex. Each time she tells me to have faith in you, to be patient and everything will be fine."

Alex pulled her into the warmth of his arms. "I thought Honora would approve of you. You were concerned that my family hated you because of your name, and here my mother's spirit has been counseling you."

Tears ran down Maura's face. "How is it possible,

Alex, that I could see her, hear her?"

Alex shrugged. "How is it possible that your mother sees things before they happen, lass? I canna explain, but I do know there are too many unexplainable things that happen not to believe anything is possible."

"I suppose I would have to believe that since the likelihood of you and I marrying is quite incredible if you think about it."

He smiled at her. "Your father tells me he has always known that we would marry."

"You must mean my mother," she corrected.

"No, lass. Just this evening he told me that."

Maura smiled as she lovingly caressed his face. "We never stood a chance, my love. It seems everyone had our life planned for us."

"Aye, 'tis the truth of it," he said, kissing her ear.

"What will you do about Glenna?"

"I will have a talk with her."

"Be kind, Alex. I truly feel sorry for her. She will know misery enough with her conscience and her desolation."

"Aye, you are probably right. Perhaps she did us a favor. At least this should cure Simon of his passion for her."

"I hope that is the case," Maura said softly, "but why she would prefer a black-hearted rogue like you over your sweet brother I do not know."

Alex suddenly shifted positions and deftly rolled her over on her back. "Then perhaps I should be showing you, lass, since you seem to forget so quickly," he challenged, a fire in his mocking eyes.

"Perhaps you should, Alexander MacLaren," she said, pulling his mouth down to hers.

Let all thy joys be as the month of May,
And all thy days be as a marriage day:
Let sorrow, sickness, and a troubled mind
Be stranger to thee.

Francis Quarles

Chapter Twenty-One

By the next morning the walls of Dunraven Castle rang with the boisterous festivities which inevitably attended a Highland wedding. Pipers strutted before the castle, saluting their chief and his lady. Streamers and flags blew in the breeze, adding color to the courtyard and surrounding buildings. Games were set up everywhere in the courtyard and surrounding fields, and the young men of various clans were already competing. There was fencing, wrestling, and archery, and even a footrace or two in between the horse racing.

Dressed in a dove gray silk gown trimmed with lavender velvet, Maura stood with her mother on the steps of the courtyard, trying to take in everything, while Alex greeted the guests who were arriving in droves.

"How was so much accomplished in so short a time?" she asked in disbelief.

"Alex has a very capable staff," Anne answered. "The kitchens were already well stocked and the wine cellars filled to the beams. It seems all they had to do was announce that the MacLaren was taking a bride, and the clan took care of everything else."

"'Tis incredible," Maura said in awe. "They even managed to have a beautiful spring day for our celebration."

"You can see how much the MacLaren is respected." Anne smiled. "Even God is celebrating with us."

"Where will all these people stay?"

"Dunraven will hold many people," Anne laughed. "Besides, the men will not need rooms. They will stay up celebrating until after the vows are said tomorrow, and they will expect Alexander to join them."

Maura looked at her mother. "Are you saying my husband will probably sleep on his wedding night?"

"You know him better than I do, my dear. What do you think?"

Maura smiled. "He will not sleep."

"I was sure you would say that," Anne said as she hugged her daughter. "Maura," she said, becoming very serious, "what would you think of my returning to Rockhenge to live with Donald?"

"Oh, Mother, I think that would be wonderful," she exclaimed happily. "I have been waiting for you to decide to do just that, since I know Father has wanted you back with him from the first day we arrived here."

"Perhaps this time we can be happy and grow old together," Anne said hopefully.

"I know you will be happy, Mother. And just think, you won't be far from me and your grandchildren. It will be wonderful!"

"Grandchildren already, my dear?" Her mother laughed.

"'Tis something Alex and I both want very badly. I hope to give him many bairns."

"I have no doubt you will, my sweet."

The mention of bairns reminded Maura of her confrontation with her cousin the night before. Apparently Glenna had decided not to face Alexander with her ludicrous accusation. "Mother, have you seen Glenna this morning?"

"No, I haven't, dear. Perhaps she is helping Mary. Do you need her for something?"

"No," Maura said, glancing around. "Would you look at Father." Maura pointed out. "He is in his glory. If we are not careful, he'll be running in one of those races."

"And well he should be in his glory." Anne smiled. "You've made a dream come true for him, my dear: his only child marrying the man he admires more than any other."

"I am glad he is pleased. From what I've been told he had the whole thing planned all along."

"Aye, that is the way of it."

"Have you known this would happen, Mother? Have you known all along I would marry Alex?"

"Aye. I began to see it when we arrived at Dunraven."

"What else have you seen, Mother?"

"This is not the time, Maura. We will talk this evening."

"No, Mother. Tell me now," Maura insisted. "What else have you seen?"

Anne looked into her daughter's eyes, knowing there wasn't any sense trying to put her off. "You and Alex will have to overcome many obstacles, Maura, but as long as your love is strong, your marriage will survive."

Maura clasped her mother's hands. "That is all I need to know. Someone else already told me I must always have faith in him, and I will, Mother," Maura swore, tears brightening her violet eyes. "I firmly believe I was meant to be loved by Alexander MacLaren and no other, and he shall have my love and trust until the day I die."

Anne glanced at the carriage that pulled up in front of the steps. "I believe one of those obstacles has just arrived, my dear."

Maura followed her gaze. "I can handle Leanne MacPhee."

"Aye, but can you handle Iain MacPhee?" her mother asked as they descended the steps to greet their guests. "Be very careful with him, my dear. The young man can bring disaster to you and Alexander."

"Do you know how, Mother?"

"No, not yet. Please, just be very cautious around him."

Leanne MacPhee purposely avoided having to speak to her, but unfortunately she wasn't as lucky with Iain. After she had greeted Lady and Lord MacPhee and their daughter Katherine, Iain pulled her aside.

"I must speak with you right away."

"Of course, Iain. What is it?"

"Not here. Where can I meet you privately?"

"I do not believe Alexander would appreciate us meeting in private, Iain. If you have something to discuss with me, please feel free to do it here."

"My God, Maura, how can you act this way? When I left here a few days ago I thought you and I had an understanding."

"You were mistaken, Iain. I am sorry if I gave you that impression."

"Did my warnings mean nothing to you? Alexander MacLaren is a notorious outlaw with a reward on his head. Think of the danger you will be in once you become his wife."

"Alexander can take care of himself, and I am sure he can take care of me," Maura said firmly.

"He will be captured and hanged, Maura," Iain predicted. "What will you do then?"

Maura's eyes flashed. "I thought you were an honorable man, Iain, but I wonder how you can come here and accept the MacLaren's hospitality and friendship while stabbing him in the back."

"My father is Alexander's friend, not me."

"Then why are you here?" she asked angrily.

"I came to convince you to change your mind."

"There is nothing you can say to change my mind. I love Alexander MacLaren, and I will be his wife 'til death."

"I am truly sorry to hear that, Maura. I fear you will live to regret that decision."

"Perhaps, but that doesn't change how I feel. If you wish to stay here as my friend, Iain, I would be pleased to have you, but we will not discuss this subject again." Maura walked away towards Alex before Iain could say anything.

"These buffoons were just asking me if it was true you beat one of the King's knights in a horse race," Alexander said as she joined him.

"Aye, 'tis true." She smiled at those gathered around Alex.

"Would you like to race against us, lass?" one of Alex's men invited. "We would be honored."

"'Tis very kind of you to ask, but I am wise enough to know there is a vast difference between racing an Englishman and racing a Scotsman. I believe, to save face, I will pass, gentlemen."

They all cheered her, while slapping Alex on the back and congratulating him on his choice of a wife. "She will make you a bonny wife, Alex," one of them exclaimed.

Alex drew her aside, his arm around her shoulders. "Be careful charming my men, lass, or I will have them challenging me for your hand. 'Tis bad enough my own brothers accuse me of stealing you from them."

Maura laughed. "'Tis only fair, m'lord, since I am forced to keep an eye on all the fair maids in Scotland. Faith, I cannot believe how they pursue you."

"'Tis all in the past, lass. I only have eyes for you now."

"And you best remember that, Alexander MacLaren, or I'll prove to you how adept I am with a dirk," she warned with a teasing grin.

"You just stay away from Iain MacPhee, lass, so I am not forced to show you the way of it. I saw him drooling all over you as soon as he arrived."

"You have nothing to worry about there, my darling. He has become a pest, I fear, but I can handle him."

"Well, God's love, lass, just use some of that temper on him the next time he comes after you. I dinna know why I should always suffer the brunt of it. I think you will find out our friend Iain prefers his women weak and cowardly, so that would certainly leave you out."

She glared at him, but could not help but laugh. "I thought you'd offer to come to my assistance and protect my honor."

"Lass, one of the first things I learned about you was that you could take care of yourself. A man doesna stand a chance who gets on your wrong side. I pity poor Iain." He laughed.

"Go on with you, Alexander MacLaren," Maura playfully pushed him away, "before I have to slap your arrogant face in front of your guests."

"Aye, I believe I could use a hearty draught of ale after doing verbal battle with you, lass." He quickly snatched a kiss. "I'll return soon. Try not to kill any of my guests with your sharp tongue."

"Alex," she laughed in exasperation.

Maura wandered among the crowd of well-wishers, stopping occasionally to talk with Alex's friends. She was amazed by their warmth towards her. Glancing across the courtyard, she noticed Glenna attempting to get someone's attention. Following the direction of her interest, she was surprised to see Iain hurrying towards her cousin. When he reached her he grabbed her by the arm and pulled her away from the crowd. Curious, Maura continued to watch, trying to read the expression on Iain's face. Perhaps since Glenna hadn't spoken with Alex she planned to confront Iain with her accusations.

Suddenly Iain stormed away towards the stables and Glenna hurried after him. Maura started to follow them, but Katherine MacPhee placed her hand on her arm.

"Maura, I wanted to express my happiness for you and Alexander," she smiled timidly.

"Why, thank you, Katherine. 'Tis very kind of you. Perhaps yours will be the next wedding," Maura said quietly, noticing Colin standing off to the side.

"I would like nothing better," Katherine admitted, smiling at Colin. "Particularly if he would look at me the way Alexander looks at you."

Maura glanced at her husband-to-be who was surrounded by a group of his men. He was listening to what was being said, but his eyes were on her.

"I dinna believe anyone else could ever have tamed the

MacLaren," Katherine said in admiration.

Maura turned back to the young girl and took her hand. "I have not tamed him, Katherine, nor do I wish to. Alexander's strength is what makes him the MacLaren, and I would have him no other way."

"You are very wise in the ways of the heart, Maura," Katherine said with awe in her voice. "I think I could learn much from you."

Maura laughed. "Oh, Katherine, I am flattered that you think I am wise in these matters, but I am not. I am simply a woman in love."

"I believe a better description would be a woman who courts disaster," Leanne MacPhee said from behind them.

"Have you taken to eavesdropping on private conversations now, Leanne?" Maura asked.

"I overheard you filling my sister's head with your nonsense, but you neglected to tell her that you are the sworn enemy of the MacLaren and MacPhee clan and your marriage will do nothing but bring trouble to us all. Possibly even bringing Cromwell down on our heads."

Maura smiled at Leanne. "Do you never give up, Leanne? I think Alexander knows who his enemies are, and I am certainly not one of them."

"Alexander is obviously under some kind of spell," Leanne said caustically. "I have heard all about your mother's ways with potions."

Maura clenched her fist, trying to control her anger. "You are a guest at Dunraven to attend *my* wedding, Mistress MacPhee, and if you wish to stay and enjoy the festivities, you are welcome, but let me warn you, I will not tolerate your snipes and insults."

"This should be my wedding," Leanne spat.

"But it isn't," Maura retorted. "'Tis mine, and I will not let you or anyone else ruin it."

"Is there a problem, my love?" Alex asked as he appeared beside Maura, purposely placing his arm possessively around her.

"No, Alexander. Everything is fine," she answered.

The smile that touched Alexander's mouth did not extend to his level gray eyes as he stared at Leanne. He had no doubt she was making mischief, and after knowing what Maura went through with Glenna, he did not want her troubled further. "I am pleased to see that you wish nothing but the best for my bride and me, Leanne."

"I was not—"

"I was about to take my sister inside for a cool drink," Katherine said, cutting off Leanne's biting comment. "Please excuse us."

"Are you all right, lass?" Alex asked when they were alone.

"Of course." She forced a smile. "I was enjoying Katherine MacPhee's company. She is a sweet young lady."

"Aye, I believe Colin agrees with you," he said as he led her through the crowd.

"Do you approve, Alex?"

He smiled down at her. "She is innocent and without guile. I suppose she would make Colin a good wife if she loves him."

"She does."

Alex laughed. "Now how do you know that? God's love, but you were only talking to her for a few minutes."

"'Tis the way she looks at him, Alex, and the way he looks at her."

Alex smiled and kissed her nose. "I will take your word

241

for it. Now tell me, lass, do you think we could find a few moments privacy so I can steal a proper kiss?"

"I dinna believe there is a private place at Dunraven at the moment, m'lord."

Alex sighed. "I believe you are right, but by tomorrow afternoon you will be mine, Maura Campbell, and I will seek my pleasure with you when and where I please," he warned with a twinkle in his eye.

"I knew one day I'd end up being ravished by the MacLaren," she teased. "I would have been safer had I stayed in the tower of Beaumaris Castle."

"You may have been safer, lass, but I doubt you'd have been as happy."

"Your arrogance knows no bounds, Alexander Mac-Laren." She laughed. "What makes you think I am happy with you?"

"You glow, lass," he said, pleased with himself. "Aye, you positively glow, and my arrogance leads me to believe I have something to do with that."

Maura smiled warmly. "Your head is already big enough. I will not add to it. Now tell me, will we be able to find a moment's privacy after our vows are said? I would not like to spend my wedding night entertaining your clan."

"Do not worry about a thing, lass. I have it all planned," he promised.

They say that Hope is happiness;
But genuine love must prize the past;
And memory wakes the thoughts that bless;
They rose the first—they set the last.

Lord Byron

Chapter Twenty-Two

By the evening meal Maura was exhausted from fending off Glenna, Leanne, and Iain. The evening had started out being a joyous occasion when Alexander presented her with his mother's beautiful jewels. She had chosen to wear the emerald and diamond necklace with her green velvet gown to dinner, unknowingly giving Leanne's fury cause to erupt again.

"So that is why you are marrying him," Leanne hissed when she was alone with Maura. "I should have known you were after the MacLaren jewels," she said, unable to take her eyes off of Maura's bejeweled neckline.

"I assure you I knew nothing about the jewels," Maura said in disgust. "Why don't you find someone else to annoy?"

Leanne was not to be put off. "Everyone in Scotland knew the elder MacLaren presented his wife with a fortune in jewels when they were in France."

"Is that why you wished to be the mistress of Dunraven?" Maura asked. "For the jewels?"

Leanne's aplomb faltered momentarily. "I love Alexander, and a match between us would strengthen our family and clan."

"If Alexander felt that was most important then he would have married you long ago, Leanne." Maura sighed. "Now if you will excuse me, I believe I will seek some pleasant company."

"Do not look so stricken, my sister," Iain said as he slipped into the seat Maura vacated. "I still have a plan or two up my sleeve."

"Well, you better do something quickly," she hissed, "because in a few hours they will wed. Then you and I will both be out of luck. If nothing else works, contact your English friends in Edinburgh. I am sure Lord Randolph would be pleased to know where his betrothed is."

"No!" Iain said angrily. "I will not place her back in that butcher's hands. She will belong to me, Leanne, and if I find you dare tell anyone she is here, you will do so with your last breath," he warned between gritted teeth. "Do I make myself clear?"

"Very clear," she retorted. "You are as big a fool as Alexander. What could you possibly see in the bitch? Glenna is much better suited for you, and I thought you were interested in her."

"That was when I thought she would be inheriting Donald Gordon's lands. Now I will have his lands and his beautiful daughter."

"I can understand you wanting the Gordon lands, but why would you want to marry Maura Campbell, Iain. She would only bring you trouble. The clans may not cross Alexander MacLaren about his Campbell bride, but you would never get away with it. At least with Glenna you could keep peace."

"I hate to disappoint you, sister dear, but Glenna is too

much like you for my tastes. 'Tis bad enough to have had to live with your deception and devious ways for all these years."

"Damn you, Iain."

"Come, come, sister, we must be allies now. I suggest you use your feminine wiles on Alexander again, though I doubt it will do little good. In the meantime I will try to put some doubts in Maura's mind."

Maura slipped into the chair beside Alexander, clasping his hand beneath the table. The smile he gave her made her forget her antagonists, and she was quickly caught up in the heated discussion about politics and intrigues.

"King Charles was a fool," one of the chiefs was saying. "He preferred trying to play his enemies against each other instead of showing his loyalty to the Scots."

"Aye, but no matter what we Scots thought of his methods," Alexander pointed out, "I dinna think anyone cares for the execution of a Stuart king."

Maura glanced at Iain as he took a seat at the table next to his father. He had been very polite to her since she threatened to tell Alexander of his treachery.

"Nor do we care for the garrison of English troops Cromwell has left in Edinburgh," her father was saying.

"You mean, 'the Lord Protector, Oliver Cromwell,'" Simon pointed out, and everyone laughed. "He goes by the title 'His Highness' yet he claims to despise all kings and their way of life."

"Aye, let him come to the Highlands and we will give him a taste of what he gave Charles Stuart," Angus MacPhee said, lifting his tankard of ale. "With the

MacLaren to lead us we will run the English out of Scotland."

Maura stole a glance at Alexander's rugged, chiseled face, and knew that he was troubled. With all his arrogance and pride, she knew that he realized he was only a man, a mere mortal who wore a long sword at his side and a wicked dirk in his belt, a man who felt anger, boredom, indifference, who loved and hated as other men, who stood taller than most and who held his dark head high with pride, giving all around him the impression he was invincible. Yet for the first time, she could see in his face that he knew he could die in a moment's time like other mortals, that he could languish in prison, or hang at the end of a rope. And now that he had chosen to take a bride, the torment was there in his gray eyes, the dark violence and disquiet that had seethed through the Highlands since the beginning of time was now a threat to more than just the laird of the MacLarens. It now was a threat to his soul, his heritage, and once again, his loved ones.

"I dinna know about you lads, but I prefer the cheerful company of a beautiful woman to a debate about Cromwell," Alexander said, coming to his feet. "My dear, would you honor me with a dance?"

"It would be my pleasure, m'lord."

They danced for only a moment before Alex led her toward the hallway. "I need a breath of air to clear my head," he said, leading her up the tower steps. "All this talk of war and politics on the night before my wedding is sobering."

"Aye, I have had enough of intrigues and insults myself."

"Insults, lass?" Alex asked, glancing at her shadowed face.

"It was just an expression." She quickly laughed.

Once they reached the parapets, Alexander pulled her into his arms and kissed her deeply. "Oh God, how I've longed to do that all evening."

"And I have longed for you to do that," she said, laying her head against his chest. "I believe this has been the longest day of my life. I should have agreed to handfast with you."

Alex laughed and placed a kiss atop her head. "Now you tell me, lass. Here, I have something else for you," he said, reaching into the pocket of his black leather jerkin.

"You have given me enough already," she protested. "I have already been accused of marrying you for your wealth."

"God's love, how could anyone think that when I have had to fight the ladies off from Edinburgh to Dunraven. Surely you'd agree they were after more than my riches?" he said, laughter in his voice.

Maura smiled at him, thinking his moods were like quicksilver. "Aye, I'd have to agree, though it galls me to admit it."

"I imagine it does, lass," he said with a grin. He opened his hand to display a beautiful jeweled dirk. " 'Tis a miniature given to my mother by King James," he said softly. " 'Tis small enough to fit into your bodice, but deadly enough to kill someone if the need ever arises. I want you to keep it with you always."

"Why your concern now, my love? Earlier today you implied I could kill someone with my sharp tongue."

"This is in case the tongue does not do the trick, lass. I pray you never have cause to use it, and I should add, never, I repeat, never think about using it on me."

"Never give me cause, Alexander MacLaren, and I

247

promise the thought will not cross my mind."

"'Tis a bargain, then," he said, pulling her back against him. "I love you, lass. If anyone had told me how deep my feelings could be for you, I'd never have believed it."

"Aye," she sighed. "I know the feeling. I never imagined I could be this happy."

"I pray I never give you cause to regret your decision to become my wife, Maura," he said softly.

"There is nothing you could ever do to make me regret marrying you, Alex."

"If you just promise to comfort me through all this madness, love," he said, anguish in his voice.

"Alex," Maura said, looking up into his face, "our love will overcome anything. Please believe that. Not the insanity of war, nor the jealousy of those around us can diminish what we feel for each other as long as we stand together. Our love will be something for our children to talk about for years to come, perhaps for ages."

He could not find words to tell her how he felt. His arms encircled her, drawing her against his hard chest, while his mouth took possession of her, showing her without words that he believed what she said was true. They could face anything together.

After spending some time alone with her mother and father, Maura decided to leave the celebration and seek the peace and quiet of her room. She enjoyed a leisurely bath and one of Mary's hot toddies, then climbed into bed, hoping to get a good night's sleep.

She fingered the jeweled dirk, wondering if Honora MacLaren had it with her when she was attacked by the

248

Campbells. The thought made her shiver. Slipping the dirk beneath her pillow, Maura pulled the covers up over her head, trying to block out the sounds of the revelers coming from the courtyard.

Unaccustomed to the sounds that filled the castle, Maura slept fitfully. One such sound brought her straight up in bed, sure she had heard her door open. "Is someone there?" she asked, trying to see in the inky darkness.

Telling herself her imagination was running away with her, Maura lay back down, but still the hair on her neck stood on end. "Honora . . ." she whispered in the darkness.

A large hand clamped over her mouth, stilling her scream. She stared in paralyzed terror at the face only inches from her.

"I will let you go, if you promise not to scream," Iain whispered, "but if you make a sound I will be forced to hurt you. Do you understand me?"

Maura nodded.

Slowly he removed his hand from her mouth, but he continued to hold her down with his weight. "That's better. Now you and I will talk without any interruptions."

"You are out of your mind," she whispered, her chest straining against his suffocating weight. "Alexander will kill you if he finds you in my bedroom."

"How will he find out if we don't tell him?"

"This is madness, Iain."

"It is madness for you to marry Alexander MacLaren, Maura. Why can't I make you see what a worthless individual he is? Besides being an outlaw he is a womanizer. Are you aware Glenna carries his child? Your own cousin carries the child of the man you will call husband. Can you live with that, Maura?"

"She lies," Maura protested.

"Come now, love, be reasonable," he said as he slid his hand inside her nightgown. "I am well aware your father arranged this marriage, hoping to keep you safe, but I can keep you safe, Maura. I have contacts that can take care of your problems with Cromwell and Randolph. We can be married and live in London, and I will spend my life making you happy."

"You are insane," she exclaimed. "Why would I want to do that? I told you I love Alexander."

"No!" he said tersely. "Put Alexander MacLaren from your mind. He is no good for you. Now listen to me very carefully. I will let you up so you can dress, and we will leave here tonight."

"I will not go with you!" she screamed.

"Damn you, be quiet," he warned, clamping his hand over her mouth again. "I am doing this for your own good," he said as he began to fondle her breasts. "I am an excellent lover, Maura. I will make you happy and you will make me happy. I don't want to have to force you, but I will if that is what it takes."

"Never," she mumbled beneath his suffocating hand. When she stopped struggling against him, he slowly released her again.

"I will trust you to get dressed," he said as he stood up. "Now hurry."

Maura slowly sat up, slipping her hand under the pillow at the same time.

"That's better," he said, thinking she was going along with him. "You will not be sorry."

"But you will be if you do not leave the castle now, Iain," she said as she clasped the dirk in her hand. "Be gone from Dunraven this night or I shall inform Alexander of your treachery."

"You little fool!" Iain grabbed her by the wrist, twisting it painfully. "I tried to be patient with you. Now I will just have to carry you from here unconscious."

When he raised his hand to strike her, Maura raised the dirk and met his blow. He screamed in pain as the knife slashed across the palm of his hand.

"Bitch!" he howled as he stared at the blood dripping from his hand. "Damn you!" he swore as he started toward her menacingly.

Suddenly the door crashed against the wall startling both of them. Alexander stood there, his wide shoulders filling the doorway. Without saying a word he crossed the room and grabbed Iain by the throat, choking off any words of protest.

"No, Alexander," Maura screamed, trying to pry him away from Iain. "Do not kill him. Please do not start our marriage off this way," she begged. "There has been enough violence. Make him leave here, but do not kill him."

Suddenly Alex threw Iain against the wall where he lay gasping for breath. "Take your sister Leanne and leave here, and if I ever lay eyes on you again I will kill you," he warned, each word ringing with his bitter rage. "Do I make myself clear? You live only because my wife pities you."

Iain struggled to his feet, holding his bloody hand to his body. "You will both regret treating me this way."

Alex grabbed him again, shoving him hard against the wall. "My wife may pity you, MacPhee, but I still would like nothing better than to choke the life from your spineless body," he said between gritted teeth. "What is it to be?"

251

"I will get my sister."

"Are you all right, love?" Alex asked when they were alone.

"Aye," she answered, numbly staring at the bloody knife in her hand. "He was trying to take me away from here."

"I was a fool not to realize he was dangerous," Alex said, taking the knife from her hand. "You should have let me kill him. Knowing MacPhee we haven't heard the last of him."

"I could not let his death at your hands ruin our wedding day," she sighed, sinking to the edge of the bed. "I don't believe he is dangerous, Alex. I think he is just confused. I did lead him on that first day I met him. I was trying to make you jealous, and look at all the trouble it has caused. My God, I stabbed him," she said with a shudder.

"I am sure you would not have if he hadn't threatened you, lass. Believe me, all this started long before you came into my life. Iain MacPhee has always been a thorn in my side. His greed has been a source of worry to his family and friends, particularly since he has taken residence in Edinburgh where Cromwell's troops are garrisoned. There is no telling what he would do for money and position."

"He will not bother us again, Alex, I am sure of it. He and Leanne will leave here tonight and tomorrow we will have a beautiful, peaceful wedding."

"I should never have allowed him to come here," he growled.

"Alex, please . . . just hold me."

There is only one happiness in life,
to love and be loved.

George Sand

Chapter Twenty=Three

Regardless of the evils of the night, the morning sun shone on Dunraven. The skies were fair and clear, and the thorn trees surrounding the courtyard blossomed just for the wedding of Alexander MacLaren and Maura Campbell—or so he told her in a note he sent with a crown of heather.

"You look beautiful," Katherine MacPhee exclaimed as she helped Maura into the lovely white and silver satin gown. "Your dress is fit for a queen. I have never seen anything like the work Grizel does."

"Aye, when Alex sees you it will take his breath away," Mary agreed. "You are the most beautiful bride I have ever seen."

"Thank you both," Maura said, tears in her eyes. "Thank you for being here with me. I am a nervous wreck. Has anyone seen Alex this morning?"

"Aye, I did," Katherine said with a giggle. "He's as pale and nervous as a bridegroom should be. Colin and Simon were with him so I'm sure they are helping him get ready at this very moment."

Mary patted Maura's cheeks. "Dinna worry about a thing, my dear."

"I'm trying not to," she answered vaguely. "Where is the crown of heather Alex sent?"

"Right here," Katherine said happily. "Oh, I pray the man I marry will be as thoughtful. One of the girls in the kitchen told me she saw Alexander leave at dawn this morning to pick these. Your mother says they will bring you luck."

"I hope she is right," Maura said as they placed the lavender flowers on her hair. "Where is my mother? I thought she said she'd be right back," Maura said, wringing her hands.

"She will be, my dear. She wanted to be sure your father was ready. Now stop worrying about everything."

"I wish I could," Maura sighed. "Are all the guests in the chapel already?"

"Yes, my dear. All they need is the bride and groom. Now stand still while I place these beautiful diamonds around your neck," Mary instructed. "Oh, how I wish Honora MacLaren could see you," she said, standing back and inspecting Maura. "She would be so happy for her son."

"Perhaps she can," Maura said softly, fingering the chain of diamonds. "I know if she were here I would tell her that I will try always to make Alexander happy."

"Are you ready?" Anne asked as she burst into the room. "Alexander and Donald just—" She stopped in midsentence as she stared at her daughter. Tears came to her eyes and she could not voice any words. Instead, she hugged Maura, then gently touched her face. "You look like an angel."

Maura wiped away a tear and laughed. "But Alexander

already knows I am anything but that. Now the three of you go on. I want just a moment to compose myself."

When she was alone, Maura picked up the jeweled dirk and turned it over in her hand. "I pray you approve of my marriage to your son, Honora. I must tell you, even though I am honored to be wearing a gown made of the material you meant for your daughter's wedding dress, I feel very strange about it. And your jewels . . ." she said softly, her hand going to her throat to touch the slender chain of diamonds.

A faint chill went through her and she struggled against the involuntary urge to shiver, as though she stood in a cold draft. The diaphanous figure suddenly appeared.

"I would have chosen you for Alexander myself, my child. 'Tis a spirited, passionate woman like yourself that he needs. Go to him now, and know that I trust you with my son's happiness and future. Together you and Alexander can guide my other sons to their happiness. I can leave you now."

"But I—" She was alone again.

Maura moved slowly down the stairs, the rustle of her satin gown as loud as thunder in the silence of the castle. Her father stood at the foot of the stairs waiting for her, the smile on his face lighting up the hallway. Together they moved down the long corridor past the well-wishing servants, to the family chapel at the far end of the castle.

"Are you ready?" her father asked as they stood just outside the doors.

"I am ready." She smiled as she gave him a quick kiss. As soon as they entered the candlelit chapel her eyes met Alex's warm gaze. She relaxed and gave him a radiant smile when he winked at her. He looked so handsome, she thought proudly. He wore a doublet of black velvet lined with white; the sleeves elaborately slashed in the Spanish style and heavily embroidered with gold thread. His dress sword hung at his side in a black velvet scabbard trimmed with gold tassels, and around his neck hung the gold crest presented to his family by James V of Scotland.

Alex could barely breathe as he stared at his bride. The lustrous white and silver satin gown emphasized her tiny waist and the lovely curves of her breasts. Her gleaming black hair cascaded around her shoulders in a cloud, and the crown of heather he'd picked this morning highlighted her bright eyes, as he knew it would. There was a radiant happiness about her that seemed to spread through the whole chapel.

When they reached him, Donald placed Maura's trembling hand in his, and he gave her a reassuring smile. They knelt side by side, speaking their vows in clear, unhurried voices that even those who crowded outside the chapel could hear. The sun fell softly through the leaded-glass windows, striking their bent heads as they were pronounced man and wife.

Alex offered her his hand and helped her up, pulling her into his arms to give her a possessive kiss to the cheers of his clan and family. "I will expect many more of those later, Lady MacLaren," he whispered before he released her.

"Aye, m'lord, I shall look forward to it myself." She laughed as they rushed up the aisle, their faces beaming. Before they reached the great hall they were surrounded by a crush of well-wishers. Maura was pulled in one direction while Alex was led off in another by his men.

People she couldn't even remember seeing before hugged her and congratulated her. Someone else placed a goblet of wine in her hand, and toasted to her fertility, while several small children surrounded her, touching her gown in awe. She glanced around, hoping to find a familiar face and was relieved to see her mother and Katherine MacPhee trying to make their way towards her.

"Faith, I am glad to see you," she said breathlessly.

"You were so beautiful," Anne exclaimed, embracing her daughter. "I never saw such happiness in a bride's eyes."

"And in Alexander's," Katherine said excitedly. "Oh, Maura, I envy you. It is written all over his face how much he loves you. I am sorry Leanne and Iain had to leave so suddenly. Maybe Leanne would have finally realized how Alexander really felt about you and stopped her nonsense."

Before she had a chance to comment, another group of guests surrounded them, everyone hugging and crying. Maura glanced across the room and caught sight of Alexander with his brothers and her father. They were laughing and raising flacons of wine in a toast, and she thought they looked happier than she had ever seen them. All thoughts of intrigues and battles were put aside for this wedding day. God, let this happiness last forever, she prayed silently.

"You must be starved, Maura," her mother said, guiding her towards the banqueting tables that had been laid for the lengthy feasting that would take place the rest of the day. "I know you did not eat a thing this morning."

"I must admit I am starving, and I just made the mistake of drinking this wine on an empty stomach."

"Come, let's get you a plate before the crowd finds the table. These Scots have a hearty appetite."

Before she had time for more than a bite of food, Alexander was at her side. "'Tis time I formally introduced you to my men, love."

Maura glanced beyond him and noticed that his men had encircled them in order to be introduced to the new mistress of Dunraven. "Dinna be afraid of them, lass, even though they are a motley crew," Alexander said loud enough for them all to hear. "Of course, you already know my brothers . . ."

"Not so fast, Alex," Colin protested. "'Tis tradition we all get to kiss the bride."

"If I catch anyone of you giving her more than a chaste brotherly kiss you'll answer to me before the sun sets," Alexander warned with laughter in his eyes.

"Who would ever have guessed the MacLaren would be a jealous husband?" one of his men laughed.

The kisses certainly weren't chaste, but it was all done in good fun, and as soon as Maura had accepted the last one's dying devotion and loyalty, Alex swept her away towards her parents.

The fear that Alex's friends and family would not accept her because of her Campbell connections was quickly forgotten. She was now a MacLaren, and obviously with the name came respect and loyalty—from everyone except Glenna. When she was alone for a moment, her cousin slipped into an empty chair beside her.

"You think you have won," she said in a slurred voice, "but you have not. When I have this child I will have Alexander."

"I am not a fool, Glenna," Maura said in disgust. "If it were Alexander's child you would have already told him. Your omission proves you lie. If you carry a child at all, I pity the poor bairn. He will be born to a mother who lies and cheats, and will not stand a chance in this harsh world."

Rage twisted Glenna's features. "You will regret marrying him, Maura. I swear if 'tis the last thing I do, I will make you regret it," she said, stumbling to her feet.

Maura quickly came to her feet and grabbed Glenna by the wrist. "Now let me give you a warning, cousin. I am tired of being threatened by the likes of you and Leanne MacPhee. If you ever do anything to interfere in my life with Alexander, I swear I will make you regret you were ever born. Do I make myself very clear?" she asked, her violet eyes blazing angrily.

Glenna's eyes widened in fear. "Let me go! You are a madwoman."

"Aye, when it comes to the people I love I would do anything to protect them. You would be wise to remember that. Now go and be out of my sight," Maura said icily. "You make me sick."

"I heard only part of that conversation," Anne said as she joined her daughter. "I am sorry she has put you through this on your wedding day."

Maura shrugged. "She came to me two days ago with her accusations. Alexander says he has not slept with her in six months, so 'tis not possible. 'Tis a last desperate attempt on her part."

"It is such a shame. If she had not gotten so greedy she could have married a wonderful man like Simon."

Maura laughed bitterly. "I think Simon is very fortunate her true colors came to the front before that ever happened. She would have surely ended up making his life miserable one way or the other."

The day seemed to wear on endlessly. Maura could tell it was already getting dark outside, yet the festivities seemed in full swing with no thought of ending. Alexander was kept busy with his men, who seemed to try to outdo each other with their endless toasts and jests. The musicians had been playing for hours, but most of the men were too preoccupied with drinking to notice, and only a few young couples danced.

Maura smiled when she noticed Colin and Katherine slip from the room. She was a dear, sweet girl, she thought, and her parents seemed loyal to Alexander even though their son was not. Perhaps Colin and Katherine would marry, then there would only be Simon to find a wife for, she thought, remembering Honora MacLaren's parting words. Finding a suitable woman for Simon would be a little more difficult. He had more of Alexander's pride and intensity about him than the younger brother did. Colin always seemed to be able to find the humor in a situation, which endeared him to her immensely.

Suddenly the music changed to the boisterous Volta, and she noticed Simon inviting one of the young ladies to dance. Strange, she thought, he seemed to be making an immense effort to draw everyone's attention to them.

She glanced across the room to where Alexander stood. She found him staring at her, and it seemed she could feel the warmth of his gray eyes from across the room. He nodded towards the door that the servants used to bring food into the great hall, and she smiled and nodded back, anxious for a few moments alone with her husband.

"Was that all planned?" she asked, rushing into his arms when they met in the small hallway.

"God's love, I had to do something." He laughed. "I was afraid you were going to get caught up in Simon's ruse, and not notice me trying to get your attention."

"There was no chance of that," she assured. "I only had eyes for you, my husband," she confessed, placing her hands on each side of his face. "I thought I was never going to have a chance to have a moment alone with you."

His kiss was soft and tender, promising of things to come. "Oh God, Alex, I cannot bear to go back inside and have you taken from me again," she moaned.

He touched her cheek, his eyes full of laughter. "That's what I like, a woman anxious for my touch."

"A woman?" she said indignantly. "You are an insufferable, arrogant Scotsman. I am your wife now, and there'd better be no other woman ever anxious for your touch."

Alex laughed. "Come along, lass. I have no intention of going back inside. You are mine now."

"But the celebration . . ."

"We have our own celebrating to do, unless you want my clan to be part of it," he laughed. "Have you forgotten the age-old custom of bedding the bride and groom? I have already heard snatches of conversation about what they plan to do, and I can tell you I have no intention of letting them be part of my wedding night. I have had enough of these customs for one day. I want to be with you alone, my lovely wife."

261

Maura giggled. "Your argument is well taken, m'lord Where are we going?"

"Someplace where no one will bother us," he said pulling her along. "Grab up those skirts, woman, or we'l never get there."

Maura did as he ordered, smiling as she realized they were on the cliffs heading for his ship.

How silver-sweet sound lovers' tongues
  by night,
Like softest music to attending ears!
                              Shakespeare

Chapter Twenty-Four

There was no sign of anyone on the ship, yet candles had been lit in Alex's cabin, and an elegant supper had been laid out, complete with French champagne. The beautiful bed under the wide stern window had been turned back, exposing gleaming satin sheets.

"You thought of everything," she said breathlessly. "It is all so beautiful."

"I tried to, love. I wanted this day to be everything you could possibly hope for."

"It has been, Alexander," she said, tenderly touching his face. "It has been the most beautiful day of my life. You really didn't have to go to all this trouble for me. Being with you is all I need to be happy."

He smiled sheepishly. "Actually, I felt rather guilty having already made love to you, so I wanted to make this night as special as possible. As if it were our first time."

She smiled sweetly as she wrapped her arms around his neck. "Alexander, my love, don't you know that everytime with you will be like the first time."

Alexander took a deep breath, feeling desire flood over

263

him as she leaned her pliant body against his. "God's love, what your touch does to me, lass."

He lowered his head and kissed her gently at first, then more deeply, parting her lips with his tongue. When he raised his head he smiled down at her. "Aye, love, it will always be like the first time. You have this hold over my emotions that I believe some would call sorcery."

Maura suddenly pulled away. "Don't say that, Alex. Don't ever say that."

Alex grabbed her by the arm and pulled her back to face him. "Maura, I was only teasing you. Why should that make you so angry?"

"'Tis nothing," she sighed. "I am famished. Shall we enjoy some of this delicious food."

Alex wouldn't let her go. "Not until you tell me why what I said made you angry."

"'Tis something Leanne said."

"Well . . . ?"

"Why can't you leave it be?" she asked in frustration. "It is not important. I overreacted."

Alex lifted her chin, forcing her to look at him. "What did she say, love?"

Maura sighed, knowing he would not give up until she told him the truth. "She said I had you under my spell with one of my mother's potions."

His laughter surprised her. "Faith, lass, I thought it was something serious." He pulled her back into his arms. "I am under your spell, my love, but 'tis from your beauty and warmth, not from any potion."

"I knew that," she grinned as tears brightened her eyes. "But 'tis so nice to hear you say it."

"Ah, lass," he said softly, as he brushed a tear from her cheek. "Do you not know how much you mean to me?"

You alone have shown me that I have a gentle, tender side that I dinna know existed, and you have shown me there is more to life than fighting battles and harboring hatreds. With you I dare think of bairns and the future, of growing old with you at my side."

His words filled her with an emotion so poignant she could scarcely breathe, much less speak. Tenderness and love so strong it actually made her weak overcame her. "I love you, Alexander MacLaren," she whispered, "I will love you 'til the day I die and into eternity."

"And I you," he whispered as he began to slowly unhook the tiny clasps at the back of her dress.

"No." She stilled his hands. "Let me." She slipped his velvet doublet off his shoulders, then pulled his white silk shirt over his head. When she had bared his skin, she ran her tongue over his warm flesh.

"What are you doing to me, lass?" he moaned.

"Dinna you know? I believe you once told me it was called seduction. Do you remember that day at the river when you proved how expert you were at it? You claimed to be able to master my body. Well, now, my husband, 'tis my turn."

"Temptress," he groaned as she shoved him back on the bed to remove his boots and breeches.

"It would serve you right if I had a piece of grass or a feather," she said as she ran her fingers lightly over his bare legs. "But I am sure I can improvise . . ."

"Love," he moaned as he reached for her.

She laughed and quickly sidestepped his hands. "Just lie still, Alexander," she gently ordered as she finished undoing her gown. She slowly let it drop to the floor in a rustle of satin.

Obeying her, Alex placed his arms behind his head and

watched her undress, his eyes glowing with love. "God's love, but I believe I've died and gone to heaven."

She smiled seductively at him. "As I've already told someone today, I am not an angel, and you better than anyone knows that, m'lord."

"Aye," he gave her a devilish grin, "and that makes me the luckiest man in the world. But he warned, my lovely temptress, do not ever turn your charms on anyone else, or I shall have to deal with you in my own way."

Maura leaned over him, letting her dark hair trail over his chest. "Shall we have a pact, m'lord? I swear to you no other man shall ever touch me, if you in turn will swear you will never touch another woman."

He moved his hands up and down her arms, caressing as she stared down into his face. "That is easy, my love. Shall we seal our pact with a kiss?"

"Oh no." She laughed. "You and I both know what your kisses do to me, and I have plans for you, my love," she warned, trailing her fingers over his hard, flat stomach. "'Mastery,' I believe you called it."

"Maura, this is not the time to prove what powers you hold over me," he moaned as she lightly touched his pulsing shaft. "God's love, lass, no man deserves such punishment."

"I believe it is the time, my love, and we shall see if you consider it punishment when I am through."

Alex's flesh was like warm crushed velvet beneath her exploring hands and mouth. She paused at the nasty scar on his side, touching it first with her gentle fingertips, then with her searing mouth. "I want to know all of you, as you do me. I want to feel you and taste you."

Alex stiffened as her warm hot tongue traced patterns along the inside of his thigh.

"Oh God, lass, I dinna know how much of that I can stand," he warned hoarsely.

"All you have to do is beg for mercy, my love . . ."

His body gave a convulsive leap at her words, and he moaned from the pleasure and pain her mouth and hands elicited as she thoroughly seduced him, imprisoning him in her sensual web.

The surge of love and tenderness he felt for her as he held her in his arms afterwards brought tears to his eyes. He felt humbled by her sweet, selfless giving. She had used his own methods of lovemaking to pleasure him with loving and profoundly touching ability. She encircled him with her tenderness, her gentleness, so different from the hard, ruthless world he was used to. He had never had a woman who was willing to give as well as take. And now she snuggled against him like a warm kitten, basking in the pleasure of pleasing him, ignoring her own needs.

But what Alex didn't realize was that Maura never felt more satisfied. As she cuddled against him, she was still savoring the feel of power she had held over him. She had been able to make him feel all the wondrous pleasures he had made her feel. Happiness flooded through her like hot liquid. He had made her a woman—his woman—and she had never imagined feeling so satisfied and so loved.

"Are you through seducing me, love?" he asked as he brushed her hair away from her face.

"For the time being."

Alex laughed deep in his chest. "Good God, at this rate I will be an old man before I am forty."

Maura poked a fist into his ribs. "Are you complaining, m'lord? Because if it is a prim and proper wife you want, one who lies beneath you stiffly and allows you your pleasure before she makes her escape to her chambers, then you have chosen the wrong woman for your wife."

Alex grabbed her hand and kissed it. "I picked the right woman, lass. I have never been more certain of anything in my entire life."

Suddenly Maura became very serious. "This is going to sound very strange, Alex, but your mother came to me just before the ceremony. She said she thought I would make you a good wife, and that now she could go in peace, trusting us to see that Colin and Simon were guided to their happiness."

"Aye, she came to me also," he said, staring at the ceiling. "I believe she is at peace now."

"Aye, I hope so," she said, quickly kissing him. "I believe I am ready for some of that champagne."

"Oh no," he laughed, pulling her back against him before she could move off the bed. "Not yet, my love. There will be plenty of time for champagne. This time is for you. . . ."

> But to see her was to love her,
> Love but her, and love forever.
> Robert Burns

Chapter Twenty-Five

They spent two heavenly days aboard the *Nightwind*, two days of lovemaking and getting to know each other, before they ever came on deck. They never saw another human, yet an abundant amount of food was always left for them just outside the cabin door.

Maura wandered the ship, wearing only Alex's shirt. "Are you sure we are alone?" she asked, glancing around.

"I am sure," he laughed. "I told the crew to take off for a couple of days, and only Simon and Colin knew we were coming here."

She raised her arms above her head, reaching towards the sky. "'Tis such a beautiful day."

"Personally I was hoping for rain."

Maura looked at him, surprise on her face. "Rain? Why in heaven's name were you hoping for rain?"

"It would force us to remain in the cabin," he answered with a grin.

"You are insatiable," she said, wrapping her arms about his neck, "but I like that."

"Aye, lass, where you're concerned I am. 'Tis your fault though. You fill my days with endless wonder."

"I fear I have spoiled you, Alexander. If I am not careful you will tire of my attempts to please you, and send me on my way back to England."

He grinned down at her. "I think not. Call it my male ego, if you like, but I rather like the idea of you wanting to please me. If I had more control over my obvious lust for you, I would pretend to be unaffected by your lovely body, but alas, it is not to be, for as soon as you are near, I am ready."

"And when I am large with child? Will you still desire me?" she asked softly.

"Ah, yes, my love," he said with such tenderness it brought tears to her eyes. "I will cherish and adore your body when you carry my child within."

She smiled at him, tenderly touching his face. " 'Tis possible I may already have your seed growing inside of me, Alexander. Faith, we have tried often enough in the last two days."

"Aye, lass, that we have, but I am a firm believer that practice makes perfect," he teased. "Shall we go back below?"

"Go on with you, Alexander MacLaren." She playfully pushed him away. "A lass needs an occasional breath of air." She walked over to the rail and looked down into the dark water. "What is it like to sail the seas, Alexander?"

Alex stood next to her, staring out at the clear sky and endless sea. "You feel a sense of freedom you feel nowhere else. You are one with the sea and the sky, an insignificant speck, depending on the irrational, unpredictable moods of nature. The sea nearly always challenges you with some quirk of her mood—a storm that threatens to tear you apart and send you to the bottom of her murky depths, or a lull in the wind where you drift endlessly and aimlessly, making you realize the loneliness of life at sea."

"You have felt all these things while at sea?" she asked, awe in her voice.

"Aye, and since you have come into my life, I fear the loneliness of being away from your would kill me."

"Then you will have to take me with you."

"That thought has crossed my mind, lass. As a matter of fact, before I decided we would stay aboard *Nightwind* for our wedding night, I had thought about us sailing to France. I still keep a residence there."

"What changed your mind?"

"I did not want to share you with my crew," he answered, omitting the fact that he did not want to leave while the threat of Cromwell was so near. "Staying aboard ship was the only way I knew for us to have total privacy."

"You made the right decision," she smiled at him. "This has been wonderful. I have been to France and it didn't compare."

"I am pleased you feel that way, love," he said as his mouth brushed her cheek. He lifted her long raven hair and pressed tender kisses on the sensitive area of her throat. "Do you know, lass, if I should die tomorrow, I would die a happy man."

"Aye, I cannot imagine ever feeling more content," she agreed as she returned his kisses.

"Are you ready to return to Dunraven and sleep in a bed that does not toss back and forth?"

She stared at him, disappointment obvious on her face. "I dinna know . . . I mean, it has been so wonderful here,

271

but I know we cannot stay here forever."

"Lass, we will stay wherever you wish. I thought you'd be tired of being isolated aboard ship, and I knew everyone would be gone from Dunraven by now, including your mother and father. They planned to return to Rockhenge yesterday, so you see we will still have our privacy."

"Would I have to share you with your men or clan yet?"

Alex laughed. "You dinna have to share me with anyone, lass. I am all yours."

"Fair enough. I better go get dressed," she said, suddenly excited about returning to Dunraven.

"God's love, lass, you could pretend to be reluctant a little longer," he shouted after her.

She turned around and laughed at him. "Now that you have mentioned it, I am anxious to see your brothers again. I have missed their handsome faces."

"Maura . . ." He chased after her while she shrieked with laughter.

Maura had dreaded facing everyone, sure that a lot of teasing would go on, but everyone acted as if she and Alexander had gone for a walk and just returned. The men in the courtyard continued the work in which they were involved. Jane, the cook, greeted her with a delicious cookie, telling her that she hoped the food that had been left for them the past few days had been agreeable, and that she had a delicious meal planned for their first evening home. Mary softly told her that her things had been moved into Alexander's room, and if she'd like a hot bath, just to let her know.

Maura turned tear-filled eyes up to Alexander while she continued to clutch his hand. There was a lump in her throat that gave her voice a rough husky tremor when she spoke. "They are all so wonderful."

"Aye, they are," he answered proudly. "I have always found a contented clan is more likely to be loyal."

"You are a very wise man, m'lord."

"He is not so wise," Simon greeted from behind her.

Maura turned around, giving her new brother-in-law a warm embrace. "How wonderful to see you again, Simon."

Simon kissed her cheek. " 'Tis pleased I am to see you returned, m'lady. This place has been very dull without you."

"Am I supposed to tolerate this obvious display of mutual admiration?" Alexander asked, laughter in his voice. "God's love, but the lass married me, Simon. I dinna remember that giving you any special rights involving my wife."

Simon put his arm possessively around Maura's shoulders. "Then you better review the rights of the brother-in-law, Alex, because I do have special privileges. I get to hug her, accompany her on occasional outings, sit next to her at meals—"

"The hell you do!" Alex laughed as he pulled Maura from his brother's arms. "Go find yourself a wife, brother. This one is mine, and I've worked hard for her. Faith, I can see life is going to be different around here. 'Tis going to be a constant battle to protect what belongs to me."

"Nonsense. We are going to be one, big happy family," Maura said. "You and your brothers have had free rein long enough. Now that I am here we will turn Dunraven

273

into a gentle, cultural home," she announced, laughter in her eyes. "And from now on there will be no fighting here."

"No fighting?" both men exclaimed in unison.

"God's love, Alex, she is going to have us doing needle-point," Simon snorted. "What have you gotten us into?" He threw up his hands in defeat. "She's your wife; you best do something to control her. I can see us both bouncing babies and feeding them porridge."

"The devil take both of you," Maura said, giving them both her best look of disdain. "I am going to enjoy a hot bath."

When they were alone, Alex and Simon headed towards the stables. "Where is Colin?" Alex asked.

"He rode with Donald and Anne to Rockhenge. He'll be back this evening. You should have seen Donald. He was certainly a different man than the one we brought here a few months ago."

" 'Tis amazing what a woman's love can do for you," Alex said with a smile, thinking about his wife taking a leisurely bath.

"I wouldn't know," Simon said, slapping his brother on the back, "but I can see from the expression on your face that you know what you are talking about."

"Aye, I heartily recommend it, lad, but only if it is with the right woman."

Simon suddenly became very serious. "You dinna have to worry about Glenna any longer, Alex. She left here the day after the wedding, and no one is sure where she went."

"I have a very good idea," Alex said in disgust.

"Well, perhaps you would tell me?"

"I dinna know. . . ."

Hearing the hesitation in Alex's voice, Simon laughed. "You might credit me with enough sense to know I made a bad mistake, Alex. I am certainly not going to go after her."

"Did you know she told Maura she was pregnant with my child?" Alex asked.

"No!"

"I never lied to you about her, Simon. I did take her to my bed when I visited Donald at Rockhenge, but only the one time, and that was many months ago."

"And she wouldna give me the time of day, so it was not my child," Simon mused. "Then who?"

"My guess is that if she is actually carrying anyone's child, it's Iain's. I saw her confront him in the courtyard. They seemed to be arguing about something. If I am right, she has probably joined him in Edinburgh and that can only mean trouble."

"Particularly after your confrontation with him," Simon said. "I wouldna put it past him to turn you in for the reward just to get even."

"Aye, we will have to be very careful. I want some extra men put on guard around the castle. There is no sense taking any chances. Also alert our men in Edinburgh to keep a close eye on Iain."

"I dinna like it." Simon shook his head. "I always knew Iain MacPhee was not to be trusted, but now . . ."

Alex laughed, putting his arm around his brother's shoulder. "I've a sharp nose for survival, without which I'd have lost my head long ago. Dinna worry, brother, I have more reason for caution now than ever. Which reminds me, my lovely wife is enjoying a bath. I think I will join her."

"Go on," Simon feigned annoyance. "I've other affairs to attend to, but I would appreciate it if you dinna gloat so much."

Alex laughed as he took the steps three at a time. "We'll find you a wife, Simon, I promise."

There is something in the wind.
Shakespeare

Chapter Twenty=Six

Maura brushed at something that seemed to crawl across her face, then she pulled the quilt up over her head.

"Wake up, sleepyhead." Alex laughed as his attempts to waken her with tickling failed. "Faith, are you going to sleep this beautiful day away?"

Maura woke slowly, reluctant to leave the deep contentment of sleep. She stretched lazily, smiling even before she opened her eyes. "If you would let me sleep a night through I would not have to lie abed in the morning."

"Ah, it has begun," he sighed dejectedly. "You are tired of my loving already."

She touched his face, tracing the jagged scar. "I will never tire of your loving, m'lord."

"Splendid. Then come along, lass," he said, leaping from the bed. "We have things to do. It is a beautiful spring day."

Maura laughed as she sat up. "What role do we play today, m'lord? Shall I be the mistress of Dunraven, a seaman, or a highwayman?"

"That is for you to discover, m'lady," he said, pulling her from the bed. "If I tell you now you'll have nothing to anticipate."

"But how shall I dress?"

"Dress in the clothes you usually wear for your adventures, lass," he said with a grin. "You know, the ones you wear when you fall off mountains."

"You!" She threw a pillow at him. "Am I allowed to have something to eat? I am famished."

"I anticipated that, my lovely wife," he said, gesturing towards the table before the fire. "Your tea and breakfast are served, m'lady. Now eat quickly, because I have a gift waiting downstairs."

"Not another gift, Alexander," she lightly scolded. "I keep telling you it is not necessary to lavish me with gifts."

"Umm," he mused, "I know that's what you say, but I think you will like this one."

"What is it?" she asked, her curiosity piqued.

"You will see in a few minutes," he answered, stealing a piece of her buttered roll.

Maura ate quickly, then took a drink of her tea. "I don't know why you can't tell me," she said with her mouth full. "You know I hate these guessing games."

"I will tell you this," he teased. "It has something to do with you coveting my horse."

Maura nearly dropped her teacup. "You are going to give me Dubh Sith?" she asked, wide-eyed.

"God's blood, lass, you would take my horse again?" he exclaimed in disbelief, nearly choking on a piece of roll. "I canna believe I have to protect him from my wife. What am I to do, keep him under lock and key?"

Maura laughed. "What is it then?"

"I suppose if I am to have any peace, I am going to have to tell you," he sighed in mock exasperation.

"Precisely, my love," she said, coming to her feet. "You know how determined I am."

"Well, tell me, lass," he smiled mischievously, "would you settle for one of Dubh Sith's offsprings? He produced a beautiful young filly two years ago who I think would make you a fine riding horse."

"Oh, Alexander," she exclaimed, throwing her arms around his neck. "This is the best gift of all. You are too generous."

Before he could return her embrace, she was out of his arms and rummaging through the chest where she kept her breeks, shirt, and boots.

"I'm pleased you think so," he smiled. "I hope you will take the time to show your appreciation a little more this evening."

"I will, Alex, I will. I'll be ready in just a moment, love," she said as she threw clothes all over the room. "Where are those boots? I'm sure I told Mary I wanted them kept right here. Here they are," she laughed as she came up with them. "Is she broken to ride?" she asked as she pulled the breeks on. "Does she look like Dubh Sith? Was she in the stables when I was there before? I don't remember a filly that looked like Dubh Sith."

Alex laughed as he watched her struggle with her boots. "Aye, she has been broken, she looks just like Dubh Sith, and she was not at the stables in the courtyard when you were last there. She has been grazing in one of the fields. Does that answer all your questions, love?"

"I can't wait to see her," she exclaimed as she slipped

279

her dirk inside her boot. "Oh God, look at my hair. It's a mess. I need something to tie it back," she said, looking through the combs and clips on the dressing table. "Here, this will do," she said as she pulled her hair back and tied it with a piece of velvet ribbon. "Do I look all right?" she asked as she turned before him.

"You look beautiful to me," he said, pulling her into his arms, "but I dinna know if the filly will approve."

"Oh, Alex, you think I am daft, don't you?" she asked, chagrined.

A smile drifted across his face. "Just a little, but I pray you never change."

"Oh, Alex, you cannot imagine how happy you make me."

"'Tis all I need to hear, lass," he said, kissing her briefly.

"Hurry, Alex," she urged as she rushed out the door and down the steps ahead of him.

"The horse isn't going anywhere, love. Slow down before you break that lovely neck of yours."

Ignoring his plea, Maura was out the door and across the courtyard. Alex grinned at her excitement, thinking she was like a child about to be presented with her first horse, yet she had already told him she had ridden some of the best horseflesh in England.

Colin was just coming out of the stables leading the beautiful black mare, and Simon followed with Dubh Sith.

Maura froze in her tracks, her hand going to her mouth. She gasped as she took in the beautiful, sleek animal. "Oh Alex," she said in a choked voice. "She is the most beautiful thing I've ever seen."

"I'm glad you like her, love." He smiled warmly.

Maura rushed towards the filly. "Oh, my beauty," she exclaimed softly, rubbing the velvet nose and muscular flanks. "You and I will have such a wonderful time together. We will ride like the wind across the hills and moors."

"I think you have made a terrible mistake, Alex," Simon teased. "Sounds to me like your wife already prefers the filly's company to yours."

Maura released her hold on the horse and turned to give her husband a kiss. "Don't pay any attention to him, my love. You will always be first in my heart," she assured.

He smiled at her. "'Tis glad I am to hear that, love." He returned her kiss.

Colin grinned. "I suppose since you two are more interested in each other I'll just put the filly back in the stall."

"No," Maura exclaimed. "Oh Alex, please, I want to ride her."

"All right, Colin, go ahead and saddle her."

"You're going to have your hands full with Dubh Sith," Simon pointed out. "He's strutting about playing the proud sire."

"You have every right to be proud, Dubh Sith," Maura said, patting the muscular neck of Alex's stallion. "She's a beauty, just like you."

"Do you have a name for her, lass?" Alex asked.

"I think . . ." Maura rubbed her chin as she studied her horse. "Perhaps Lady Rebel. What do you think?"

Alex laughed as he strapped his sword on. "I think it suits both of you."

"Do you want Colin and I to ride with you?" Simon asked.

"No, it isn't necessary," Alex answered. "We willna go any farther than the loch."

They had ridden for an hour before stopping at the edge of the loch to rest. They walked along the water's edge, leading their horses behind them, and enjoying the beauty of the day. They talked of the clan and how to give each clansman a decent mode of living, of farming and how to increase the yield of each barren acre, and of the family they hoped to have. The rushing water was loud and it covered the sound of approaching horses.

Suddenly Alex froze. He hadn't really heard anything, but something in the air warned him that danger was near. Dubh Sith raised his head and whinnied.

"Maura, mount up," he said quickly but firmly.

Before she had a chance to do as he ordered, they were surrounded by the sound of thundering horses. "Get behind me," he shouted to her, knowing it was too late for her to ride. She stood in stunned silence as he raised his arms, giving a deafening shout in Gaelic at their horses, sending them back towards Dunraven in a wild gallop.

She prayed they were not in danger, but then she saw the men draw their swords as they slowly circled them.

"What do you want?" Alexander asked.

"You're coming with us," one of them said.

Maura glanced at Alex. His eyes were hard and steady as he assessed the situation. There were four riders surrounding them, and another rider waited just beyond the trees.

"What do you want with us?"

"There is a generous reward for you, MacLaren," one of them answered.

282

Maura laughed, surprising even Alex. "You think this is the MacLaren?" she asked. "I am Jeannie Campbell, and this is my cousin Duncan Campbell. Faith, mon, anyone in the Highlands knows the MacLaren is our enemy."

The men looked at one another, confused. "What are you doing on MacLaren land?"

"Campbells go where they please," Maura answered boldly.

The riders moved about, uncertain what to do. Then the other rider who had been sheltered by the trees moved forward. "You fools!" Iain MacPhee shouted. "She lies to you. This is Alexander MacLaren. Take him!"

Before they could react, Alexander pulled his sword and swung at the nearest rider, knocking him from his horse. In the next second he sidestepped the charging horse of another, and caught the man in the stomach with his sword. "Run, Maura!" he shouted as he fought like a man possessed.

Maura had picked up a limb and was swinging it at one of the other men who was attempting to circle Alex. She caught his horse in the leg sending the huge animal stumbling forward, discharging his rider over his head, but the man came up with his sword swinging. She ran forward to help her husband anyway she could, but before she reached him, Iain swept her up into the saddle before him, holding her in a fierce grip as she struggled to get away.

"Bastard," she screamed. "You will pay for this. Traitor!"

He slapped her hard, stunning her for a moment. When the numbness wore off, she watched in fascinated horror as Alex lunged and parried at his attackers. He swung his blade, landing a slashing cut across the shoulder of one of the men. The man fell, blood staining his clothes. The clash of steel rang out in the still forest, echoing over the hillside. She prayed the horses had returned to Dunraven and help would be on the way. Blood was running down Alex's arm and from a wound in his thigh, making her wonder how long he could hold out against his attackers. The men he fought were also covered with blood, but they continued to attack undaunted.

"Take him!" Iain screamed. "God's blood, he is only one man! Kill him, if you have to!"

"Bastard!" Maura screamed, as she elbowed her assailant in the ribs. When Iain doubled over in pain, she jumped from his horse and removed the dirk from her boot. With the small jeweled weapon in her hand, she ran towards Alex's attackers and leaped on the back of one of the men, stabbing him in the shoulder and neck.

The man screamed in pain and fell forward, but at that moment, one of the others turned and lunged towards her. She saw the flash of steel, heard Alexander's scream of anguish even before she felt the burning sensation in her side, then there was darkness, silence.

The time of my intents are savage-wild,
More fierce and more inexorable far
Than empty tigers or the roaring sea.
                                        Shakespeare

Chapter Twenty-Seven

Alexander MacLaren lay on the cold damp floor of the overcrowded prison cell, in Edinburgh Castle, his wounds unattended. His skin was hot and his lips were cracked and raw. He knew he was probably dying, but it didn't matter. Maura was dead, killed before his eyes. He closed his eyes tightly against the sight of her blood seeping out on the ground. He had been powerless to save her. He tried to remember the trip to Edinburgh, but her lifeless body was all that he could remember.

"MacLaren," someone whispered. "Do you want a sip of water?"

"Water . . . Aye, water." Gathering his strength, he struggled to a sitting position and leaned against the damp stone wall, grimacing in pain as he did. Someone handed him a metal cup of foul-tasting water. He quickly downed it, nearly choking as he did. "Thank you."

"How did they capture you, MacLaren?" the voice asked from the darkness.

"Treachery," Alexander said between gritted teeth. "Who are you? I canna see in this darkness."

"Gavin MacDonald," the voice answered. "We fought together at Inverlochy a few years ago."

"Inverlochy," Alexander repeated. "Aye, I remember. You have a brother named Cameron."

"I had a brother named Cameron," he answered bitterly. "He was hanged a few weeks ago on Cromwell's orders."

"I am sorry," Alexander said, his voice weary. "He was a good man. I hope 'tis a better place we all go to."

"Aye," Gavin agreed. "It has to be better. I just pray there are no English there."

"And no traitorous Scotsmen," Alexander said coldly. "If I had but one wish to make before they place that rope around my neck, it would be to choke the life from Iain MacPhee with my bare hands."

"So one of your own turned you in for the gold." Gavin shook his head in disgust. "A friend who betrays you is worse than an enemy."

"For the gold and for my wife," Alexander said, the pain obvious in his voice. "I suppose there is a blessing in everything. At least she dinna have to suffer at his hands." He rubbed the back of his hand across his eyes. "God," he moaned, "why didn't I kill him the night before my wedding?"

"Do you mean he killed your wife?" Gavin MacDonald asked in disbelief.

For a long moment Alex didn't answer. He thought with pride of how Maura had fought. She'd not become frightened or hysterical. She had stood beside him like the wife every Highlander dreams of, an avenging angel, fighting to help her man.

"MacLaren, you dinna answer me. Did this MacPhee fellow kill your wife?"

"Aye, or at least one of his men did," he answered in a choked voice.

The unseen figure gently touched his arm in a gesture of sympathy. "I will pass the word around, MacLaren. Even if you can do nothing to avenge your wife, someone here will get MacPhee sooner or later, I promise you. We have quite a network you will find, and not everyone here is to be hanged. Some will be released after serving their time, and they will do the deed."

"MacPhee was here yesterday," someone who had been listening from the opposite side of the room said. "The mon was checking to see if you were well enough to hang. He seemed rather anxious, he did, but the officer who was with him told him he was going to have to be patient." The man chuckled. "Told him that they do not hang unconscious men."

"Do you hear that, MacLaren?" Gavin MacDonald said excitedly. "Maybe you will have your chance to kill him with your bare hands. All we have to do is get the bastard back here."

Maura opened her eyes to the grim anxious face of a woman she'd never seen before. A single candle guttered and flickered, shedding a dim light from the far side of the room.

"Where am I?" she asked in a weak voice.

"You are at Lord MacPhee's house," the woman who sat on the bed answered.

"Angus MacPhee?" Maura asked hopefully.

"No, lass, Iain MacPhee's residence in Edinburgh," the woman answered, patting Maura's hand as she talked. "Ye gave us a fright, ye did, lass. You ha' been out of your

287

head for days now."

Maura attempted to sit up, then fell back in pain. "Oh God," she moaned.

"Ye must be very still, lass. You'll be opening that gash in your side if you move about. Lord MacPhee said 'tis a miracle you lived through it. You lost so much blood."

"Blood . . ." Maura laid her hand on the rough bandage binding her side. Suddenly it all came back to her. The ambush, the battle, Alexander fighting off his assailants. "My husband . . . Where is my husband?" she asked hoarsely.

The woman stared at Maura, confusion on her face. "I am sorry, lass, but I know nothing of your husband. Lord MacPhee brought you here alone in the dark of night. He never mentioned anyone else. He said he knew you were in danger and when he went to offer his help, he found you like this. Weren't you fortunate he found you?"

"Where is Iain now?" Maura asked, trying to keep the hatred from her voice.

"He will be here soon, lass. He went upstairs to try to get rid of some unwelcome company. He dinna want anyone to know you are here. He thought it best for your reputation. Poor man, he has been very concerned about you, staying at your side day and night."

Maura closed her eyes, biting back her words of hatred for Iain MacPhee. Instead she concentrated on prayers for Alexander. He had to be alive. . . .

"Do you think you could eat some broth, lass?" the woman asked. "You need your strength."

"Aye, I need my strength," she agreed, accepting a spoonful of the clear liquid. I need my strength to kill Iain MacPhee, she thought.

"I am sure Lord MacPhee will be glad to fill you in on

ll that has happened, but you must not excite yourself.
t will take at least a week for you to heal enough to even
walk around."

"Leave us!" Iain ordered, suddenly appearing in the
room.

The woman scurried away from the bed, bowing before
ain as if he were some member of royalty.

"I am pleased to see you finally conscious, Maura. I
vas becoming concerned."

"Where is my husband?" she asked, trying to contain
her rage.

"Have you no warm welcome for the man who saved
you from death?" he asked.

"Bastard! It was because of your greed and treachery
that we were attacked," she spat viciously. "Now I want
o know where my husband is."

"You could show a little gratitude for my hospitality,
my dear. I could have left you in the mountains to die,
but I have risked my good reputation to bring you here,
even though you betrayed me."

"Betrayed you?" she asked in disbelief.

"I tried to warn you what would happen if you married
the MacLaren, but you would not listen," he said angrily.
"Now you will pay, and pay dearly."

She fixed him with a venomous glare. "We've been
through this before, Iain. I told you how I felt about
Alexander."

Iain grabbed her chin between his thumb and finger,
bruising her face as he forced her to look up at him.
"Bitch, I would have been pleased and honored to have
married you when I first met you. I would have given you
everything you could possibly want—wealth, respecta-
bility, anything you desired—but instead you married

that devil, panting after him like all the other sluts. Well, look where it got you, my pretty. Now you will live here as my slut, my slave, never to see anything but this dark, dank room, these four walls. You will be at my mercy. Do you understand me?"

"You are insane," Maura hissed.

"Am I?" he laughed. "Everyone thinks you are dead, Maura. No one will ever know where you are. This room is below the house with an entrance that only I and that addle-brained woman know about, and Norah knows I will kill her if she tells anyone."

"My God, what happened to you?" Maura gasped. "I canna believe you would do this. . . . Your father is Alexander's friend."

"Believe it, my love. I will finally have my revenge on Alexander MacLaren. Not only did he deny my suit for his sister years ago, but he took you away from me."

"I love Alexander MacLaren," she said weakly, her strength ebbing. "I have loved him from the first moment I met him."

"Well, my sweet, when I tire of you you can return to whomever you wish, but by that time I doubt anyone will even recognize you, much less want you."

Maura began to tremble violently. "Where is my husband?" she asked weakly, fighting back the tears.

"He is dead," he answered bluntly.

The room began to spin around her. "No . . . No . . . He is alive. I know he is alive. . . ." She sank into merciful darkness, Iain's laughter ringing in her ears.

Alex was dreaming, lost in the memory of their time at the cottage. He could smell the sweet scent of her hair, feel the velvet softness of her skin, hear her beautiful laughter.

Suddenly he opened his eyes and stared around him at the dirt and filth. Pain enveloped him, bringing with it all too vividly the memory of Maura's death. Why couldn't it have been him? Why did she have to die, his sweet, brave wife?

Would Simon and Colin realize what happened to them? he wondered as he struggled to lean against the cold stone wall that soothed his hot flesh. Hopefully they had found her body. He closed his eyes. At least grant me that, God, he prayed silently.

He took another sip of the brackish water and forced it down. If only Simon and Colin would remember what he had instructed if his imprisonment ever came about. They gave him their promise they would immediately sail for France, yet somehow he had the feeling his two head-strong brothers would forget their pledge when they realized his fate. He knew it as well as he knew the chances of getting out of this prison alive were next to nil.

"Here, lad," someone whispered to him. "Rub this powder on your wounds. It will help fight the infection."

"You wouldna have a dirk on you, would you?" Alex asked, accepting the small container of strong-smelling powder.

"I wish I did, lad," the man chuckled. "I would use it to take a few of these bloody English with me to hell."

"I thought this was hell," Alex snorted.

> When life is so burdensome, death
> has become for man a sought-after
> refuge.
>
> Herodotus

Chapter Twenty-Eight

Simon paced the room, fingering the small jeweled dirk they had found at the edge of the loch—along with two unidentified bodies.

" 'Tis a good sign that they were not there, don't you think?" Colin asked as he tried to comfort Anne. "If they had been killed they would have been left there with the others."

"Colin is right," Donald agreed. "It must have been the English come for them. Alex had the foresight to send the horses back here so we would know something foul had happened."

"Then we ride to Edinburgh to find out," Simon said firmly.

Suddenly their attention was drawn to Anne who suddenly began to moan. Her eyes were open, but she was staring unseeing past them. Her hands gripped the arms of her chair, her knuckles turning white, and her breathing seemed labored. "I see her. . . . She is alive. Oh God, there is blood. . . . She is hurt . . . and a prisoner, a prisoner in a room without doors. . . . She is alone—no, I

293

see a face . . . a strange woman, and . . . Iain. . . . My God, I see Iain MacPhee. His face is distorted . . . angry. Oh my God . . . oh my God," Anne screamed, her eyes rolling back in her head before she fainted dead away.

"Iain MacPhee," Simon exclaimed. "By God, we should have known he'd have something to do with this," he said, tossing the knife aside. "I'll kill the bastard!"

"But what did he do with Alex?" Colin asked, feeling a chill of apprehension crawl down his spine. "Surely if he had killed him we would have found his body with the others."

"She's coming around," Donald said, offering his wife a sip of sherry. "Are you all right, dear? Here, let me loosen your collar. Breathe deeply now," he instructed.

"I am all right. Thank you, Donald," she said, sipping the sherry. Then she turned her attention to Simon. "What are we going to do? We have to find Maura," she said, tears running down her face. "She is in grave danger."

"We'll find her, Anne, I promise you."

"Anne, what about Alex?" Colin asked. "Did you . . . I mean, do you have any idea where Alex is?"

Anne rubbed her temples. "I saw only darkness, nothing more. I am so sorry I can't be of more help. Maybe something will come later."

"We will go to Edinburgh and see what we can find out on our own. Alex has several men there. Perhaps they already know something," Simon mused.

"We canna just ride into Edinburgh," Colin pointed out. "They'd have us arrested before we could dismount."

"Not if we are disguised," Simon smiled. "Who would

294

bother a couple of old men who drink too much?"

"It may work," Colin mused.

"It has to work," Simon answered, "and I think it is what Alex would do."

Suddenly they heard a horse enter the courtyard. All rushed towards the door, hoping to find Alex. Instead Katherine MacPhee was dismounting from her horse with the help of one of the guards.

"God's blood, I forgot," Colin exclaimed. "I was suppose to go riding with Katherine."

"Get rid of her, Colin," Simon ordered.

Colin stared at his brother angrily. "Damnit, I happen to be in love with the lady, Simon, and she loves me. She would not betray me or my family."

"Not even to protect her brother?" Simon asked coldly. "At this point we canna trust anyone. After we find Alex you can see whoever you wish, but for now a MacPhee is the last person we need around here."

"Perhaps Simon is right," Donald agreed. "Just explain to her that something urgent has come up and you have to go to Edinburgh, but dinna say anymore."

"Aye, just give me a few minutes with her," Colin said grimly.

Colin met Katherine on the steps and quickly led her away towards the stables where they could talk. "I am sorry, Katherine. I know you were expecting me to come to MacPhee Castle for you, but something has come up that my brother and I have to take care of immediately."

"I was afraid it was something like that." She smiled warmly at him. "I thought if our ride was off, I would visit with Maura for awhile."

"Maura?" he asked, stunned. "Ah, Maura is not here.

She and Alex went riding."

Katherine gave him a puzzled look. "Is something wrong, Colin? You seem very uneasy."

Colin shrugged. "Simon and I are riding to Edinburgh in a few hours, and I never feel comfortable going there."

"It is something else," she stated. "You are not telling me everything, Colin. Something is wrong here."

"Katherine, there is something wrong, but I canna tell you or anyone else. Please, just go home and as soon as things are cleared up, I'll come to you. I promise."

"How long will you be in Edinburgh?" she persisted.

"I dinna know. It could be days."

"Then I will go visit my brother there. That way if you need me, or anything else, you can come to his house. You know which one it is, don't you?"

"Aye, I know the house," Colin said thoughtfully, wondering if this could help them in any way. "I will try to see you while I am there, Katherine, but I canna promise anything. Please just be patient."

"I will be patient, Colin. I just wish you would trust me."

"I canna trust anyone right now, lass," he said, kissing her hand. "Please understand, 'tis for your own good."

Leaving their good mounts with a family just outside of Edinburgh, Simon and Colin entered the town on two old nags. Their clothes were no more than rags, and they were covered with soot. As they had hoped, no one paid them a bit of attention as they slowly made their way towards one of the taverns near the Edinburgh Castle.

Hitching their horses to a post, they took a few minutes to glance around. The Scottish town was filled with English soldiers, wandering about as if they owned the place.

"God's blood," Colin whispered, "'tis a nest full of the English bastards."

"Aye. Even if we find Alex, 'tis not going to be easy getting him out of town."

"You never said what you thought of Katherine's invitation to visit her at Iain's house," Colin commented as he pulled his ragged cape closer around him.

"It could come in handy," Simon said, taking a swig of whiskey. "Come along, little brother, 'tis time for our act."

For a very short time during the day, and if the sun was shining, a small stream of the golden light managed to peek through a crack in one of the walls. Everyone gathered around it, curious to see what each prisoner looked like. Alex noticed many of them were without a stitch of clothes, and some were in worse shape than him, with infected wounds.

"The prisoner from Aberdeen is dead," someone said, discovering the body in the sliver of light. "God's blood, he's as stiff as a board. He must have died days ago."

"Who could tell with the stench in this place?" Gavin MacDonald said. "We are ankle deep in our own excretion. I wonder if you ever get used to it?" He shuddered.

Alex said nothing. Days ago he would have thought it impossible to breathe the air in this place, but breathe it he did, while he concentrated on the sweet smell of his wife, or of the spring heather in the fields.

For the first time Alex noticed a young boy leaning on a crutch against the wall. "What's your name, lad?"

The boy looked at him, but didn't answer.

"The lad has not spoken since they brought him here.

297

I'm not sure he can speak."

"God's blood, he canna be more than eleven or twelve What could the English want with the lad?"

"Aye, what ha' any of us done to deserve death?" someone else said in disgust. "I would not give them my cattle, but they took it anyway, killing my two boys in the doing."

"Quiet," someone hissed. "The guard comes."

Everyone in the room fell silent, watching, wondering which one of them would be taken this time to be tortured or killed.

Alex stiffened as he recognized the voice of Iain MacPhee. Slowly he made his way toward the wooden door with the barred window. He listened, praying the guard would unlock the door. All he needed was a second. . . .

The guard slid the small window covering open instead of unlocking the door.

"MacLaren, get over here to the window," the guard ordered.

No one moved or spoke.

"There is someone here to see you, MacLaren. Come on, we know you've regained consciousness."

Alex bit his lower lip until he tasted his own blood Patience, he told himself as rage threatened to send him over the edge. Just open the door, he thought. One second is all I need. . . .

"I don't need him to come to the door."

He heard Iain's voice, smug and arrogant. He could stand no more. "Bastard!" he screamed, grabbing the bars of the door and shaking them until the door rattled.

"Get back! Get back!" the guard ordered, fearing the door would come off the hinges.

"You killed her, you bastard. You killed her and you re going to pay. As God is my witness, I swear you will ay," he screamed like a madman.

Iain's laughter froze him. He stared through the barred vindow into the face of his enemy. "Face me like a man, ain," he growled. "For once in your life be a man instead of a sniveling coward."

"You stand there in your own filth and tell me to be a nan," Iain sneered. "I put you there, MacLaren. I was nan enough to do that."

"You sent your butchers after me. You let them kill ny wife. How does that make you a man?"

"It doesn't matter how," he laughed. "I always knew 'd get you sooner or later. Patience is one of my finer points, wouldn't you say? I have been waiting years for his, MacLaren. Since the day you laughed in my face when I asked for your sister's hand. You and your father old me her marriage would be to a Stuart. Do you emember that, MacLaren? I wasn't good enough for her. remembered, and I waited . . . patiently waited to have ny revenge. Then Maura came into the picture. Beautiul, desirable Maura. I could see in your eyes you wanted her, but I had other plans for her."

"You killed her, you bastard!" Alex screamed, rocking he door on its hinges again.

Iain's sadistic laughter echoed off the stone walls. 'She is not dead, but she'd be better off if she were."

Alex stared at him, hatred emanating from every pore. "Where is she, MacPhee?"

"She is living with me. She is my mistress, my slave, MacLaren. I want you to imagine it. To think of the hings I do to her while you rot here, waiting to hang. When I tire of her I have promised the guards they can have her, but that will be awhile yet."

Alex's body jerked unnaturally. Reaching through the bars, he tried to get to Iain. He uttered a loud unearthly wail that could be heard throughout the prison compound, before he sank to his knees, where he sat rocking back and forth and repeating Maura's name over and over.

My only hope lies in my despair.
Jean Racine

Chapter Twenty-Nine

"Dear Lord, let me be dreaming," Maura said in the darkness of her strange room when she woke the next time. "Alex . . . Oh God . . ." She pressed her palms to her temples, trying desperately not to think of what Iain had said. She would know if Alex was dead, she was certain of it.

Slowly she sat up, gripping the bedpost for support. She struggled to light the candle next to the bed, then glanced around at her meager surroundings. How long had she been there? she wondered, and how had she gotten to this horrid little room with no doors?

Ignoring the burning pain in her side, she felt around the walls, sure that Iain had come through where empty bookcases lined the wall. "What kind of room was this?" she whispered to herself. There had to be a way out, but she could find no secret buttons or panels. Her strength ebbing; she stumbled back to the bed and sat on the edge. She looked around her, hoping to find something she could use for a weapon when she was stronger, but the room was absolutely bare. He has thought of everything,

301

she thought dejectedly.

Suddenly the bookcase moved aside and Norah stepped into the room, the wall closing behind her. Maura stared at her, thinking she didn't look very strong, but looks could be deceiving, and she wasn't strong enough to overtake anyone just yet.

"I thought you might be hungry for something other than broth," the woman smiled.

"Aye, I am hungry." Maura returned her smile. "Thank you for your kindness, Norah. It is so nice to see a friendly, concerned face."

"You just put yourself in my hands, luv," the woman said. "I will take care of you like you was one of me own. Lord MacPhee and I will have you stronger in no time. I am sorry about the lack of a knife and fork, but Lord MacPhee dinna want you to have them yet. Said you might do yourself harm."

Aye, I would use them on him, she thought bitterly. "Do you have children, Norah?"

"Aye, I had four children, m'lady, but they are all dead. Died of the fever, they did. I just have Lord MacPhee now, but he is like a son to me."

Maura's heart sank. "I am sorry to hear that," she said as she picked at the roasted bird on her plate. Iain said she was addle-brained, but she was also loyal, which won't help my situation any, Maura thought in frustration.

"I have a good life here, my dear," Norah continued. "Lordie, I was living in the streets of London when Lord MacPhee found me. Now he and I take good care of each other. I have a lovely room upstairs, and all the food I can eat. He even pays me a small wage, he does."

"Norah, why does he have this . . . this room without doors?" Maura asked.

"The previous owner of the place had it built, I'm told. Lord MacPhee said the man had some strange, perverted ideas. Doan' know much about it," she shrugged. "Never came down here until he brought you here. He said it would be a good place for you to hide until you're well. You see that small mirror over there? From the other side of the wall you can see in here without anyone knowing it. Isn't that something? What will they think of next?"

"Norah, I must get out of here."

"Now, now, deary, don't you fret. Lord MacPhee is just trying to preserve your reputation. I am sure he will give you one of the nice rooms upstairs soon. I will come often to keep you company and bring you goodies."

Suddenly the wall opened again and Iain appeared. "I'm glad to see you are feeling better, my dear. A few days of Norah's excellent cooking and you'll be on your feet."

"I want out of this prison," Maura said sharply.

"Now, now, my dear, I told you we are only keeping you here for your own good. Isn't that right, Norah?"

"Aye, it 'tis, m'lord, but I do not believe the poor little thing likes this room."

"I'm sure she doesn't," he smiled at Maura, "but you and I both know she has to stay here to save her reputation. It would surely be the scandal of Edinburgh if anyone learned she was living with me without benefit of marriage."

"You just listen to Lord MacPhee," Norah said, patting Maura's hand. "He knows what is best for you."

"Leave us now, Norah. I will bring Lady Campbell's dishes up when she is through."

"I am Lady MacLaren," Maura corrected, but no one paid her any attention.

When they were alone, Iain turned to her, a sneer on his face. "I warned you, Norah will be the one to suffer if you continue protesting your treatment here. She only wants what is best for you."

"And what do you want, Iain?"

"I only want what is mine."

"Yours?" Maura asked in disbelief. "What here is yours?"

"You are, my dear," he said as he sat on the side of the bed. His hands moved to her neck and under the back of her hair. "The sooner you realize that the better off you'll be."

Maura could not still an involuntary shudder. "Keep your hands off me," she spat.

"You may as well learn to enjoy my touch, Maura. I plan to use your lovely body often. 'Tis true, we have had no holy words said over us, but you belong to me now. You will be my wife, without the privileges you could have had if you had listened to me and not married Alexander MacLaren."

"You are insane," she said in disgust.

"I dinna think so, my sweet." His mouth came down on hers, hard and punishing.

Maura thought she would gag. She kept her mouth and eyes tightly closed and her fist clenched.

Suddenly he shoved her away from him. "Before long you will beg for my favors," he said, his voice harsh and angry. "Particularly when you realize your precious life depends on my kindness, and my kindness will come only with your cooperation."

"You will never have it," she said, wiping the back of her hand across her mouth.

He laughed. "When you get hungry enough or thirsty

nough, you will change your mind, my love," he said, unning his hand inside her shirt.

Maura slapped him across the face with the little trength she had. "Curse you to eternal damnation," she creamed at him. "Spawn of Satan . . ."

He grabbed her wrist and painfully twisted it. "I like pirit in my women, my sweet, but if you ever slap me gain, I will make you suffer unbelievably."

Suddenly the panel reopened and Norah stood in the oorway. "What do you want?" Iain shouted at her.

"I am sorry, m'lord, but you have visitors upstairs. our sisters."

When Maura was alone, she painfully left the bed and an her hand along the sliding panel. "How did he open ?" she screamed in frustration. She beat on the wall ntil her hands bled, praying someone would hear her. urely Katherine would come to her aid. "Help me, lease. Someone help me. . . ."

Alex sat in the darkness, oblivious to everything round him. He could endure anything, death, torture, ut not the thought of his beautiful Maura in Iain 1acPhee's hands. Somehow he had to get a message to imon and Colin before he was put to death. If Iain was elling the truth, someone had to know about it.

Suddenly he felt someone slide down the wall next to im. He was surprised when he heard a child's voice, pparently that of the youngster who had not spoken ince he'd been brought there.

"Maybe he lied to you," the child said, trying to offer omfort.

"Aye, maybe he did," Alexander answered.

"You must love your wife very much."

"Aye." Alexander could not say anything more.

"You asked me why I was here," the boy continued. "I killed a soldier who raped and killed my mother."

Alexander was silent for a long moment. Then he held his hand out to the boy. "I am proud to know you, son. My name is Alexander MacLaren."

"Aye, I know of you, m'lord. I'm Rory Donlevy of Inverness. My father was Jamie Donlevy. He spoke of the MacLaren clan often."

"Where is your father?"

"Dead. Killed by the English when he tried to stop them from cutting down his forest."

"How old are you, son?"

"Eleven."

Alexander felt a rage well up within him. Then it ebbed, leaving him weak, as he realized his helplessness to aid this boy or anyone else. Yet also at that moment, without his realizing it, a determination to live and somehow get his revenge took over. He picked up the maggot-infested piece of meat that had been thrown to him earlier and chewed on it.

> It is natural for man to indulge in
> the illusions of hope. We are apt
> to shut our eyes against a painful
> truth. . . .
>
> Patrick Henry

Chapter Thirty

Simon sat at a table in the back of a tavern across from Edinburgh Castle, listening to conversations around him. Many of the patrons were guards at the castle prison, and there were even a few English soldiers present, their accents foreign in this Scottish tavern.

He and Colin had spent the past two days frequenting places like this, trying to learn something of the prisoners held in Edinburgh. Just this morning they had had their first breakthrough. One of the guards had mentioned that the Lord Protector, Oliver Cromwell himself, was coming to Edinburgh in a few days for the hanging of an important prisoner. Simon knew without a doubt it was Alex they spoke of, even though they didn't mention him by name. He picked up his mug of ale and sipped it. They had contacted the men who served Alex in Edinburgh, and they were now gathering information about whom on the guard staff could be bribed to get a message inside.

In the meantime, Colin headed for Iain MacPhee's residence, hoping to learn if Maura was being held there. He and Simon had decided it would be best if he showed up alone, asking to see Katherine. They didn't want to tip off Iain that they knew he was involved just yet.

He walked down High Street, past Candlemaker Row, then turned into the narrow street of grim, leaning houses where Iain resided when he was in Edinburgh. He stopped and glanced around, trying to remember which one was Iain's. One of the city's dour inhabitants pushed past him, with ill-concealed irritation that he would block the narrow way. He felt like everyone was looking at him, yet he knew they weren't. They were too busy in their own little worlds to pay him any mind.

It was a cool, dreary day that seemed appropriate for this dirty, dismal town, Colin thought. The stench of offal in the gutters was nauseating, and several times he had had to duck to keep from being hit by pails of refuse thrown from windows. "God's blood, why would anyone wish to live in the city?" he mumbled as he made his way towards Iain's house.

"Get out of my way, old man," a coachman shouted as he nearly ran over Colin in the narrow street.

Colin ducked into a doorway when he realized it was he the man yelled at. Lost in thought, he had forgotten he was dressed as an old man.

Before he reached the door of a gray stone house, Katherine came racing down the steps and rushed past him. "Katherine," he hissed, trying not to draw too much attention to himself.

She turned and stared at him. Then recognition dawned on her face and she gasped. "In the wynd over here," she said, rushing ahead to the dark, twisting lane. When she stopped, she glanced around before rushing into his arms. "Oh, Colin, I'm so happy to see you. I was coming to look for you. Faith, but you smell terrible,"

308

she suddenly exclaimed, taking a step back.

Colin laughed. "I am sorry. I've been living in taverns and pigsties the past few days, lass. Now tell me, why were you looking for me?"

"My brother will not let Leanne and I stay with him," she said, near to tears. "I had hoped to be of some help to you, but he insists we return home in the morning."

"Do you know why?"

"No, but 'tis very strange. He's acting like a madman. He was furious at us for coming without telling him, yet I dinna believe we have ever told him ahead of time before."

"Katherine, do you really want to help me, even if it means defying your brother?"

"Aye, I am very fond of you, Colin. I think you already know that."

Colin glanced around to be sure they were alone. "What I tell you must be kept secret. It is a matter of life and death."

"You have my word."

"Alex and Maura disappeared four days ago. We believe Alex is being held in the prison of Edinburgh Castle, but Maura's mother, who has the gift of second sight, saw Maura being held by your brother."

"By Iain?" she asked in disbelief. "But why would he do that? He is very fond of her."

"Aye, 'tis part of the problem. Iain left Dunraven the night before the wedding because he went to Maura's room and tried to convince her to go away with him. When she rejected him, he swore revenge. Then Alex confronted him, and swore if he ever caught Iain near Maura again that he would kill him."

Katherine twisted her hands nervously. "But where

would he have her? I dinna see her at the house."

"All I can tell you is what Anne saw. She said Maura was in a room without doors. Do you know of any such room in Iain's house?"

"No." She shook her head.

"Damn," Colin swore. "I had hoped you might have a clue."

"Wait—I just remembered. There are rooms downstairs that I have never seen. I came upon the door to the basement once and it was so damp and dark I never went near it again. I was sure I heard rats scurrying about down there." She shuddered.

"That could be where he's keeping her," Colin exclaimed. "Can you get me inside without anyone knowing it?"

"It is too dangerous. You would have to spend too much time searching and would surely get caught. Let me try to find out if Maura is in the house. If I find her, I will put a candle in the front bedroom window on the second floor, a signal to meet me at the servants entrance at midnight. Then I will lead you to her."

"I will forever be in your debt, Katherine," he said, clutching her hands. "Faith, I would like nothing better than to kiss you right now, but I willna do that to you in my state."

"I will look forward to it when you are yourself again," she smiled at him. "Be careful now, Colin, and dinna forget to watch the window after it gets dark," she said as she hurried back towards her brother's house.

"You be careful, my love," Colin whispered as he watched her leave.

*   *   *

Two men slipped into chairs at Simon's table and ordered ale. "This is Thomas Collins," Alex's man, Gilmore said, introducing the Englishman. "He has a lass he'd like to impress, and could use a few extra shillings."

"You can trust me," the Englishman said noticing Simon's hesitation.

"I know I can," Simon answered. "You and I both know you'll find a dirk between your ribs if you betray me."

"Aye, I figured as much. What do you want of me?" he said, picking up the mug of ale the serving wench set on the table.

"We need to find out if Alexander MacLaren is a prisoner in the castle, and if he is we need to get a message to him."

"He's a prisoner, all right," the man stated knowingly, "but getting a message to him may not be easy. He's in with men who will all be hanged in a few days, and they watch 'em like a hawk."

Even though the news was dire, Simon felt hope for the first time in days. Alex was alive. "Is he well?" he asked the guard.

"I thought he was dead when they brung him in, but I heard the other day he near tore the cell door off its hinges when a visitor taunted him, so I suppose he's well enough."

"Do you know who the visitor was?"

The man rubbed his chin in thought. "No, can't say that I do. Some fancy-dressed lord."

"Are you ever on guard duty over these prisoners?"

"I haven't been yet, but I may be able to trade with someone who's on duty tonight. I know this fellow who likes his ladies and his drink more than his work. It would

311

cost you a little extra though."

"Get a note to the MacLaren and I'll double you money," Simon promised.

"You got it, mate," the man smiled, as he rubbed hi hands together greedily.

Simon removed the note he had been working on from his pocket and folded it into a small square. "Meet me here this time tomorrow and let me know if you were able to pass it to him. Here is half your money. You'll get the rest when I know Alex has the note."

"Done," the man said, getting to his feet. "Anytime you want anything done, you just ask me. They don't pay me enough around here to deserve my loyalty."

"'Tis good to hear, my friend. I think we may be able to pass some more business your way soon, but remember dinna mention this to anyone."

"You got it, mate."

Simon watched the Englishman leave. "Follow him fo awhile just to be cautious," Simon told his man. "He seemed greedy enough to work out, but you can never tell."

As Simon was finishing his ale, he saw Colin hurry in His brother glanced around and then headed in his direc tion.

"I have some news," he said, taking a seat across from his brother. "I met Katherine, and she is going to investigate the rooms in her brother's house."

"God's blood, Colin!" Simon exclaimed angrily.

"A moment, Simon. I know you dinna trust her, but I do. She wants to help."

"I swear if she betrays us, I'll deal with you myself,' Simon hissed between gritted teeth.

"You sound more like Alex every day," Colin growled

"I wish the two of you would give me some credit for having a bit of sense. Now do you want to hear the rest of what I have to say?"

"Go on."

"She is going to search the house this evening, and if she finds Maura, she will leave a candle in a second-floor bedroom window. If that is the case, I am to meet her at midnight, and she will lead me to Maura."

Simon drummed his fingers on the wooden table. "You dinna think it is a trap?"

"Simon," Colin moaned in exasperation, "Katherine loves me. She is not going to do anything that would endanger me."

"I hope for all our sakes that is the case." Simon shook his head. "Now, would you like to hear my news?"

Darkness falls with steely rain
Silver droplets reflect the pain,
And whisper secrets of hidden fears,
Mocking silent, icy tears.
From a song by Chris Bullard

Chapter Thirty-One

"Did you hear 'King' Cromwell himself is coming to see you hanged?" Gavin MacDonald whispered to Alex.

"Where did you hear that?"

"'Tis what the guards are saying."

"God's blood, but I'd like to disappoint him," Alex laughed bitterly.

"Wouldna we all, but at least your presence here makes it easier, Alex. We are proud to die at your side."

"I wish it could be on a battlefield, instead of a gibbet," Alex said.

"Aye, if that were the case we'd at least take a few of them with us to the grave." There was a few moments of silence before Gavin spoke again. "I dinna think the boy could bear up under all this without you. Faith, 'tis a miracle the way he speaks now."

"He is a brave lad," Alex said, wishing there were something he could do to save the boy from hanging. "I'd like nothing better than to send him to Dunraven to be raised by my brothers."

"Guard coming," someone hissed.

"MacLaren, get over here to the door," the guard ordered.

"Do you think that fool MacPhee has come back?" Gavin whispered.

"I hope so. Maybe this time I can get my hands on him," Alex said, slowly getting to his feet. The wound in his thigh had healed, but it left him with a stiff leg.

"I'm MacLaren," he said when he reached the door. "What do you want with me?"

The guard glanced around, then whispered, "I got a message for you, MacLaren," handing Alex the basket of bread. "It's in the bottom of the basket. Hand out the bread then give me back the basket."

Alex dug around in the basket until he came up with the piece of paper, then he passed the basket to Gavin. "How the hell am I supposed to read this in the darkness?" he asked caustically.

"Listen, MacLaren, I told your brother I'd deliver the message, that's all. What the hell do you want from me?"

"My brother?" Alex froze. He had thought Iain MacPhee was up to some trick. "I want you to read it to me."

The guard sighed in disgust, taking the piece of paper from Alex. He glanced around, then began to read in a whispered voice.

"All it say is, 'Have faith, brother. You are not forgotten.'"

Alex leaned his head against the bars. "Young fools! They're going to get themselves killed."

"Your brother struck me as a man who knows what he is about, MacLaren."

"Are they both in Edinburgh?" Alex asked.

"I doan' know about that. I just met with Simon

acLaren. He had a couple of men with him, but no one
id who they were. Do you have an answer? I'm going to
e him again tomorrow."

"Aye, tell him to forget about me. I want him to find
aura. Tell him MacPhee claims to have her. He'll know
hat to do."

The guard repeated the message. "Good luck, Mac-
aren," he said as he moved away. "You're going to need
."

"What was that about?" Gavin asked.

Alex sank down next to his friend and bit off a piece of
e moldy bread. "Trouble, I fear. It was a message from
y brother telling me I am not forgotten."

"That sounds hopeful," Gavin said. "Maybe they are
lanning a way to get you out of here."

"You and I both know that's next to impossible. The
ools will get themselves killed."

Gavin chuckled. "Are you saying you wouldna try to
nd a way to help them if they were in here?"

"Aye," Alex sighed. "I suppose I would, but I have had
ore experience at these things."

"Give him a chance, Alex. God's blood, I can tell you I
el better knowing they are out there."

"Aye, 'tis true," Alex pondered. "I canna lie; I feel a
read of hope, but if we were all killed it would be the
nd of the MacLaren clan. None of us have sons to
arry on our line."

"Have faith, Alex," Gavin said, placing his hand on
lex's shoulder. "You have to give them credit for
lready finding a guard they could bribe. You know, I just
emembered something my brother once told me. He
elieved you MacLarens had some special powers," he
ughed. "He claimed the birds sang louder, the trees

were taller, the flowers bonnier, and the stags were fatte
on the MacLaren land."

Alex laughed, thinking of his beautiful land. "Aye,
swear what he said is true. God's love, you have m
believing anything is possible."

"Maybe you'll consider taking a few friends with you
you get out of here."

"Hell, I'll take all of you," he swore, feeling a tinge (
hope even though he knew his brothers were up again:
more than they realized.

Katherine listened to her brother and sister argu
about his decision to make them return home. Sh
sighed, wishing Leanne would cease and go to bed
Perhaps Iain then would go out for the evening and giv
her a chance to investigate.

"I will not continue to discuss this, Leanne," Iai
shouted. "I told you I am expecting important guest
tomorrow and there will not be room for you, nor woul
it be proper for you and Katherine to be here."

"Katherine had her heart set on doing some shopping
That's the reason we came. Faith, we both get tired o
being so isolated at MacPhee Castle. You should under
stand that."

"I do understand that," Iain said in exasperation, "bu
this is not a good time. You can both come back at the en
of the month."

"The end of the month!" Leanne fumed. "Why that'
nearly three weeks away."

"It is all right, Leanne," Katherine finally spoke up. "
can shop the next time we come to Edinburgh. I under
stand Iain's predicament."

318

"Thank you, little sister," he said, raising his glass to her. "I am glad I have at least one understanding sibling. Now, if you ladies will excuse me, I have to get ready to go out. I have an appointment to keep."

"And what are we supposed to do?" Leanne asked irritably.

"My dear, I could care less what you do. Just be sure you are ready to leave first thing in the morning. John has already been told to have the carriage ready for your departure," he said as he left the room.

"He has become unbearable," Leanne raged. "When we return home I'm going to tell Father how terribly he treated us. I wouldna be surprised if he doesn't cut off Iain's allowance."

"I suppose we should have let him know we were coming, Leanne," Katherine said, picking up a book and flipping through it. "I think I'm going to retire and read for awhile."

Leanne came to her feet. "Well, I'm going to bed, since there doesn't seem to be anything else to do."

Katherine blew out the candle next to her bed and listened at the door to hear when Iain left his room. She didn't have long to wait. Slowly she opened her door and peered out into the hallway as he headed for the stairs. She could hear him telling John, his valet and groom, that he would be out front in a few minutes, after he had attended to something first.

Katherine slipped into the hallway and stood at the top of the stairs. Iain laid his gloves on the table in the hallway, then glanced around as if he were expecting someone. Moments later Norah appeared and handed him a glass of brown liquid. He opened the door that went to the basement and disappeared while the housekeeper headed back to her room.

"Oh my God," Katherine gasped, as the realization hit her that her brother must really have Alexander MacLaren's wife in a lower room. But she had to know for sure. Surely Iain was going to go out, or he wouldn't have had John bring his horse around front. She heard the clock strike ten. There should still be time to explore downstairs, then get a candle in the window to signal Colin.

Maura painfully moved around the room, trying to find some way of escape. She jumped in fright as she heard Iain's voice from the other side of the wall.

"Move away to the bed," he ordered.

Maura backed toward the bed, watching as the wall slid aside, yet still giving her no clue as to how it worked.

"Well, well, I am pleased to see you are up and about, my dear. My patience was wearing thin. I am looking forward to enjoying your lovely body."

"Iain, please, let me return to Dunraven or Rockhenge." Maura decided to try a different tack. "I swear I will never mention any of what has happened here."

Iain laughed as he set the glass on the table. "You will never tell anyone because you aren't going anywhere, Maura. You may as well accept your new home and position. Tomorrow evening we shall enjoy our wedding night."

A chill of apprehension slid down her spine as he approached her. "You will come to crave my touch, my sweet," he said, pulling her robe off her shoulders, baring

320

er breasts to his hungry eyes. "Before long you won't be able to remember what Alexander MacLaren looked ike."

"Don't!" She scrambled back against the headboard, rying to get out of his reach.

"Don't?" he repeated, his eyes glazed with anger. "You dare tell your husband not to touch you?" His and whipped out, slapping her hard across the face before she had a chance to defend herself. "Never oppose me again, Maura. Do I make myself perfectly clear?"

She could taste her own blood, yet still she glared at im defiantly, hatred in her eyes. "If you expect me to dmit to defeat, you will have a long wait. You will have o kill me before I willingly submit to you. Alexander MacLaren is my husband, and will be my only husband. I vill never forget him."

"You are a fool, Maura," he growled between gritted eeth. "If I had the time now, I'd teach you a little espect, but that will have to wait until tomorrow. Think bout that, my love," he said, running his finger down er neck and over her breast. "Anticipate what will take lace in our marriage bed. I promise, you will never resist me again."

"I will always resist you, and I will kill you," she spat.

Iain grabbed her by the hair and painfully pulled her ead back. "Drink this," he ordered, pouring the liquid own her throat.

Maura choked and gasped, swallowing the foul-tasting iquid against her will.

"That will keep you quiet for awhile. I can't have my uests hearing you snivel down here. What would my ttle sisters think?" He laughed. "Although I doubt eanne would be disturbed by your situation. You did

321

steal her only love. Perhaps someday I will tell her how I avenged her honor."

Maura's head was already swimming. She struggled as he removed her only piece of clothing, her robe.

"I hate to disappoint you tonight, my sweet, but I don't have time to stay with you. I just want to see you. You don't need any clothes on down here anyway. Your lovely body is for my eyes only."

His mouth came down on hers in a brutal kiss while he ran his hand over her body. Maura fought against his groping hands, but she was suddenly too weak to do more than feebly protest. "Bastard," she hissed when he released her.

Katherine watched her brother come through the door, pick up his gloves, and leave. Hurrying down the stairs, she picked up the candle on the hall table and opened the basement door. Slowly she made her way down the rickety steps, shivering as she heard something scamper across the floor in front of her. Even though she had seen her brother come down here, she still prayed he wasn't holding Maura prisoner. He had always had a cruel streak, but she could not believe he would go so far as to hurt another human being.

She thought of a time he had strangled a rabbit she had found just to make her cry, and another time when he had beaten his own pony until it bled, because it hadn't done what he wanted it to. Suddenly she froze, as another memory surfaced, a more terrifying one. Tears came to her eyes as she remembered when she was only five, and her big brother had held her hand on burning peat. Oh

God, he could do this! He could hurt Maura, she thought wildly.

The lower portion of the house was like a maze. She wandered down a hallway, opening doors, only to find most of the rooms were used for storage. Suddenly she heard a door open above, then footsteps coming down the stairs. Quickly she blew out her candle and stepped back into one of the rooms and watched from the darkness. She was surprised to see Norah, her brother's housekeeper come down the steps with a tray in her hands. Norah turned in the opposite direction and went down another hallway.

Katherine slipped from her hiding place and cautiously followed, but the housekeeper had totally disappeared. She moved along the darkened hallway, feeling for a door, but she could find nothing but solid walls. Where could the woman have disappeared to? she wondered in frustration. There had to be a door someplace in the hallway. Suddenly her eyes adjusted to a faint light ahead of her. She couldn't tell if it was an open door, or—

Katherine froze as she stared through an opaque piece of glass. "Oh God," she moaned, closing her eyes against the sight before her. Maura lay totally naked on the bed, except for a bloodstained bandage that was around her middle. There was also dried blood on her face, and she looked thin and pale.

The housekeeper set the cup of tea on the table and started back towards her. Katherine quickly flattened herself against the wall and held her breath. A panel in the wall slid aside, then quickly closed. The woman headed for the stairs, unaware anyone had been watching her.

Katherine felt along the wall for a button or lever, but she could find nothing. "Maura," she whispered as loud as she dared. "Can you hear me?"

When there was no answer, Katherine decided she better get upstairs and place the candle in the window for Colin. Surely he could find a way into the strange room.

I sometimes hold it half a sin
To put in words the grief I feel;
For words, like Nature, half reveal
And half conceal the Soul within.
                    Alfred, Lord Tennyson

Chapter Thirty-Two

"God's blood, I dinna believe it," Simon whispered as he and Colin watched Katherine place a candle in the second-floor window. "I knew the man was greedy, but to betray Alex and to hold his wife prisoner . . ."

"Aye, and since we received word from Donald that Glenna's body was found just a short distance from Dunraven, you can be sure Iain also had something to do with that. He's a dangerous man, Simon, and I fear for the safety of Katherine since she has helped us."

"Angus MacPhee is loyal to Alex, no matter what his son has done," Simon pointed out. "When he learns of Iain's crimes, he'll punish him, and protect his daughters."

"If he does not, I will. I wish the bastard hadn't gone out," Colin growled. "I'd like to get my hands on him. I'd show him what we do to those who betray us."

"I'd have to agree with you there," Simon said as he slipped Maura's small dirk in his belt. He had brought it with him to give back to her when they found her, but it just might come in handy now, he thought.

"I just hope he hasn't harmed Maura," Colin said "Come on, we better go now. Katherine will be expectin us at the back door presently."

Katherine flew into Colin's arms when she saw him "Oh God, Colin, 'tis terrible," she cried. "She's locke downstairs, and she's hurt! I canna believe it . . . my ow brother."

"Shh," he comforted her. "We'll get her out of here Is there anyone else still up?"

"No, I dinna think so. Leanne went to bed about a hour ago and there's only the housekeeper and Iain' valet. I think both have retired."

"Take us to her then," he instructed. "We need to ge her out of here while Iain's gone from the house."

Katherine picked up a candle and led them down th steps. "I dinna want to believe it," she whispered. "The I saw her with my own eyes."

"Was she conscious?" Simon asked.

"No. I dinna know if she has been seriously hurt or i Iain has been keeping her drugged. She has a blood stained bandage around her middle, but I also saw hir carry a glass of dark liquid down to her that could hav been a drug," she whispered, her voice trembling. "Thi way."

"What the hell is this place?" Colin asked. "I though there would be rooms."

"You are not going to believe it," she said, clutchin; his hand tightly. "I could not find a way into the roon where Maura is. I searched all over."

Colin glanced at her, his expression puzzled. "Ther how do you know her condition?"

"Look in there." She pointed to the glass pane in the all just ahead of them.

"I'll kill him!" Simon said, slamming his fist on the ass. "The bastard . . . the perverted bastard. There will hell to pay when I get my hands on him!"

"Sweet Jesus, she looks like she's dead," Colin whis-red, his voice choked with emotion. "What has he ne to her?"

"I am certain she's alive, Colin," Katherine said, uching his arm. "Earlier I hid right here while the usekeeper brought her nourishment."

"How did the woman get in and out?" Colin asked, eling along the wall.

"The wall just slid open, then closed behind her. I nna see her touch anything or use anything. As I said, I arched for several minutes, but found nothing. I even ied to call to Maura, but she could not hear me."

"Have you any suggestions?" Colin asked his brother he continued searching.

"We could drag the housekeeper out of bed and force er to show us how to get in, but I'd rather not have nyone else know we're here," Simon said, still feeling gainst the wall.

"Do you think we could kick it in? Or maybe break at small pane of glass?" Colin asked.

"Aye, the glass may be our answer. Perhaps there's a tch we could reach from inside once we break the ne," Simon said, taking his sword from its sheath. Katherine, step back a few feet."

As he raised the hilt of his sword to break the glass, the all suddenly opened.

"Simon," Colin exclaimed, "it was in the floor. atherine must have stepped on something that opened the door."

"Both of you stay right here while I get her," Simo[n] instructed.

"Maura, can you hear me?" Simon asked as he slipp[ed] one of her arms into the robe. "You are going to be fi[ne] now. I swear I'll make that bastard pay for doing this [to] you."

"Is she all right?" Colin asked from the doorway.

"I canna say for sure," he answered as he tied the sas[h] of her robe. "She's unconscious."

"Simon, have you thought about what we're going [to] do with her? We canna carry her into an inn like that."

Simon ran his hand through his hair. "You have [a] point, little brother. We would surely raise suspicion.[”]

"I am returning home in the morning. Perhaps the[re] would be someway to hide her in the carriage," Kath[e]rine suggested.

"No, if Leanne discovered her she would surely expo[se] us," Simon said.

"Is there enough time for me to take her back [to] Dunraven?" Colin asked.

"No, Cromwell is supposed to arrive in Edinburgh th[e] day after tomorrow. Besides, she is obviously in no sha[pe] to make a trip of any kind."

"Simon, doesn't Charles Campbell live just down th[e] street?"

"Aye, as far as I know, but Jesus, Colin, a Campbel[l] Donald would surely kill us."

"I agree that would be the case with most Campbell[s] but Charles and Alex have had some dealings, Simon. [I] remember one time we met him on the road, and h[e] apologized to Alex for Angus Campbell's barbaria[n] behavior. Besides, he is a relative of Maura's. Surely h[e] ould want to help her."

Simon rubbed his chin. "At least we could try to get
im to take her back to Rockhenge. I suppose we have no
ther choice, Colin," he said, picking Maura up from the
ed. "Let's get the hell out of here."

"No one's going anywhere!" Iain said from behind
em. "Get upstairs, Katherine. I will deal with you
ter."

"Iain, please let them go. This is wrong—Maura needs
elp," Katherine entreated.

"Do as I said!" he screamed at her, brandishing his
word like a lunatic.

Katherine cautiously moved around behind him, but
e remained in the hallway.

"Put her back on the bed," he ordered Simon.

Simon gently laid Maura back on the bed, slipping his
and to his belt and palming her small dirk as he did.
You won't get away with this, MacPhee. You are going
 have too many bodies to explain."

"I am not going to have to explain anything to any-
e. The English will be delighted to have the other two
acLarens, whether you're dead or alive."

"Do what you want with us," Colin said, his hand
sting on the hilt of his sword, "but at least let Kathe-
ne get Maura a surgeon."

"She doesn't need anyone's help. She belongs to me
ow and I will take care of her."

"Iain, please do what Colin asks," Katherine begged
om behind him.

Iain swung around, screaming at her to get upstairs. As
e did, Simon threw the knife, embedding it between
ain's shoulder blades. Iain stumbled forwards, trying to
each the blade protruding from his back before falling

dead on his face.

Katherine screamed and fell to her knees next to her brother. "Oh God, Iain. Why?" she cried.

Colin bent over and pulled her to her feet. "He's dead Katherine. You must leave here now."

She stared at him, her eyes glazed. "Leave here? canna leave here. Leanne is upstairs."

"Then wake her and tell her you want to go home Katherine. Tell her you're sick, anything, but get out of here. Let the servants find him."

"But he's my brother, Colin. No matter what he' done, I canna just leave him down here. You go on. promise no one will ever know how this happened. I' just tell them I found him this way."

"God's blood, Katherine, I canna leave you to face thi alone," Colin exclaimed.

"Please, Colin, just go. I will take care of everything, she pleaded.

"What do you think, Simon?" Colin asked, reluctar to leave her.

"All I know is we've got to get out of here," Simo said, picking Maura up from the bed. "We've truste Katherine this far. We'll have to trust her a little longe Just know, lass, our lives are in your hands. If you betra us, we'll both hang."

"You have nothing to worry about. Now hurry, befor someone comes," she said, quickly kissing Colin. "Com to me at MacPhee Castle when this is all over."

"I will, Katherine, I promise."

Cruelty has a human heart;
And Jealousy a human face;
Terror, the human form divine,
And Secrecy, the human dress.
                              William Blake

Chapter Thirty-Three

Maura opened her eyes and stared at Simon as he laid
er on the bed. She was certain she was dreaming until
e heard his voice.

"'Tis all right, lass. You will be safe here. Charles
ampbell has assured us he will take you to Rockhenge as
oon as you can travel."

"Charles Campbell . . ," she repeated, her brain still
umb from the drug.

"Aye, lass. He was the only one in Edinburgh we could
o to. He has assured us we can trust him."

"How did you find me?" she asked weakly.

"It was a combination of things. Your mother saw you
eing held prisoner, and she saw Iain's face. Then Alex
ent us a message that he thought Iain was—"

"Alex?" She struggled to sit up, her head swimming as
e did. "Alex is alive? Where is he? Oh God, where is he,
imon?"

"Aye, lass, he's alive, but he's being held prisoner at
dinburgh Castle."

"Oh, God." She collapsed back on the bed. "Iain told

me he was dead, but I never believed it. I prayed. . . You know it was Iain that led the attack on us," she sai close to hysteria. "I tried to help him."

"Quiet now, lass. You need your rest. Janet Campbe just finished examining you, and she said the nasty swo wound in your side is slowly healing, but you'll have to l very careful not to reopen it."

Maura wiped the tears from her face and sniffed. "Ho can we get Alex out of prison, Simon?"

"You're not to worry, lass. Colin and I are working c it," he assured. "I promise, we will all be back Dunraven soon enough."

"I want to help."

"The only way you're going to help is by getting well. he said firmly. "Besides, there would be hell to pay Alex found out we let you get involved."

Maura clutched his hand. "Do they—I mean, what c they plan to do with him?" she asked in a tremulo voice.

"Maura, why don't you rest now."

"Tell me, Simon. I want to know," she persisted.

Simon ran his hand through his dark hair. "They pla to hang him, but we are not going to let that happer More than twenty of his men have already come int town to help, and more are on the way, so everything well in hand."

Maura stifled a sob, closing her eyes against the pair "How long do we have to get him out?"

"The rumor is that Cromwell is coming to witness th hanging. Some say he'll be here the day after tomorrov others say not until the end of the week. It doesn't reall matter, because our plan is to make our move when the transport him to the gallows."

"Oh, God, Simon, if it doesn't work . . ."

"It will work, lass. Trust me."

"I'll go to Cromwell and plead with him. Maybe I can ke him understand."

"No, lass. Cromwell has wanted Alex for a long time. s not going to listen to a woman's pleading. Now you d to rest, and Colin and I have a lot of details to attend

"You will come back tomorrow?"

"Aye, one of us will check in on you. Sleep well, lass."

Charles Campbell stood with his back to the window ing Colin. "I dinna like this at all. You are placing my ily in great danger."

"Maura is a relative, Charles. Surely you can see why decided to ask for your help, and you agreed to give

"Aye, but I've had time to think of the consequences, w that you tell me she's married to the MacLaren."

"Aye, she is, but there are no MacLarens in Edin- rgh and you well know it. We have to depend on you, arles."

"We canna turn the lass away, Charlie," his wife said. he needs rest and good food to help her recuperate."

"Tell me, Colin," Charles Campbell said, "While we e care of the MacLaren's wife, what are you going to be ng?"

"I think it would be safer for us all if we dinna discuss t, Charles."

"Ah, just as I thought," he said, throwing up his hands disgust. "You're going to be helping your brother ape, and probably getting yourselves killed in the

333

process. Then what the hell am I supposed to do with girl when that happens? Or if you're successful help your brother escape, maybe you expect me to give h shelter. God's blood, mon, you ask too much."

"Calm down, Charles," Simon said as he entered room. "The only help we ask of you is to let Maura s here for a couple of days. I swear to you we will involve you in anything else. Besides, you agreed to that the girl was taken to Donald Gordon as soon as s could travel."

"Aye, I must have been out of my mind to agree that." He shook his head. "If my clan finds out that I' been conspiring with MacLarens . . ."

Alex sat staring off into space, praying his brothers h found Maura and taken her back to Dunraven. Home, thought longingly. Home, where morning creeps up the Highlands, sprinkling shiny diamonds upon t hillside and on the trees. He closed his eyes and imagin the mountains still wet with the gauzy mist off the s and of his ship bobbing at anchor—waiting for him waiting to take him away from this hell. He pictur Maura on the deck of his ship, her raven hair blowing the wind. He could almost feel her touch, smell t sweetness of her.

"MacLaren," someone shouted from the barred do "You are to come with us."

Gavin gripped Alex's arm. "Don't go with them," whispered.

Alex laughed bitterly. "What are my options, n friend?"

"I've never known anyone to come back."

334

"Dinna worry. I am sure I'll be back. You did tell me omwell was traveling all the way from London to see e hang. Why would they kill me before he gets here?"

Gavin released his hold on Alex's arm. "Aye, I suppose u're right."

"I am certain I'll be brought back here, Gavin, but just case something happens, the next time the guard mes asking for me, send a message to my brother that e gone to a better place."

"Alex . . ."

"Take care of the boy. Give him your strength."

"God go with you," Gavin said, embracing him.

Alex stiffly walked between the two guards. They had aced iron fetters on his ankles and bound his wrists hind him.

"Where are you taking me?" he asked.

"All I know is Lord Somebody from London wants to e you," one of the guards volunteered. "I don't know hy they can't just leave us alone down here. They ways got to be sticking their nose in our business. I was ght in the middle of a card game. Had the winner, I did."

"Aye, I was in the middle of tea," Alex snorted. "Why n't we just leave the bastard to wait and go out for a ink?"

Both guards laughed. "Sorry about that, MacLaren, it we got our orders. Nothing personal, you know."

"Aye, I know."

The guard opened the door and led him inside. The an behind the desk stood up, a black look on his ugly ce. "Leave us," he ordered. "Wait outside until I call r you."

He stood up and came around the front of the desk, staring at Alex as he tapped his riding crop against his leg. "So you're the infamous MacLaren. You don't look so dangerous to me."

"Chains and shackles can do that to a man," Alex answered. "Do you mind telling me who you are and what you want with me?"

"I am Lord James Randolph."

Alex raised one dark eyebrow. "Lord Randolph," he said, giving a mock bow. "I am Lord Alexander MacLaren, but then you already know that."

"Enough of your games, MacLaren," he said coldly. "Last night I had an interesting conversation with a friend of yours. He informed me that you were the one who kidnapped my betrothed, Lady Maura Campbell."

"Of course that would be Iain MacPhee," Alex said in disgust. "Did he also tell you that the lady is now my wife?"

Randolph paled and his hand stilled. "Your wife?" he repeated incredulously.

Alex laughed. "So, he dinna tell you everything. Iain must be up to something, m'lord, or maybe he was afraid you'd take your anger out on him."

"You bastard!" He raised the whip and brought it down hard against Alex's face, leaving a bloody gash.

Alex stared at him, his gray eyes turning to steel. "You'd better be sure they kill me, Randolph, because if I ever get my hands on you . . ."

Lord Randolph laughed, but he had the sense to move back to the other side of the desk. "You're not going to do a thing, MacLaren. You're going to die, hanged from the neck until every last breath is choked from your body, and then you'll stay there for all to see, and for the birds to feast upon. I look forward to seeing that, you bastard."

Alex laughed. "If a man had just told me he had married the woman I desired, I'd call him out. I wouldn't leave it up to someone else to deal with him. But then maybe you haven't the guts, Randolph."

"Nice try, MacLaren, but it isn't going to work. Cromwell has waited too long to see you pay for your rebellion. I'd hang beside you if I took that pleasure from him. Though there is nothing I'd like better than to cut you down piece by piece for taking the lady from me on my wedding day."

"'Tis a small matter to me how I leave this earth now, Randolph. I have had the lady's love. I can die a happy man," he taunted.

Randolph's eyes blazed angrily. "Guards," he shouted. "Come in here. Hold this man," he ordered when they entered the room. "He needs a lesson in humility."

"M'lord, the man is already shackled," one of the guards said in disbelief.

"I ordered you to hold him," Randolph shouted as he raised the crop and brought it down across Alex's bare chest.

What is love? 'Tis not hereafter;
Present mirth hath present laughter.
What's to come is still unsure;
In delay there lies no plenty . . .
                              Shakespeare

Chapter Thirty=Four

Maura stared out the window that overlooked one of the narrow streets of Edinburgh. She traced a raindrop as it made a path downwards, and remembered how Alex had held her in the protection of his arms when they had ridden from England. She smiled, recalling how they had fought—and how they had loved. "Alex, Alex," she whispered. "Know that I am with you in thought, and hopefully we shall be together again soon."

Suddenly the door opened behind her and Janet Campbell rushed into the room. "Simon is here. He's downstairs talking with Charles."

Maura hurried through the door and down the stairs. "What is the news?" she asked as she rushed into the room. "Have you heard from Alex?"

"Nothing directly from Alex," he answered grimly, "but Cromwell arrived this morning. It looks like tomorrow is the day."

"Oh God," she exclaimed, swaying on her feet.

"Here, sit down, lass," Simon said, helping her to a chair. "I have to explain a few things to you and then be on my way. You and Charles are going to leave for the port of Leith in just a few hours. It's only a short distance from here."

"No! I will not leave here without Alex," Maura protested, coming to her feet. "There has got to be something I can do to help. I can ride a horse as well as any man, and I can wield a sword with ample skill. Please, Simon, I have to help my husband," she pleaded.

"Maura, listen to me." He gently shook her. "This has all been planned very carefully. Together, Colin and I have tried to think of everything. If you try to do anything different now it most likely will ruin any chance we have of saving Alex. Surely you understand that, lass."

"Aye," she whispered, the strength to argue leaving her. "I just feel so helpless."

"I am sorry, lass, but it has to be this way. Now listen to me carefully. A room has been rented for you at the Black Hawk Inn. Charles will take you there, along with your luggage."

"I have no luggage," she sighed in defeat.

"Janet has taken care of that. She has shopped for you and has everything packed. Now, you will stay in your room at the inn until one of us comes for you. If for some reason that does not happen in two days' time, you are to tell the owner of the inn you want to meet with Capt. Evan Fraser, who will also be staying at the inn. He will take you to safety."

"But, Simon—"

"Listen to me, Maura. Under no circumstances are you to head for Rockhenge or Dunraven. If something goes wrong with our plan, that will be the first place the English will look for you. You should know by now they would not hesitate to hang you if they found you."

Maura struggled to hold back the tears. "If anything happens to Alex it does not matter," she murmured. "Oh God, Simon, do you really think you can save him? I dinna think I could go on if Alex is . . ." She couldn't say the words.

Simon took her in his arms. "Dinna worry, lass," he whispered. "We MacLarens are invincible. Hasn't Alexander told you that often enough?"

"Aye," she forced a tearful smile, "and I pray 'tis true. Please be careful."

"We will, lass. Have faith," he said, kissing her on the forehead. "We'll see you in Leith."

Maura glanced at the landscape as the carriage entered the port of Leith. It was like all seaports, crowded and filled to the rafters with scoundrels and rough-looking seafaring men. A good place, she supposed, for one to blend into the crowds, and she was certain that was what Simon had in mind.

The carriage stopped in front of a small inn. When the groom opened the door, Charles helped her down, then turned and told the driver to wait for him. She could hear boisterous voices coming from the tavern in the lower part of the inn. The voices sounded very gay, she thought, not having heard laughter in some time.

"Your room is above," Charles said, taking her by the arm. "We must go through the ordinary, but if you pull your hood over your face the men will not take notice."

As they made their way through the crowded room, she was glad for the strength of Charles Campbell's arm, and for the shielding cover of her hood. The loud shouts of laughter and curses filled the room, and she was relieved when they reached the safety of the stairs without mishap.

"It isn't much," Charles said, opening the door of a small, yet clean room.

Maura glanced around. There was a bed, a small table, and one chair, but a fire burned brightly on the hearth, and fresh candles had been lit, giving it a cozy feeling. "It isn't so bad."

"The innkeeper has instructions to bring you food and beverage several times a day," Charles said, glancing out through the wavy pane of the window that overlooked the harbor. "Just remember, it is only for a few days."

"Aye, I'll remember," she assured him.

"I hate to leave you," he said, concern in his voice. "Are you sure you'll be all right?"

"Aye, I'll be fine," she said, placing her hand on his arm. "I want to thank you, Charles. You and Janet have been very kind to me and I will always remember it."

"We are family," he shrugged.

"Aye," she smiled at his embarrassment.

"I must be on my way, lass. I hope things go well with you. We're no'so fond of Alexander MacLaren, but I know he doesna deserve to hang."

"No, he does not," Maura answered. "Thank you again, Charles."

She watched the man leave, then she turned away to look out the window. The sun had set and all she could make out was the outline of many slender masts, and the sparkle of riding lights being lit as darkness fell. She had never seen so many ships in one place.

She turned away to lie across the bed, thinking of the small, hidden cove where *Nightwind* was anchored. She wished more than anything she could be there with Alex t that very moment.

She thought of Janet's parting words: "What will be, will be," she had whispered, "and no matter what happens, you will have to go on with your life."

Laying her arm across her eyes, Maura swallowed back the tears. It was easy for Janet to say that. She had never felt Alexander MacLaren's warm breath on her throat, or savored his passionate kisses. She had never heard him laugh, or had never bantered with him, or had never been loved by him. "No one understands," she whispered in the darkness. "Life would be meaningless without him."

And if I lose thy love, I lose my all.
Alexander Pope

Chapter Thirty-Five

Maura dozed off and on, but the night seemed endless, and the next morning was even worse. The breakfast the innkeeper had brought still sat on the table. Even the thought of food made her nauseated in her nervous state. She paced the small room, her imagination her worst enemy as she thought about what could be happening in Edinburgh. She knew if Simon and Colin hadn't been successful, they would also be dead by now.

The morning and afternoon passed, and soon the sun began to set again over the harbor. Maura stood staring out the window at the ships. "God, what is happening," she moaned. "Not knowing is driving me mad."

She strained to get a better view of a lone rider coming towards the inn. Her heart sank as she recognized Simon—Simon all alone. "Oh God, no . . . No," she choked back a sob. "It canna be." In that moment she felt beaten, broken, exhausted to the very depths of her soul. "Alex is dead."

She heard the door open behind her, but she could not turn around and face the truth. Gripping the window sill, she tried to steady herself for the devastating words. But Simon did not speak. Her voice was a tremor when she asked. "Is it . . . is it too late to help Alex?" she asked with a sob.

"Aye, he has been beyond help since he met a fair lass named Maura Campbell."

Maura whirled around so quickly she almost lost her balance. Alex grabbed her and pulled her into his arms, kissing her all over her face.

"Oh, God, love, how I have missed you," he confessed, tears brightening his own eyes. "I dinna dare dream I would hold you in my arms again."

"Nor did I," she sobbed, touching his bruised face as if she didn't believe he stood before her. "Oh God, what have they done to you?"

"It is nothing," he answered, touching her, caressing her. "You are so pale, and your beautiful eyes are shadowed, lass. Have you been going without sleep?"

"I have spent a bad hour or two," she admitted, "but I will be fine now."

"My brothers should have told you it would take more than Oliver Cromwell or James Randolph to do me in," he said, running his thumb along her jawline.

"Aye, they did, but I found it hard to believe. So much was against us."

He raised a dark brow, a smile in his gray eyes. "Have you no faith in your mother's predictions, lass? Did she not tell us we would be together?"

"Aye, but I had begun to believe it was to be in another world."

He kissed her fingertips. "I must admit, I wondered if that was the case myself. Come, sit with me on the bed. I find I have little strength left after the harrowing activiies of this morning."

Maura sat next to him, touching his bruised and cut face, running her hand through his dark hair. "How did they accomplish it, Alex? How did they save you?"

"A lot of money changed hands. Enough to make it possible for the lot of us to escape when there was an explosion in front of the scaffold. Ironically it was thanks to Iain MacPhee's empty house that we were able to pull it off. There we were able to hide while we cleaned up and changed into clothes Simon and Colin had plundered. Then we left Edinburgh one at a time. Two of my acquaintances, a young boy and a friend named Gavin MacDonald, will be going with us, the rest were on their own."

"Incredible," she whispered in amazement. "Do you think they will come looking for us?"

"Aye, lass, I am sure of it. That is why my ship waits in the harbor to take us to France for awhile."

"Here in Leith?" she asked incredulously.

"Aye, lass. 'Tis how my men arrived in Edinburgh unnoticed. The harbor is so crowded, who would look at one more ship?" He laughed. "God, I canna wait to scrub in a hot tub. I washed at MacPhee's, but I still feel like I'm dirty."

"You are amazing, Alexander MacLaren." She smiled. "You have just accomplished the impossible, and here you stand talking about a bath."

"You flatter me, sweet, but I have to give credit to my brothers and my men. They worked out everything," he explained. "Simon and Evan are waiting downstairs now. I want you to know that our trip to France is only temporary," he assured. "We will return to Dunraven as soon as it is safe. Cromwell canna stay in power forever."

"Of course we will, my darling. Dunraven is where we will raise our sons, and they will be a force for England to reckon with for years to come."

Alexander placed his fingers to her lips. "What would pray for, my love, is that our sons are allowed to live in peace, to enjoy the beauty of their land, and to know the love of a good woman like their mother."

Maura smiled at her husband. "My father once said all you needed was a loving woman to soften your sharp edges."

"Your father is a very wise man. By the way," he said as he kissed her throat, "word has been sent to your mother and father to meet us at the cove tomorrow night. They will have a chance to tell you good-bye, or come with us. Whatever they want to do. Colin has also gone on to MacPhee Castle for his new sweetheart. He hopes that she will sail with us. He tells me she is the one who led them to you in Iain's chamber of horrors."

"I did not know," she whispered, "but I am grateful."

Alex gently touched her face, his eyes searching hers. "Did he hurt you, love?" he asked quietly.

"No," she answered with a shiver. "He touched me, but never more than that. The wound I suffered when he took us saved me from having to endure more."

"Are you healed now, sweet Maura?" he asked, gently touching her side.

"I have never been better, my love," she assured, the words burning in her throat. "Nothing else matters but that we are together again."

"Aye, Simon took great delight in telling me that you and I belong together," he laughed softly. "He claimed he had never seen two people so hardheaded and so stubborn, and if it had been left up to you, you would have

me riding down on Cromwell with your sword bran-
shed." He laughed deep in his throat as he kissed her.

"You once said you liked a lass with spirit," she
irmured, "and I would please you."

"You please me, lass," he said with a devilish grin.
Can you imagine what our children will be like?"

"Aye, Alexander MacLaren. I can well imagine," she
iiled, "and I canna think of a more fitting place to start
our family than on *Nightwind*."

"My very thought, lass," he said, pulling her to her
et. "Let us leave this place. We have a ship waiting to
ke us to freedom."

"Aye, my husband, to freedom and to paradise."

O happiness! our being's end and aim!
Good, pleasure, ease, content! whate'er
   they name:
That something still which prompts the
   eternal sigh,
For which we bear to live, or dare to die.

Epilogue

If you are ever in the Highlands of Scotland, amidst the proud hills and mist-shrouded castles, stop and listen to the voices on the wind. Perhaps you will hear Alexander MacLaren's whispered words of love to his beautiful Maura, or you may even catch the sound of laughter as Maura, Katherine, and Simon's lovely French wife watch their children play near the loch. You may even be fortunate enough to have Honora MacLaren appear and tell you that her three sons lived and prospered at Dunraven in the dark years of Cromwell's rule, and that she has hopes someday her heirs will yet see peace in her beloved Scotland.